the
Bench

the Bench

• a mother's imperfectly perfect journey •

jen brewer

SWEETWATER BOOKS
An imprint of Cedar Fort, Inc.
Springville, Utah

ISBN 13: 978-1-4621-3988-0

Published by Sweetwater Books, an imprint of Cedar Fort, Inc.
2373 W. 700 S., Springville, UT 84663
Distributed by Cedar Fort, Inc., www.cedarfort.com

Library of Congress Control Number: 2021933613

Cover design by Courtney Proby
Cover design © 2021 by Cedar Fort, Inc.
Edited and typeset by Valene Wood

Printed in the United States of America

10 9 8 7 6 5 4 3 2 1

Printed on acid-free paper

For my husband, who not only walked with me through
my own dark years of not knowing my purpose,
but also pushed me to find the answers.

For my children, who have given me much
more than I have ever given them.

But most of all, to you—the mamas in the trenches. The ones who
wonder how you can make it through another day. The ones who
maybe wonder if you should bury that deep dream you have
kept hidden for too long. I see you. I know you have a light
inside you. A light that is ready to shine (Matthew 5:16).
You've got this!

Chapter One

Within ten seconds, the extra blue line appeared.

The image of pink cheeks and tiny fingers momentarily replaced the bathroom vanity and mirror in front of Miranda. A new little one for them all to love on.

The image vanished and her smile faltered.

Four kids.

The number loomed large in Miranda's mind. As did the sleepless nights, endless feedings, terrible twos. Again.

Her chin dropped to her chest, and a lock of brown hair escaped the scrunchie, now covering her field of vision. She blew the wild strands away from her eyes and touched her abdomen. The baby weight held on longer with each pregnancy. She'd worked so hard to get her runner's body back, and now it would balloon once again. Not to mention the nine months of sickness, the heartburn. And all of that just to get the baby here.

Stop. This is what you've always wanted. So many women never get the chance to have a baby of their own. Snuggling a sweet newborn. That sweet, freshly bathed baby scent. She breathed in, almost smelling it.

She could do this.

Landon. Her stomach fluttered. He'd be over the moon. Such a proud daddy, holding their newborns in his thick, muscular arms.

They'd wanted a big family from the beginning. How should she tell him? Maybe she could hit up Pinterest for a few ideas.

No. She had enough Pinterest fails to warrant a lifelong ban. Besides, a project like that would prolong telling him. She couldn't hold it back any longer. She pulled her phone out of her pocket and snapped a picture of the pregnancy test.

Swoosh. The message sent.

Within seconds her phone dinged. *I knew it! When you ate that hot dog, I knew this was the month. Crazy cravings, here we come. Maybe this time we'll get twins.*

Her thumbs went to work. *That'd be fun, wouldn't it?* Even as she typed the words, Miranda shuddered. As a twin herself, Miranda and Landon had joked about carrying on the twin tradition into the new generation. His sentiment was sweet, but twins? Double midnight feedings? Nope. No thank you.

She could do this. Her purpose was to be a mother. She'd prayed for this. Yearned for it. Her earliest memories included a doll on her hip, playing house. And now here she was, privileged to live out that childhood vision. She loved her children completely, loved being a mom.

But . . .

Why the hesitation? Behind the excitement lay . . . what? Guilt? Emptiness?

Selfishness.

Deep in the recesses of her mind, it tugged. Her decade-old promise to herself. Fading, but there. She quickly shoved it back to the fringes.

Four kids. How had Mom handled six, and done it with such grace? What Miranda wouldn't give to dial her number right now.

She searched her phone to text Jess. Mid-text, a call came through.

The high school attendance number.

No . . . not now. Not again. Hadn't they taken care of this the first time?

Miranda's stomach dropped as her thumb hovered above the answer button. Did she really want to listen to another automated call from Brendon's school? Her first born, good-natured, good-looking, and getting good at ditching his freshman English class. She frowned and pocketed the phone. She'd save that headache for later.

A glance at the clock, time to pick up Isabella. A grin crept to her face. Would her spunky four-year-old dance out of preschool again? Miranda turned to leave the bathroom but caught sight of her reflection in the mirror and pivoted toward the closet. Show up to playgroup in a hoodie and sweats? Never.

———

"Is it playgroup day?" Isabella's curly blonde hair bounced as she lunged into her car seat.

"It sure is." Miranda forced her chattering teeth into a smile as she leaned in to click her daughter's straps.

"I love playgroup." Isabella kicked and arched her back, causing the strap to flip out of Miranda's hand.

"Careful, honey. It's cold out here. Let me get this buckled." She clenched her teeth against the blasts of the frigid Minnesota wind. She stomped her frozen feet on the snow-covered ground to get her sluggish blood moving again. She closed the door and jumped into the driver's seat, blowing warm breaths into her hands.

As she started the car, she reached for her phone to pick a song for the ride. The voicemail icon blinked with the waiting message. Miranda clicked on the voicemail, then pulled the car onto the road.

"This is an automated message from Bridgeport High School informing you that your child, Brendon Williams, had an unexcused absence in the following period: three. If this was an error, please have your child—"

Miranda disconnected the phone as tension spread across her forehead. The only error was Brendon's judgment. When would he learn that the decisions he made now would affect his future? She'd head to the school later and get him straightened out.

The light in front of them flipped from yellow to red. Miranda slammed on the brake. Her hand flew to her abdomen as her eyes darted to the rear view. "Are you okay, Izzy?"

Izzy giggled. "That was fun! Do it again." Thanks to Landon's interesting driving, Izzy treated any car ride like a roller coaster. Miranda took a drink from her water bottle and smiled. With the news from this morning, Isabella would soon be dethroned from her royal status as baby of the family, but they wouldn't tell her about the infantile coup d'état yet. Isabella understood time two ways, "now" and "not now." Miranda wasn't ready for the daily questions of when the baby would be here.

The green light urged the van forward again. Miranda glanced once more in the rear-view mirror and studied Isabella a beat longer. Then again, maybe a little prep wouldn't hurt.

"Hey Izzy, what would you think about having a baby join our family?"

"A baby sister? Yes! I always wanted a baby sister. Can we get one, Mommy? Can we? Please?"

"What about a baby brother?" Miranda took another sip of water.

Isabella wrinkled her nose. "Nooo! Boys pee in the air."

Miranda's burst of laughter sprayed water across the steering wheel and onto her coat. "What?"

"When I played at Donna's house, her mommy changed baby Allen's diaper, and he did that. It was gwoss. We need to get a baby sister so she won't pee in the air."

Miranda chuckled as she eyed the wet splotches on her coat and pants. "You do have a point." But as she pulled into the parking lot of the rec center, a knot formed in her stomach and strangled the laughter.

Talking and laughing while finding her motherhood tribe had been her hope when she signed Izzy up for the indoor playgroup. Why hadn't that happened? With the brutal Minnesota winters, indoor activities became the only way to ward off cabin fever. Camaraderie with other moms would come, wouldn't it?

Wrong. If Isabella didn't love it so much, Miranda would've stopped attending long ago.

"Mooooommy!" Isabella's shout broke Miranda from her momentary pause while opening the door. "Let's go, let's go!"

She pushed the door open, blowing her breath into the cold burst of air. "It'll be so fun." At least she could try.

Inside, Isabella scampered off to play with her friends. Miranda squeezed her way into the cluster of chairs with the other moms.

"Hi, Miranda. It's good to see you." Sheila's high-pitched, sugar-coated welcome failed to cover the up-and-down perusal she gave

Miranda's green sweater and last-year's jeans, almost dry from the water spots. Perhaps this outfit wasn't right either.

"Hi, Sheila." Miranda found an empty seat next to a woman she didn't recognize. "Hi, I'm Miranda." Maybe she could forge a new friendship and make the playgroup more bearable after all.

The woman twirled a piece of her long chestnut hair with one finger while extending the other hand. "I'm Penelope. Good to meet you. Alexa told me about this group—some mommy therapy each week."

"It's a great group." Miranda's jaw twitched, threatening to reveal her lie. "I hope you find a home here." That was true. She wouldn't wish her experience upon anyone. She didn't fit the mold. Why? Her mom had. Mom would've been at the center of every conversation, talking fashion and child-rearing. Teaching them how to prepare a seven-course meal in under an hour.

"Ouch!" Four-year-old Zack, dressed like a miniature model, tugged on a scooter with Isabella on the other end of the battle. He backed away and faced his mom with a pout.

Sheila rushed to him. "Honey, what happened?"

"She pushed me." His accusing finger pointed straight at Isabella.

Sheila glared at Miranda then returned to comforting the *victim*.

Miranda turned her back on the gawking crowd, rolled her eyes, and strode to Isabella. "Did you push him?"

"He pushed me first!" Isabella put her hands on her hips and pursed her lips.

"He wouldn't push." Sheila hugged Zack. "We don't use physical force in our family. We follow the Lovingly Logical Parent guidelines. He knows not to use violence to get what he needs."

Definitely a first-time parent. Miranda took a deep breath. "Izzy, we don't push. You know that's not the way to treat other people." *Even if someone pushes you first.* "We use our words. You need to tell Zack sorry."

Isabella scowled at Zack, mumbled, "Sorry," and scurried away.

Sheila's stare demanded something more, but Miranda was too tired to attempt advanced parenting techniques with a group of pre-schoolers. She crouched to Zack's level. "Sorry, bud." Without waiting for Sheila's approval, she stood and headed back to her chair.

As Miranda approached the group of women, she forced a half laugh. "You can tell Izzy's used to standing her ground against older siblings." She sank into her seat.

Alexa lifted a hand in the air with a shrug. "Kids. They can be best friends one minute and worst enemies the next."

The words of the random conversations buzzed around Miranda. She studied the women in the room. Everyone seemed so happy. So . . . connected. How could she sit in a room full of women who were at a similar stage in life and still be isolated? She checked the clock. Only one hour left. She painted on her best Sunday smile. She could do this. For Izzy.

As the minutes ticked away, she mentally scanned her to-do list. Fill the gas tank. Stop at the grocery store. They were out of detergent—death to any multi-child laundry room. She should grab some milk too. And eggs. They always needed eggs—

" . . . Mom of the Year committee. Isn't that great?" Alexa smiled, her straight teeth dazzled against her olive skin.

Miranda snapped back into focus. "What did you say about Mom of the Year?" *Don't do it. Don't go there. You don't stand a chance.*

The image of Mom smiling down on her bolstered her courage. She could follow in her footsteps.

"Penelope's on the nominating committee for Minnesota's Mom of the Year contest. We're helping her brainstorm people to nominate. It's usually someone who has older kids. Someone with experience." Alexa's brown eyes lit up. "Miranda, you have kids the right age. One in high school, and how old is your other daughter?"

"Olivia's in fourth grade . . . "

"They should nominate you." Alexa nudged Miranda.

Miranda tried to laugh it off, too forcefully. They'd never suggest it if they were privy to the high school's attendance record.

But this was only Brendon's third time skipping class. She'd put an end to it before it became a habit.

She bit the corner of her lip. She shouldn't. But before she could command them to stop, the words burst out. "My mother was Idaho Mom of the Year about"—quick calculation—"twenty-five years ago. She was one of the national finalists that year as well."

"What?" Penelope reached into her bag and retrieved a packet. "The committee would love to promote a story like that. Passing the torch from one generation to the next." She handed Miranda the papers. "This contains the criteria from this year's nomination. It probably won't change much for next year. The nominations begin next fall, so you have plenty of time to look through it and start filling it out. Anything you can do ahead of time helps our selection. Wouldn't it be great if you won and your mom presented the award to you?"

As if seventeen years hadn't passed, Miranda's chest constricted. Yes. Her mother would've loved to see her daughter walk in her own footsteps. Only the footsteps she left were fading away too quickly. Perhaps this would be a way to revitalize her mother's memory.

"I'm sure my mother would've loved that. Unfortunately, she passed away."

There it was. The awkward pause. The head tilts of pity.

"It's okay. It's been almost twenty years. She's in a better place. I have my dad and brothers. We've all stayed close. My kids adore their uncles." She'd repeated the lines enough times, they flowed like second nature.

There. That usually untilted the heads and restored the smiles.

Alexa's daughter, Vivian, ran over, her golden hair styled with an intricate braid pattern. "Mommy, I'm hungry." Her purple patterned top coordinated with the stylish patch sewn into the tiny Levi's.

Out fashioned by a three-year-old. Good grief. Add to the list: update wardrobe. Stat. Well, nine-month stat . . .

"Speaking of siblings, my mom and sister are coming this weekend." Alexa pulled a bag of dried blueberries from her red purse and handed them to Vivian, who ran off to join Isabella in play. "I've been counting down the days. Our annual girls' trip starts on Monday."

Miranda smiled even as her soul wept. *Stop. It's been seventeen years. Get over it.* Seventeen years since she'd counted down the days for her own mother-daughter trip. A trip that never happened. Canceled by a death.

A death that was her fault.

Chapter Two

"Auntie Jess!" Isabella squealed when the door opened and their long-time neighbor burst in. She leapt into Jess's outstretched arms and twirled the purple-streaked curls in Jess's otherwise blonde hair. "Oh, Auntie Jess. You have purple hair. I love purple. Mom, can I get purple hair?" With each season, Jess sported a different color.

Miranda closed the door against the arctic breeze. "Not today."

Izzy's full lips formed a pout. "Please, Mommy? Purple's my favorite."

"I thought pink was your favorite." Miranda took the bags hanging from Jess's arms as Izzy hopped down.

Izzy studied Jess's violet waves. "I like pink *and* purple."

Jess unbuttoned her red down coat. "Tell you what, busy Izzy, the next time you come over, we can spray some fun colors in it."

"Yes! Can I, Mommy? Please?"

Miranda took Jess's coat and admired the white Sherpa sweater hanging on Jess's slender frame. There were a lot of colors in Miranda's wardrobe, but white was noticeably absent. At least any unstained white.

She ran her fingers through Izzy's blonde curls. "You bet. That sounds like fun." Fun that she could wash out the next bath time.

Izzy clapped and hugged Miranda's leg. "Thank you, Mommy."

"How was playgroup?" Jess spoke to Isabella but eyed Miranda.

"It was fun. I played with Vivian. We rode scooters, and Zack pushed me." She gave another pout, which brought a kiss on the cheek from Jess.

"I have the perfect remedy." Jess's deep brown eyes danced as she pulled a bag of marshmallows and a can of whipped cream from her bag, "Who wants marshmallows *and* whipped cream in their hot chocolate today?"

Isabella jumped up and down. Her blonde curls bounced into her face. "Me, me, me! I do! I want both. Please. Please can I have both?"

Those twinkling eyes, how could she say no? Miranda lifted her hands and shrugged. "If Auntie Jess brought them especially for you, you can have both."

Isabella wrapped her arms around Jess's leg. "You're the best auntie in the whole world."

Jess flicked her hair while raising her chin. "I'll take that status."

"I gotta go potty." Isabella shot down the hallway toward the bathroom.

Miranda nudged Jess as the two made their way to the kitchen. "As mad as I am at you"—she lowered her voice— "you're going to be in the doghouse with the kids when you break the news."

"You haven't told them yet?" Jess whispered back.

"Are you kidding? Me, be the bearer of such a tragedy? No way. You're the one abandoning us for a life of adventure halfway around the world. You have to break it to them." Miranda steeled herself against the familiar twinge and set about making sandwiches for the next day's lunches.

When Steve, Jess's husband, became the director at Save the Children, a move to London had become inevitable. Miranda smiled on the outside, but losing a ten-year friendship . . . Her chest constricted, stealing the air from her lungs. She couldn't think about that now.

"Mommy, can you wipe me?"

Miranda sighed. "And I thought I'd get a break from poop duty once she was potty trained." She set down the half-made sandwich and walked to the bathroom. Jess would go save the children, Miranda would stay and wipe their behinds.

Good grief, stop. Miranda's chin dropped. Jess and Steve had wanted their own children. After years with no baby, they'd launched into humanitarian work.

The charity world wasn't all warm fuzzies. Miranda had heard many heartbreaking stories. Budgets didn't always add up. Governments didn't always cooperate. Programs didn't always work. But here, leaning over the toilet wiping her daughter's bum, Jess's world sounded glamorous. And . . . fulfilling.

"Let's wash hands." Miranda twisted the faucet handle and scooted the stool over for Isabella.

They entered the kitchen as Jess pulled a blue binder from her bag. "As requested, the latest draft."

"Oooh, I've been waiting for this." Miranda grabbed the binder and leafed through the pages. "Did you wrap up the resolution yet?"

"I hit another snag."

The hot chocolate machine chimed. Miranda put the binder on the counter while Jess grabbed three mugs from the cupboard. She held one out, and Miranda filled it with the steaming liquid.

"Here's your favorite, my dear." Jess handed Isabella the painted-by-a-preschooler mug they'd made together on an Auntie Jess outing the previous winter.

"Maybe you can work your Miranda magic again on this draft. Oh, and come up with one of your catchy titles while you're at it." Jess grabbed the can of whipped cream.

"I want a bunch of whoopy cream." Isabella hopped into her chair. "Put in a *bunch*. And marshmallows. Lots of marshmallows."

Jess plopped a few marshmallows into Izzy's hot chocolate and swirled a white mountain on top, then settled into her chair. "None of my books would be ready to send off without your help. I'm telling ya, you missed your calling as an editor."

Isabella grabbed a handful of marshmallows and shoved them into her mouth.

"Easy there." Miranda scooted the bag out of Isabella's reach. Isabella smiled back, marshmallow slime oozing through her teeth.

"Lovely, Izzy. Lovely." Miranda made sandwiches for the next day's lunches, smearing peanut butter and jam on the last of her home-made bread. She'd need to bake another loaf after school pick up. "It's not my magic you need. It's another week of walking the streets of London, talking to your sources." Miranda punctuated her sentence with a stab of the knife in the air, and a glob of the strawberry stickiness plopped onto her arm.

"Besides"—Miranda licked the jam from her sleeve— "I'm called to be a wife and mother." Why did that sound hollow? *What's wrong with me?*

"You have that one down." Jess sipped from her mug.

"Do I?" Miranda washed off the knife then leaned against the sink. "Then why do I feel . . . I don't know . . . like something's missing?"

Jess shrugged. "Why don't you get a job? Or volunteer?" Never one to filter her thoughts, Jess could call out a problem, pinpoint a solution, and implement it before most people knew what had happened. Including Miranda.

"I've volunteered for anything and everything. PTA, Little League, you name it. I don't think that's it."

"So, get a job."

"It's not that." How could she make Jess understand? Or understand herself? "I don't want to get absorbed in a career. Once Brendon came, I welcomed leaving the workforce." She picked up a fist full of napkins and strode to the table. "Izzy, here's a napkin for your face." Miranda motioned to the table. "And another to wipe up those hot chocolate splotches."

She sat next to Jess. "It's just . . . I feel like there's something I'm supposed to do with my life. Like a piece of me isn't quite right."

"I could've told you that the first day I met you." Jess nudged her before taking another sip from her mug.

Miranda laughed, then gazed out the window. A piece of her *was* missing. Yet each time she searched for it, a haze formed inside, making it impossible to step forward.

Jess set her mug down. "You know your problem? You've spent so many years filling everyone else's needs that you've lost touch with your own soul's yearnings. You don't know what you want—or who you are right now."

"You and your deep author prose." Miranda folded her arms, covering the flinch. "You should write that down. You could use it in a novel someday." *Or as a counterargument for why I shouldn't try for Mom of the Year.*

Jess laughed. "I have enough on my plate trying to finish that." She motioned toward the manuscript on the counter. "My editor's breathing down my neck. I'm a week past the deadline."

"When have you ever been on time for a deadline? I don't think you're in jeopardy of losing your job anytime soon. She knows you always deliver in a big way." Miranda finished wiping Izzy's hot chocolate splotches. "As much as I want to be mad at you for leaving, London will give you more inspiration than Bridgetown. Especially now." Miranda nodded out the window at the overcast skies.

The gray exterior mirrored Miranda's mood. This was the end of an era for these kindred spirits. Though they talked about visits and future get-togethers, they were on different life trajectories, and though neither of them said it out loud, their talk of meeting up after the move was just that . . . talk.

Miranda's phone alarm rang. She snoozed it and finished her hot chocolate.

Jess eyed the phone. "It's early today."

"Brendon skipped class, for the third time. I'm meeting with his teacher to end it before it becomes a habit." Miranda walked to the sink and rinsed her mug.

"Remind me not to tell you how many classes I sluffed." Jess popped a marshmallow in her mouth.

"He's not as focused as he should be. It's high school. If he wants to be an engineer, he needs to realize his actions count now, more than ever." She cleared the other mugs from the table.

Brendon. If only she could motivate him. School. Scouts. At almost fifteen, he should be finishing up his Eagle. He wasn't even close. All five of her brothers earned theirs by the age of fourteen. Mom wouldn't have had it any other way. How did she do it?

If Miranda worked overtime, she could line everything up for Brendon before his birthday. Difficult, but feasible. She could make it happen.

The alarm buzzed again.

Jess handed it to Miranda. "Hey, Izzy, want to come play at my house while your mom does her crazy mamma bear thing?"

Isabella jumped off her chair and ran to Miranda, hugging her legs. "Can I go with Auntie Jess?"

The image of the two of them playing tugged Miranda's heartstrings. There wouldn't be many more opportunities like this. "That's a great idea." Best friend and insta-babysitter. Jess to the rescue.

As Izzy reached up to hug her, Miranda caught Jess's eye and mouthed *Thank you*. She dug in her purse for the keys, avoiding more eye contact. This move would leave a sting.

———————

"Honey?" Miranda pulled back the covers and crawled into bed while Landon brushed his teeth in the adjoining bathroom. The earlier conversation with Jess kept running through her mind. "Do you think I should finish my degree?"

Landon paused. "What? Finish your degree?" He quickly spit in the sink and took a drink. "Honey, this is a little out of the blue. I don't understand. What would getting a degree do for you at this point?"

"I don't know." She honestly didn't. "I hate that I went so far but didn't finish. I've always seen things through to the end. It makes me sad . . . Well, not really sad. Just disappointed in myself."

"After all you've done for the kids, how can you feel disappointed?" He flipped off the bathroom light and walked toward the bed.

"No, it's not that. I . . . sometimes I think about the time I took off to go to Niger and wonder if it was worth it. I didn't realize the time I spent there would keep me from graduating. Sometimes, I wish I could go back in time and tell my younger self to put my head down and get through school . . . to not get sidetracked."

"But you've always said how impactful the Peace Corps was on your life." Landon slipped into bed beside her. "Would you give that up for a degree? A degree you wouldn't have used anyway?"

"I know I wouldn't have used it." *But that's not the point.* She sighed. Why had she chosen that major anyway? Mechanical engineering wasn't the most motherhood-friendly field. "It's just . . . it would be nice to have finished those last two semesters."

"You don't need a degree to be a mom. Our goal is to raise a family, and you've always wanted to stay home with the kids, right?"

Tension climbed up Miranda's neck and into her temples. *Why did it have to be one or the other?* "I love being a mom. But sometimes I feel . . . I don't know . . . empty. Or maybe . . . lonely?"

"What are you talking about?" He patted her stomach. "With three, almost four, other bodies in the house, lonely would be the last thing you'd be." Landon took his glasses off, the signal to turn out the lights.

Miranda gave up and forced a laugh. "That's true. Mother of three and pregnant doesn't exactly scream lonely."

Yet here she was. So surrounded, yet so alone.

Chapter Three

As the first buds of spring poked through their long winter sleep, the months of dreary gray withered away. Miranda opened a front window and breathed in the fresh, crisp air. Ah, to see green emerge once again.

She surveyed the snow-free neighborhood. There it sat, the same, yet different. Jess's house, which was no longer Jess's house. Had it really been four months? She swallowed past the lump in her throat. Why did it ache as if Jess had just left?

The garage door opened to Jess's—the new neighbor's—house. Miranda ducked away from the window. She'd delivered a plate-of-cookie greeting when the new couple moved in, but something about seeing Jess's living room invaded with foreign furniture repelled Miranda from visiting again. She couldn't bring herself to move beyond the friendly wave from her car. She'd left her number on the welcome note, and the neighbor texted her an invitation to get together sometime. She needed to respond to that. She would . . . as soon as it stung a little less.

The alarm of her phone dinged, and she jumped.

Miranda took a deep breath. The pity party was over.

She rushed to the bottom of the stairs. "Time for church. We need to be out the door in five minutes. Let's go."

Landon's office door opened, and he stepped out, scriptures in hand. "I'm ready. Let's go."

Easy for him to say. He was only in charge of himself. Everyone else? Of course, that was her domain.

She plodded up the stairs. "Please hurry. We're going to be late." Miranda lost her "sweet mom" voice and switched into taskmaster mode.

Every Sunday followed the same drill. Getting the kids out the door was like herding cats. Uphill. She glanced toward heaven. "You know I'm trying, right?"

"C'mon people," she yelled down the hallway.

"Coming!" Nine-year-old Olivia's head popped out the doorway of her room. "I'm putting on my shoes. I'll be right down."

"Put them on in the car. I don't want to walk in late again."

Isabella hurried down the hallway, her unbuttoned pink taffeta dress falling off her shoulder. Miranda fastened the buttons and tied her sash. "You need shoes too. They're in your closet. Run and grab them."

Miranda strode to the room at the end of the hallway. Brendon would try any excuse to miss church. Sure enough, as she knocked and opened his door, he sat on his bed in his red flannel pants. His sandy blond hair shot in all directions, as if his curls had attended their own frat party the night before.

"Brendon." She inhaled slowly. *Stay calm. Get him to church without a fight.* "You know today is Sunday. And you know we go to church on Sunday. Why do you make me come up and practically drag you each week?"

"You could save us all a lot of trouble and let me stay here." His defiant green eyes stared back at her.

Fine. If he wanted a fight, he could have one.

"I'm not leaving without you. We'll walk in late if we have to. It's two hours. You're given hundreds of hours a week, you can give these two to God and go to church."

"Why should I go when I don't feel anything?"

"Those are the times you need to go the most." Miranda kicked her way to the closet through the mounds of dirty clothes and grabbed one of his church shirts. "If you want help in your life, you should put yourself in places where God can help you. I can't think of a better place to let that happen than church."

As she turned to hand Brendon the shirt, Landon appeared in the doorway. "Brendon. Get dressed. You're going to church. End of discussion."

Brendon rolled his eyes, then slowly got up and snatched the shirt out of Miranda's hands.

"I expect you downstairs and ready to go in four minutes." Landon wheeled around and stalked to the stairs. "Girls, let's go to the car—now."

Both girls scurried out of their rooms and down the hall after Landon.

Miranda followed. Why did it have to be such a battle to get Brendon to go? They couldn't let him stay home. What would the other mothers in church think?

Four minutes later, the minivan pulled out of the driveway. Miranda glanced behind her and caught the hard set of Brendon's eyes. He slouched in the seat, arms folded, and stared out the window. An ache gnawed at her chest.

They got to church and fumbled into an empty pew toward the back as the opening prayer finished.

Brendon slumped into the bench. He glowered at her, then closed his eyes and dropped his head for another hour of sleep.

———

After the first service, Landon gave her a quick kiss on the cheek, then flagged down a friend and caught up with him. Brendon threw Miranda one more scowl before walking down the hall toward his own class. Olivia hugged her and skipped down the hall, brown hair swaying side to side over her blue knit dress. Isabella wrapped Miranda's legs in a death grip that threatened to send them both crashing to the ground.

Miranda leaned down. "Let's get you to class, honey."

"I don't wanna go to my class. I wanna come with yooouuuu!" Isabella shoved her nose into Miranda's leg.

"I bet there will be treats in your class. Mine is boring women who talk the whole time. No games and no treats."

Rose, one of the elderly women in the congregation, shuffled by. "Hello, Miranda. It's wonderful to see you." She patted Isabella's head. "What I wouldn't give for another day of my children being small enough to hug my leg and want to be with me. Cherish *every moment* you have with them. Before you know it, they'll be grown and gone." She wagged a finger at Miranda. "You'll miss these times."

Miranda's jaw tightened as she clenched her teeth. Surely behind each "cherish every moment" comment lay a good dose of amnesia as to the day-to-day mothering of young children.

Sure, I'll cherish this grip of death on my leg, which I'm sure has now cut off all circulation. I'll cherish the glares I receive from my teenager. Cherish is the last word I would choose to describe this motherhood moment.

"Thank you, Rose. I will." Her hands worked desperately to release Isabella's grip.

The woman shuffled away, leaving Miranda in the struggle.

———

Monday morning brought another hint of spring. Miranda and Landon ventured outside for their run on the tree-lined trails that surrounded their neighborhood. Despite their huffing and puffing— and ever slowing pace with Miranda's growing pregnancy—the early morning runs remained a ritual. Their connection time, their time to talk about anything and everything on their minds.

"I didn't think we'd ever get outside." Miranda adjusted her mittens. The extra layers were a small price to pay for the fresh air.

Landon didn't need gloves. His hands were always warm. One of the many reasons she loved holding them. He found his stride easily. "I can't believe I didn't discover running until I met you. It's such a release from the pressures of work."

"What's going on?"

His muscular build flowed smoothly in sync with hers, his short brown hair bouncing with each step. "We have a high-stakes merge coming up."

With all the confidentiality surrounding many of his high-profile clients, she never got specific answers when it came to work. He worked so hard to support the family. They turned the corner into the forest that outlined the houses in their cul-de-sac. "You think it'll go to court? Is it going to be a drawn-out process?" *Please don't be a drawn-out process.* Those cases took their toll on his stress level—and their family.

"It should be an open and shut deal. The brunt of the work will be in the next week or so, then it should be smooth after that."

Good. A two-week timestamp. She could handle that.

"I'll probably need to go to Georgia for a few days next week. Make sure the details get ironed out."

Another trip. But just a couple days this time. That shouldn't be too bad. She'd hold the fort down. Again.

He turned his head in her direction and smiled the smile she'd fallen for minutes into their first date. Coupled with his green eyes and thick brown hair, that boyish grin still made her melt. "You're lucky. You get to stay home all day and hang out with the kids. No stress. No deadlines."

The skin on Miranda's neck prickled. *Hang out?* "Honey, I don't just hang out all day. There's a lot that goes—"

"I know, I know. You've told me. I only mean you're lucky you can put all your focus on one thing. You don't have a bunch of different deadlines like I do at work. You got the good end of this deal. I'd love to stay home all day."

Miranda's breathing sped up. Should she try again to explain? He'd obviously not internalized the many previous talks. She stopped. Landon kept running—and talking. How could she make him understand?

A couple steps more and he turned, then startled. Raising his hand, he beckoned her. When she didn't respond, he circled back. "What's wrong?" His eyes darted to her midsection. "Is it the baby?"

She stifled a scream. Would she ever be able to have a concern that didn't center on her role as mother? "The baby's fine." Her stomach knotted. It wasn't his fault. Anyone would assume the same.

She took a breath of bitter air. This wasn't the time to unload her package of fractured dreams. "I'm a little winded is all. Would it be okay if we turn back?"

"Works for me. I can get an early start at the office." They pivoted and slowly trotted to the house.

As their feet pounded the pavement, questions pounded her head. Hang out? That's how her role was perceived by the outside? Hanging out playing Candyland all day? As if the cooking, cleaning, laundry, child taxiing, appointment making, homework helping, and child-rearing all magically took care of themselves while she kicked her feet up and relaxed.

Landon tapped her back, their trot more of a fast walk. "Honey, are you sure you're okay? You got quiet all of a sudden."

"I'm fine. Thinking about all the things I need to do today." *Besides hang out.*

"Me too. Could we pick up the pace a bit? I want to get going on the case."

She quickened her steps. No use trying to push the issue. He wouldn't understand. "Thanks for working so hard for the family, honey. You're a great provider and father."

"And you were born to be a mom. The kids are lucky to have you." They rounded the corner to their home. "We make a great team."

A team where no one questioned their roles. March forward. Status quo. Keep everyone happy.

Miranda dropped off Olivia and Brendon at their schools. With no preschool for Isabella today, they returned home. As they turned into the driveway, the new neighbor, out walking, approached the car. What was her name, Emma? Ellie? Something with an E. She fought the urge to lurch into the garage and close the door before the woman reached them. Instead, she put the car in park, lowered the window, and smiled.

"Hello, Miranda. Beautiful day, isn't it?" Great, she remembered Miranda's name. Not remembering hers was even more awkward now.

The woman pulled an envelope from her pocket. "With the weather breaking, we thought we should get out of hibernation and officially meet the people in the neighborhood." She handed the envelope to her. "We hope you can come."

Miranda's shoulders drooped. It should be her reaching out. Instead, she hadn't even responded to—a glance to the envelope—Elizabeth's text.

"Sounds like fun." She shifted in her seat.

"Hi!" Isabella rolled her window down. "I'm Izzy. I'm four-and-a-half. What's your name?" Saved by the exuberant Izzy again. God knew what He was doing when He sent this social butterfly to Miranda.

"Hello, Izzy. I'm Elizabeth." She leaned in with a smile. "I'm sixty-five-and-a-half. We could be half twins."

Isabella's nose scrunched as she twisted her mouth. "We can't be twins, you're *old*. But we can be friends. I like old friends."

Miranda and Elizabeth both laughed.

Phew, Elizabeth had a sense of humor. "I never know what'll launch out of this little one."

"I'm hungry. Can we get a snack?" Saved from a prolonged conversation. She'd have to find a special snack for Izzy.

"I better get her inside before the hangry comes out. Good to see you. Thanks for the invitation." She should go. It would be good to get to know the new neighbors. But her heart constricted when she glanced at Jess's house. It was still too soon. She wasn't ready to open her heart to a friendship with Jess's replacement.

"Great to talk to you again." Elizabeth patted Isabella's arm. "And great to meet you, my young friend." Elizabeth chuckled again and waved as she turned to walk down the driveway toward Jess's—Elizabeth's—house.

Isabella unbuckled and ran inside. Miranda pulled out her phone as she opened the door. She tapped on her to-do list. First up—talk to Brendon about his Eagle Scout project. How could she get Brendon going on that? How could she get him going on anything?

She let out a puff of air and inclined her head. *God, I know you're sick of me and my pleadings. But I could use some help with Brendon. To be honest, I could use some help myself. I know I shouldn't ask. I need to buck up and stop whining. But if you happen to have any extra angels, I could sure use one to walk with me for a while.*

She sat in silence. Lately, her prayers bounced off the ceiling. It didn't stop her from praying. But it did increase her isolation. Why was heaven so far away?

She sighed and headed inside. No telling what snack Isabella would conjure up for herself if given the chance.

As she opened the door, Miranda paused. *We should go to the park.*

She peered outside. It was a beautiful, if chilly, day. They could both use the fresh air.

Miranda walked inside and pulled Isabella's jacket from the coat rack. "Hey, Izzy, how about we go to the park?" If she tired Isabella out, maybe she could sneak in a beloved nap before picking up the others.

"I wanna go to the park. Let's go, let's go!" Isabella ran toward the door.

"Wait, little miss. You need to put your shoes back on. And a jacket. It's not very warm out—"

"Nooooo." Isabella brushed by Miranda, knocking the jacket from her outstretched hand, and scurried to the car. Miranda scooped it up. Isabella would cry for it once she realized spring was not entirely in play. She grabbed some granola bars and Izzy's shoes and followed Izzy to the car.

Izzy downed both granola bars on the short drive to the park, and jumped out when they got there, refusing the jacket again. Miranda tucked it under her arm. Sure enough, after three steps toward the park, Isabella pivoted for the added layer of warmth.

Miranda strolled through the fresh spring grass to her favorite bench. The worn-out wood structure on the edge of the playground beckoned weary companions. Miranda smiled. The bench was already well-weathered more than a decade before when Brendon was the preschooler playing nearby. How many weary moms had this bench supported in its lifetime? She approached and melted into it.

A gust of wind blew through her thin shirt, and goose bumps appeared on her arm as she shivered. She'd forgotten a jacket for herself. Maybe she should round Isabella up and head back.

No. She was a mother. Her child was fine. She would make herself be fine too.

While searching her purse for her earbuds, a sharply dressed, silver-haired woman sat beside her.

Chapter Four

Miranda paused for a moment. Was this like the unwritten rules of airplane seating—if you inserted earphones, the message was clear, "Don't talk to me"? She wasn't in the mood to have a meaningless conversation about the weather, or about anything else for that matter.

Would it be rude to put in her earbuds after the woman sat? Probably. She internally kicked herself for not inserting them sooner. *Stop it. Be your own person.* Resolutely, she pulled her earbuds from her purse. As she brought one to her ear, the old woman cleared her throat.

"Spring's trying to spring, isn't it?" The woman pointed to the blossoms on the nearby trees that presented their pale pink heads against the brown bark.

Oh no. So much for a mental escape. Please, not more superficial talk about the crazy winter, with all the retelling of the tired Midwest Mother Nature jokes. One hour for her own thoughts. Was that too much to ask?

Miranda inwardly groaned. Then painted on her best Sunday smile. "It certainly seems like that, doesn't it?" At least she wasn't at the dreaded playgroup.

She should add something more to the conversation, but not a single comment came to mind. She leaned into the prolonged silence, savored it. Could she bribe Isabella away from the park with a promise of ice cream on the way home? Of course, without giving the impression she was one of those mothers who routinely bribed their kids with treats.

Aargh. Why did it matter? She'd never see this woman again. Why did she care so much what other people thought? Jess had been right. Miranda didn't know who she was. She was knocking on forty's door, for crying out loud. Time to become her own woman. Jess wouldn't give a second thought as to what she should do.

Miranda snuck a peek at the woman out of the corner of her eye. She couldn't be rude and abandon her now.

C'mon. God. Give me something. Anything to talk about other than the weather.

"Which children are yours?" The woman gazed toward the playground.

"The girl who climbed up the slide the wrong way, and is now scaling the wall of the fort on top—"

She cupped her hands around her mouth. "Izzy, that's not going to end well. You can't climb on the outside. It's a long drop. Stay on the inside. And let other kids have a turn on the slide."

True to form, Isabella glanced her way yet didn't change direction or slow down. Her sense of adventure, coupled with her agility, would take her far in life. If Miranda could keep her alive long enough.

"Excuse me." Miranda jumped up and started toward Isabella.

As predicted, now that Miranda was moving toward her, Isabella changed course. She squirreled down and took her place in line for the slide, giving her mother a sweet smile and two innocent blinks of her thickly lashed eyes.

Miranda eyed Isabella for a minute more. Maybe her chase gave the old woman a chance to rest and move on. Miranda turned to the bench. No such luck. There she sat, face toward the sun as if she were greeting an old friend. The woman, radiant in the afternoon light, seemed to be in a silent conversation, nodding slightly. Then she dropped her chin as if coming to some kind of decision. Maybe she suffered from dementia and had wandered off from her caregiver.

But she seemed lucid enough. Her navy-blue tweed jacket, tailored and clean, stood in stark contrast to Miranda's faded and ragged T-shirt. The shirt had survived three previous pregnancies and, like Miranda's body, was ready to call it quits with this one.

"Sorry for the interruption. Izzy has a mind of her own. Sometimes I wonder if she has an ounce of fear inside her."

"What a darling girl, so full of energy and excitement. Is she your first?"

"Oh, no, she has two older siblings and, come August, a younger brother will join the ranks." Miranda tried to smooth out the T-shirt as she rubbed her growing midsection.

"That's wonderful. Congratulations." The woman clapped her carefully manicured hands together. "How old are the others?"

"Brendon's fourteen. He started high school this year but hasn't grasped that this is when things count for the future. Olivia is nine and queen of the fourth grade."

"I remember those years well." The woman lifted her chin, her face rising toward the sky.

Noooo. Miranda leaned back against the bench, waiting for another lecture about how fast the time goes, how she should cherish every minute with them, blah blah. Not today.

"Such long days shuffling the older kids to activities while quieting the toddlers in the back seat." A smile played on the woman's mouth. "There wasn't a moment of peace—even in the bathroom. Carrying the weight of not only keeping all those little bodies alive, but training them to become successful adults, is a heavy burden."

Miranda's mouth dropped open. She cocked her head to the side and let her heart crack open. "That about sums up my life right now."

The old woman smiled. "I promised myself I'd never be one of those women who told everyone to hold onto every moment they had with their children. Motherhood, especially young motherhood, is made up of millions of moments. The blunt truth is that many days, the hard moments outnumber the good ones."

"That seems about right." Miranda regarded this woman who seemed to understand what she was feeling. The comfort of camaraderie soothed something inside.

"But the good moments do outweigh the hard ones." The woman crossed one leg and shifted toward Miranda. "When you reminisce about motherhood at my age, you view the edited version. The sweet, poignant moments that made the world, for a second, stand still in perfect harmony. The other twenty-three hours of the day get snipped to the editing floor—"

A scream sliced the air across the playground.

"Hold that thought." Miranda jumped up and hurried toward the slide. It wasn't the something's-wrong-and-I've-gotta-supermom-my-way-across-the-playground-to-save-my-child sound. It was a my-child-is-angry-and-about-to-let-loose sound. Izzy would most likely be in the mix of it.

Sure enough, Isabella stood at the top of the slide, arms and legs spread wide forming a human wall. She'd created a no-passing zone for the frustrated kids behind her waiting to go down the slide.

Miranda clenched her teeth. "Izzy, we've talked about this before. You're not the slide keeper. Take your turn, then let everyone else go."

Isabella grumbled. "Fine!" In a flash, she slid down and scurried to a new adventure in a different part of the park.

Miranda straightened her shirt and returned to the bench. This conversation might be worth having after all.

"Sorry about that. Izzy can be a bit . . . stubborn at times." Miranda sat back down.

"No apologies needed. With six children, I witnessed the gamut of personality quirks. One son was so stubborn I told my husband that the kid had two paths in life: he'd either become president of the United States or top America's most-wanted list. Another son went through a period of not caring about anything. I cared more about his future than he did."

That sounded so much like Brendon. How did she get her son to come around? Before she could ask, she glimpsed from the corner of her eye a familiar preschooler running out of the play area toward the tree-lined grove that created a C-shaped cape to the park.

Could Izzy stay in one place for five minutes?

Holding up her index finger to the woman, she turned and ran after Isabella. Who was Miranda kidding? Their run this morning had sapped her reserve energy. She now joddled, a term Landon made up for her waddle-jog, toward Izzy. After her first pregnancy, she bounced back to running without a second thought. But with each subsequent one, her coordination and stamina took longer to recover. After this pregnancy, would her passion for running become a distant memory?

Izzy stopped shy of the tree line, head tilted back, mouth open, her finger pointing in the air. "Butterfly! It's a bootiful butterfly!"

Miranda slowed to a walk and followed Izzy's finger line and found the reason for her playground exit. A huge monarch butterfly floated through the cool air just out of Isabella's reach.

Miranda caught up with Isabella and squatted to her height.

"You're right, Izzy. Isn't it graceful flying through the sky?"

"It's bootiful." Isabella jumped in an attempt to catch it. The butterfly danced out of her reach and darted high into the trees.

Miranda heaved herself back up and gently guided Isabella back to the playground. She trekked across the park and plopped down. A slight breeze floated by, the butterfly coasting on its wave. Miranda startled at its appearance. "Oh, hello again, my friend."

"That's one big butterfly." The woman stared as the monarch flitted in front of her.

"I think it's the same one Izzy chased. It's the biggest one I've ever seen. The designs on the wings are so intricate, like mini stained-glass windows."

"It's uncommon to see them this early in the season. They normally can't fly in the cold. This one must be on a special mission to change the weather." The woman's gaze followed the insect as it flittered in front of Miranda.

Miranda's eyebrows furrowed, and the woman laughed. A comforting, inclusive laugh.

"I'm sorry, change the weather? I'd love it to turn our weather up a few degrees if it's truly behind weather patterns." Oh no. Were they circling back to weather talk?

"Have you ever heard of the butterfly effect?"

"I saw a movie on it once . . . it's not a made-up thing?"

"It's real. Very real. Though when Edward Lorenz first introduced it at a science convention in the early 1970s, the crowd almost laughed him off the stage. A professor and meteorologist at MIT, Lorenz discovered that tiny changes in one part of the world could drastically affect weather patterns on the opposite side of the globe. He called it the Butterfly Effect, stating something as tiny as a butterfly flapping its wings in Brazil could cause a tornado in Texas."

Miranda folded her arms. "It sounds a little . . . "

"Far-fetched? Corny? Too much like make-believe?" The woman raised her eyebrows.

"Well, yeah. I mean, there are millions of butterflies flapping their wings in the world. But we don't hear of countless tornados across the globe. It's a stretch to connect the two."

"True. There are many butterflies, which create many small movements. Not all of them correlate with large outcomes. Each flap doesn't automatically cause a huge change. But given the right circumstances—being in the right place with the right wind speed and so forth—small variations in weather patterns indeed have huge effects."

"I guess I could see that. Kinda like saying small changes can make a big difference." It still didn't make much sense.

"Small changes can make a world of difference." The woman paused and shifted her mouth to the side. She stared at Miranda for a moment, then continued. "They can also change our own lives, or the lives of those next door to us. The ones who don't make headline news are often the most important. Sometimes, one statement or chance encounter can change the trajectory of a person's life."

She paused again, and Miranda leaned in.

"Years ago, a famous author and illustrator visited an elementary school. He wandered into a classroom where the students were drawing a picture of his main character. As he walked by one desk, he paused, tapped the picture, and said, 'Nice cat.' Then he moved on." The woman shifted in her seat.

"That boy internalized the comment and started drawing more. His whole career later centered on illustration and writing. He published the award-winning series about a lunch lady superhero and an academy for Jedi."

"Are you talking about Jarret Krosocska?" What were the chances . . . ? "He wrote the Jedi Academy series, right?"

"That's the one."

Miranda reached into her bag and pulled out a book. "These books launched my son, Brendon, into the world of reading. He hated reading for the longest time, and then he discovered graphic novels. The Jedi Academy was the only thing he'd read. He now loves to read more than anything else." Miranda thumbed through the book.

"Olivia, my nine-year-old, loves these books too. I always keep one with me for her."

"And the butterfly effect from 'nice cat' continues today, even touching your family." The woman smiled as if she'd just proved the theory correct. "The irony is that we seldom see the impact of our own flaps in life. Moses and Susan Carver helped save the life of one slave child over a hundred years ago. By 2009, those efforts to save and raise him as their own child had saved the lives of over two billion people."

"Say what?" Now the woman was stretching. A story like that would've made headline news.

"You don't have to take my word for it. You can find the connection for yourself. Search the link between Moses and Susan Carver and Norman Borlaug. It's a fascinating study in the butterfly effect."

"I'll do that." Miranda dutifully nodded, as she did to all people who recommended movies or books. The chances of her following through on such requests were slim to none.

"If you're anything like me, you'll want to jot down the names, as a reminder. I tend to forget details the minute I leave a conversation for something else."

Miranda pursed her lips. Did this woman just assign her homework? Miranda dutifully reached for her phone. She'd comply to make the woman happy. She stepped into people-pleasing mode and typed the names.

Isabella ran to Miranda. "Mommy, I'm hungry. Can we get lunch?"

The growing tension in Miranda's shoulders released at the welcome interruption. "Sure, sweetie. Five more minutes, then we'll head home."

"Noooo! I want to go home now." Isabella slumped over Miranda's lap.

"At least I can rest assured—" Miranda patted Isabella's back but directed her comment toward the woman. "—that if anything happens with Landon's job, we could put this one to work as an actress. I better get her home and fed before the scene gets any more dramatic. Nice talking to you."

"And you as well." The woman smiled as she stood. She took a few steps, then paused and turned around. "Remember, butterflies aren't born with wings. Yet everything they need to grow them is inside, waiting for the right moment." She pivoted and walked away.

Miranda sat for a moment. What an odd conversation. Yet, it struck a chord. She took Isabella's hand and meandered to the car. Who was Susan Carver, and how could raising one child have such a profound effect on the world?

Chapter Five

"Good morning. Welcome back to winter." Miranda approached Landon, then stepped back from the sizzling bacon as Landon leaned in for a kiss.

Landon opened the fridge and retrieved the eggs. "Gotta hand it to old man winter. He's not giving up without a fight this year. I think the weatherman may have gotten this one right. There must be six inches out there already."

"The poor birds are confused." Miranda gazed out the window as she prepared to chop ham for Landon's famous omelets. The robins flew from branch to snow-laden branch, fighting against the fierce wind that blew shards of snow into their bright red breasts.

Landon glanced up from beating the eggs. "I feel their pain. Mother Nature didn't get the memo that it's May. I should be out fertilizing the lawn today. But it looks like Antarctica out there." He shrugged. "I almost put the snow blower into storage last week. Glad I didn't." He went back to whipping the eggs.

"It's useless to shovel now. We can get to it this afternoon. The weatherman said the bulk of the storm should die down by then." The city council had warned everyone to stay off the roads for the next twenty-four hours. She wasn't about to head out before then. Good thing she'd done the pre-storm store run yesterday.

As they finished the breakfast preparations, Olivia bounded down the stairs. Isabella would follow soon. Brendon? They'd be lucky to see him emerge before noon.

"Yum, is that what I think it is?" Olivia gave each of her parents her usual morning squeeze-the-breath-out-of-you hug.

Landon laughed. "Your bacon beacon could pick up the scent two miles away." He turned a piece of the wrinkling meat with his tongs.

"We haven't eaten it for so long, I thought we might be following all those laws you told us about in the scriptures . . . those ones Abraham made everyone do? You know what I'm talking about?"

"You mean the Law of Moses that God gave to the children of Israel?"

"Yeah, that one. I knew it was one of those old prophets."

Miranda bit back a grin. "It's good to know that something's been sinking in from scripture time." Mental note: she'd need to do a better job teaching the ancient Biblical figures and their roles.

"If I lived back then, I would've found a way to sneak some." Olivia leaned over the plate loaded with the crispy slices and sniffed more of the aroma. She snatched a piece of one and shoved it in her mouth before he could grab it back.

Moses . . . what was it about that na—

Oh, the names that lady at the park told her to learn about. What was the other one? Miranda reached for her phone. Maybe writing them down hadn't been such a bad idea.

Miranda pulled up the names she'd written down. Moses and Susan Carver, and Norman Borlaug. One name popped up as a link. George Washington Carver. Ah yes, he was the boy raised by Moses and Susan Carver, and was a lover of botany. But how did he link to Norman Borlaug? She began a search for those two names.

Olivia's excited stream of conversation interrupted her typing. "If it wasn't Saturday, we'd for sure get a snow day."

Miranda put her phone back down. "With ten snow days so far this winter, you don't need any more. It's almost time to eat. Could you set the table, please?"

Landon placed the bacon on the table. "Since it's Saturday, I get to spend the snow day with you instead of plowing through this to work."

Olivia paused as she opened the cupboard. "You get to stay too, Daddy? Yes! Can we build a snowman and break our record from last year?"

"You bet. We can do anything you want. With this storm, we aren't going anywhere for at least twenty-four hours."

"Dr. Vance isn't going anywhere either. His car's stuck at the end of his driveway." Olivia carried the plates to the table.

"What?" Miranda and Landon both wheeled around to face Olivia.

"As I came down the stairs, I watched him out the window. He tried to drive through the snow but got stuck."

They crowded around the front window. Their poor neighbor tried in vain to dig out the tires of his blue sedan.

Miranda sprang into action. "Go wake up Brendon. Tell him to get on his snow gear and grab a shovel. We need to at least help him get back in the garage."

Isabella shot down the stairs. "It's snowing! Mommy! Look outside, it's so bootiful."

Miranda wrapped her into a hug. "It's pretty, but it's also cold and windy. We're going to go help Dr. Vance. Why don't you grab a blanket and watch us from the window?"

"I wanna help too. I can be like Elsa." Isabella ran to the mudroom and returned with her coat.

Miranda helped her put it on. "Sure, you can come. But why don't you see how it feels outside first?" She walked Isabella to the door and opened it.

A gust of snow blew in. Isabella retreated.

"I don't wanna be like Elsa. It's too cold. I'll watch you."

Miranda kept the victory smile to herself. She finished getting her gear on and headed to the garage.

One step down the driveway, the full vengeance of the storm engulfed Miranda and Olivia. Wading through the snow with the blasting wind made the short distance between the neighboring houses seem more like a mile. The snow pelted Miranda's face like a thousand tiny torpedoes. She closed her eyes and raised her arms to shield them. A gust came out of nowhere and knocked Olivia into the back of Miranda, almost toppling them.

When they arrived at Dr. Vance's driveway, each covered in a fresh layer of snow, they took a moment to catch their breath before getting to work.

Dr. Vance's forlorn face broke into a wide smile. "My rescue team! You're heaven sent. I'd hoped to get to the hospital to see a patient, but I guess that's not happening today."

"I think you're right. But we can at least get you back to the garage. We'll dig the snow out from under your car. Brendon and Landon will be here with the snow blower in a bit to clear a path to the garage."

"It didn't seem that bad from inside. It's funny what you think you can do . . . until you can't." Dr. Vance's gaze traveled to Miranda's baby bump. "You shouldn't be out in this storm. I can do this, especially with Landon's help."

Miranda laughed and heaved a shovel full of snow to the side. "I'm pregnant, not sick. A little exercise is good for the baby. If I get this guy used to the action now, he might not complain so much when it's time for him to be on shovel duty."

Dr. Vance smiled and held up his hands. "I know better than to argue with a determined woman." He dipped his head. "Thank you for your help."

Landon and Brendon soon appeared and carved a trail across the roadway with the snow blower. As he closed the distance, Landon looked back at the already-plowed connecting street. "Hey, maybe we can clear enough to get you to that road." He wheeled the snow blower back toward the street.

Another neighbor joined Landon as he began his second pass. Together, the two snow blowers cleared a car lane down the streets as Miranda, Brendon, and Olivia finished freeing the car from the snow. Dr. Vance jumped into his sedan and, with a good push from behind, slid out the driveway and headed toward the hospital.

The crew returned home, peeled off their snow-covered layers, and reheated the cold breakfast as they made plans for their grand indoor party.

Later that evening, as the family settled down to watch a movie, the doorbell rang. Miranda opened it to find Dr. Vance holding a warm blueberry pound cake.

"I wanted to thank you for your generous help today. You saved a life."

Miranda laughed and waved a dismissive hand. "We saved you a few hours of struggle, but I'm not sure it would've been your death."

"You don't understand. I have a patient who took a turn for the worse last night, the reason I was headed in this morning. Shortly after I got there, she crashed, and we took her into emergency surgery, which saved her life. Your actions today made that possible."

Miranda's mouth dropped open, then closed and formed a smile. "We were happy to help."

They said their good-byes and Miranda rejoined the movie crew. As the scenes on the TV played out, she replayed the events of the day. That old woman had been right. Small touch points could have a big impact. She and Landon wouldn't have known about Dr. Vance's car had Olivia not noticed as she came down the stairs. And the patient— what would her influence be in the world? All because a nine-year-old girl first observed, then helped serve.

How many other butterfly flaps had her actions, or those of her children, set in motion? Miranda's stomach fluttered as she imagined the future . . . a future filled with important small acts of service her children could do.

And the woman at the park? Miranda didn't even know her name, probably would never see her again.

Yet, she'd already affected both Miranda's parenting and personal perspective. Was that woman her butterfly?

Chapter Six

Miranda laughed at Isabella's large eyes as she tried to eat the fresh-from-the-oven cookie. Unwilling to wait for it to cool, Isabella simultaneously chewed while sucking in cool air.

The recipe, an old family secret passed down from her grandmother to her mother, was the perfect treat on the kids' last day of school. Miranda couldn't contain her grin. The kids would be so excited when they found the mega-packs of water balloons and the Slip N Slide she'd bought to welcome summer.

"C'mon, Izzy, it's time to make our last pickup rounds for the school year."

Izzy grabbed another cookie from the cooling racks and raced to the car. Miranda considered calling Izzy back and telling her to return the treat, but today, she'd let the extra sweets slide.

They made their way to Olivia and Brendon's schools.

The moment Olivia jumped into the car, she peppered Miranda with questions on what awaited them at home.

A few minutes later, when Brendon slid into his seat, he smiled and made eye contact with Miranda. Was that excitement in his expression?

Or maybe he was relieved Miranda could no longer threaten to come to school during the day and escort him to each class.

The Mom of the Year nominating committee would certainly check his school records. A Mom of the Year would raise kids who valued education.

The threat had worked. The absences disappeared during the last half of the year. If only their struggles had also. He'd made no progress since January on his Eagle Scout project. The constant nagging was getting old, even to her. How could she hope to follow in her mother's footsteps as a candidate for Mom of the Year if her son didn't earn his Eagle?

But this little change in him, if it wasn't her eyes playing tricks on her, perhaps signaled brighter days ahead this summer. For both of them.

Miranda popped in the traditional end-of-school playlist and, as usual, sang along at the top of her lungs.

Isabella snickered. "Mommy. You sound funny."

Miranda gawked in the mirror and clutched her heart in exaggerated dismay. "What're you talking about?" A smile broke through the vibrato. For all the car karaoke she did with the kids, Miranda couldn't carry a tune to save her life. Not that it kept her from singing anyway.

"You sound bad." Isabella crinkled her nose. Ah, children and their brutal honesty.

Olivia cupped her hands over her ears. "Could you not sing so loud? It doesn't sound very good."

Brendon laughed. "Ooooh burn. If Liv says it's bad, you know it's bad."

Miranda turned her volume up a notch and belted the next phrase even louder, provoking hollered protests from everyone.

Yes. Summer was just what they all needed.

After they entered the house, the girls grabbed the water balloons and made a beeline for outside, not waiting to change into their swimsuits. Brendon grabbed a cookie and walked past the welcome-to-summer stash, cookie hanging out his mouth, staring at his phone.

She needed to keep that spark alive. "Brendon, it's not electronics time. Put the phone down and go play with your sisters. At least for a little while." Miranda kept her voice steady. Anything to not ruin the potential memory-making moment.

Though he said nothing, his gaze darted to the phone in her hands then back at her with a smirk.

Point made. Though the family maintained strict rules for when and where kids could use electronics, Miranda didn't control her own usage of, and perhaps borderline addiction to, her phone.

She used it to set up playdates, find directions, and make appointments for the kids. But if she peeled back the layers, social media claimed most of her phone time. Some people used medication. Others counseling. Miranda, social media.

"Fine." Brendon plopped his phone into the electronics box and opened the back door. He grabbed the hose, mercilessly squirting his sisters. They squealed with delight at the uncommon attention from their older brother, even though they were drenched. She should take a picture. Maybe use it in the Mom of the Year portfolio. Or at least post it on social media.

I should join them. The idea fizzled as she surveyed the messy house. She opened the fridge. Maybe something would magically appear to lift tonight's dinner-making burden off her shoulders. No such luck. She opened the pantry. Spaghetti? Where's the sauc—that familiar message ding. Miranda lunged for her phone.

Jeremy. She sucked in a breath. Did something happen to Dad?

She tapped the screen and read her oldest brother's message. *Hey Miranda. Touching base about August. Can you guys come out?*

Shoot. She'd forgotten to check with Landon about his vacation time. She could let the message sit until she talked to Landon, her usual response when she forgot to follow through with something.

Instead, she came clean. *Hey Jer. I completely forgot to ask Landon. I'll ask him the minute he gets home and text you back tonight.*

Her phone dinged. *No worries. It'd be good for Dad. He's slipping . . . something to look forward to would help him a lot. Plus, we need to talk. Hope you can come.*

Miranda's head tilted. What did they need to talk about? Nothing urgent, obviously, or he wouldn't suggest waiting until August to discuss it.

She read the message again. *We need to talk.* The base of her neck tingled. He couldn't leave it like that. *What do we need to talk about?*

The response dinged. *Have you heard from Mark?*

Her eyes grew wide. Mark? Why was he bringing up Mark? Miranda and her twin, Mark, rounded out their family of six kids. Though a mere three minutes separated their birth, the third minute happened to be the stroke of midnight, giving them different birthdays. Along with being the only girl after five boys, this tiny detail forever dubbed Miranda the baby of the family.

Not for a few weeks. What's wrong? Her pulse quickened.

Nothing. It's not a big deal. I'd rather talk in person.

Her stomach dropped. *I'm confused. Can I call?*

She stared at her phone ready to dial.

The bing made her jump. *Not now. We're taking Dad out for the farm walk.*

A stab twisted her gut. What she wouldn't give to walk the farm with Dad. *I miss those walks with Dad. How's he doing? Can he still make the full loop?*

Ever since Miranda could remember, Dad made a daily loop around the farm. The kids loved joining him. On those walks, Miranda had gained a deep love of the outdoors and the connection that encircles every living creature.

The bing pulled her back. *Only half. But he's still the most alive and lucid in these moments.* There was a pause, then another message came through. *It'd be great for you to come and do a mini loop with him. I hope it works for August.*

Miranda's thumbs bounced across the keyboard. *I'll let you know tonight.*

She set her phone down on the kitchen counter but the nag remained. Mark had sworn he wouldn't tell the family her secret. Did he break that promise? Was it all over the family now? Did they want her to visit so they could have a family trial after all these years?

She grabbed her cell again. Maybe Mark would tell her what was going on. As she tapped her screen, a notification popped up on Facebook. She clicked on it and started to scroll.

"Mom, what's for dinner?" Olivia stood before her, dripping water onto the floor after leaving a wet trail from the back door.

"Olivia Marie! Don't just stand there. You're getting water all over the place. How many times do I have to tell you? Get a towel."

Olivia's shoulders slumped as she scurried off to comply with the demand.

As Olivia left the room, Miranda closed her eyes. Olivia hadn't deserved that. A wet floor wasn't the source of Miranda's mini explosion.

She glanced at the clock. Thirty minutes had vanished. How did she get sucked into the vortex again? She turned her unexplained wrath on a helpless onion as she slashed and sliced. Once again, she was failing. Was there ever a time, even a single day, her mom didn't have a dinner plan at the ready?

With six kids—double Miranda's current count—how did she do everything, and with a never-ending smile on her face?

She sautéed the onions and added in the hamburger. Miranda had spent countless nights at her mother's side in the kitchen, learning the tips and tricks of the family recipes. She'd peppered her mother with questions, who patiently answered every one as they prepared dinners together.

But Mom was gone. She left before Miranda could ask her the questions she desperately needed answered. Was motherhood all she'd ever wanted in life? Was being a mom truly fulfilling? Did she ever have any personal aspirations, hopes, or dreams?

Probably not. A good mother would never do anything so . . . selfish. Everything about Mom was so . . . motherly.

Miranda had believed that her own life's path would follow the same arc as her mother's. She'd eagerly embarked upon the path herself. On the outside, her life did exemplify her mother's.

On the inside, however—

"Stop it!" She scolded under her breath. *No one forced you into this.* She'd chosen it. Begged for it even.

If the nominating committee could read her mind, they'd scratch her from the list in a gnat's breath.

She wiped the renegade tear with the back of her hand, painted on a false smile, and finished the dinner preparations.

While mixing the green salad, she glanced at her phone again. She resisted the urge to pick it up and call Jeremy. She'd have to talk to Landon about August. They had to go. She had to find out what Jeremy was hiding.

Chapter Seven

As May gave way to June, one morning Izzy bounded down the stairs. "Mommy, can we go to the park today?" Isabella's wide blue eyes begged louder than her words.

Miranda glanced out the window. A bright glow replaced the drab rain from the previous two days. The warm sunshine brought a welcome change. She lingered on the bright rays a beat longer, letting them warm her soul. Yes, today would be a great day for the park. "That sounds like a great idea. We'll go after chores."

"Yippee!" Isabella squealed. "I *love* the park. Can we go to the slide park with the pretty butterfly?" The family named each park based on what the kids loved most about it. Even the older kids loved the giant swirly slide, making this park's name a no-brainer. She tugged on Miranda's arm. "Will the butterfly still be there?"

Miranda ruffled Izzy's already wild curls. "I hope so. We'll see when we get there." Izzy's excitement was contagious. Yes, a day at the park would be perfect.

Isabella scrambled upstairs. "Brendon, Livy, wake up! We're going to the slide park today."

Olivia shot down the stairs. "I love that one. I can practice my cartwheels there. Better get my chores done fast." She grabbed her list and zoomed out of the room.

Miranda climbed the stairs and slowly opened Brendon's door. "Brendon, do you want to hang at the park today?"

An indecipherable mumble wafted from his bed, along with the unpleasant odor of a teenage boy's bedroom.

"What was that, honey? I didn't get much more than 'hmmph mmmph'" She leaned farther into the doorway.

"No. I want to sleep in today." He opened one eye, then shut it again.

"That's fine. Remember to do your chores when you get up. I'll leave breakfast on the table."

Before closing the door, she paused. "We're leaving in about thirty minutes and would love you to come. Maybe you could read?" He preferred reading indoors on the couch, but she could try. "It'd be good to get outside."

He grunted and pulled the blankets up to his chin.

Well, at least he knew they wanted him.

The girls finished their chores in record time and, thirty minutes later, Miranda drove to the park.

They pulled up and, before Miranda turned off the car, the girls unbuckled their seat belts and jumped out the door. Surrounded by a plush carpet of thick green grass, the grand playset begged to be enjoyed on this beautiful summer day.

As Miranda reached for the door, her phone dinged. A quick peek brought a smile to her face. How she missed Jess.

Watch for a package coming your way. The book will hit the shelves in October.

Then a picture of the cover appeared, with Jess's name in big, golden letters.

She tapped the screen. *That's amazing. Congratulations! After all the drafts, it's finished. I'm happy for you.*

Without warning, her fingers faltered typing that last phase. She was happy for Jess. But below the smiling emoji she'd just typed lurked a twinge of . . . what? Jealousy? Hurt?

A void rested where Jess once resided. Jess. Off on a grand adventure, she was making her mark on the world. All the while, Miranda remained in the same city, taking her kids to the same parks, going through the same seasons.

The girls' squeals floated through the air as she opened the door. She smiled as she watched them scurry toward the equipment. She really was lucky to frequent these parks and have these moments with them. She walked toward her usual bench but stopped short and stared. Seated on the bench was a familiar silhouette.

The old woman's face lifted again toward the sun as if engaged in a conversation with its warming rays. She nodded her head. Was she experiencing the effects of old age and mental decline, causing her to hold conversations with inanimate objects? Miranda had heard of this sort of thing. Her father wasn't to that point yet, but his nurse warned about the possibility.

Miranda inched forward and studied the woman. She appeared perfectly sound. Her lavender blouse accentuated smooth gray hair, cut in a modern style below her chin, framing her bright, soft face. Her soft skin folded in slightly, forming laughter lines. But there was also something more . . . had it been there last time? An aura inviting people in. That, more than anything else, drew Miranda toward her.

Miranda reached the bench and paused, unsure if she should sit. "Hello. You probably don't remember me."

"Of course I do. You added another daughter to your entourage this morning." The woman nodded toward the grassy area, where Olivia practiced her left-handed cartwheel.

The woman remembered her. *Oh, of course!* She patted her bulging midsection. "I guess it's hard to forget a pregnant woman in a foot race with a preschooler." Miranda smiled. "I love summertime when the kids can get out and move."

The laughter lines deepened on the woman's face. "She was so intent on catching that butterfly. But you reached her in record time, if I'm not mistaken."

"I did. Though by now, she'd beat me hands down in any race." Miranda took a seat on the bench.

"The pregnancy appears to be going well." The woman nodded toward Miranda's belly. "How're you feeling?"

"Pregnant." Miranda gave the same response to everyone who asked that question. Better to keep it general and avoid going into a litany of details about her daily symptoms.

The woman leaned back. "I remember feeling like my body couldn't stretch anymore; to wake and find it another size bigger. The last few months of pregnancy are the worst . . . the only thing left is to let the baby get bigger, which means Mom also gets bigger."

Miranda laughed. "That's so true. I've hit that stage now and still have another couple of months before this last guy will make his debut." She patted her belly. "It's a pleasant surprise to see you here. I realized after our last visit I didn't even get your name."

"I get called lots of things. Some good, some not so good. You can call me Mindy." She flashed a warm, genuine smile.

What kind of response was that? Was her name Mindy? Or was that a nickname? Not that it mattered. "I'm Miranda. Nice to officially meet you." Miranda extended her hand, which the older woman shook. "I didn't think we'd see you again. Are you new to the area or visiting?" She scanned the playground. Mindy didn't appear to be here with anyone.

"I'm in town visiting family. I like to come to the park and get fresh air. It's so much like one I visited as a young mom." Mindy's blue eyes sparkled in the sunlight.

"Mom! Watch this." Olivia's voice carried across the park. Miranda turned to see Olivia in a cartwheel-ready stance.

"Okay, Liv, I'm watching," Miranda hollered back. "Go for it."

Olivia raised her arms over her head, her left leg pointed forward. Her body rocked, and she did a perfect cartwheel.

Miranda clapped and cheered. "Great job, Liv. I'm so proud of you."

She turned toward Mindy. "She's spent so much time on her left-handed cartwheel. It may seem like a little thing, but she's been determined to master it."

"Those qualities will get her far in life." Mindy pointed toward Olivia. "She exhibits a rare trait."

"What's that?"

"Engaging with a task until it's complete."

Miranda tilted her head. "I haven't thought about that before, but you're right. Olivia stays with any challenge until she masters it."

Mindy nodded. "My children learned to play stringed instruments." She leaned in and lowered her head, keeping her eyes on Miranda. "It was a harebrained plan of my husband's to get them all

45

involved in music. He read all this research linking better brain functioning in the minds of musicians."

"How many kids do you have? Was it six?"

"That's right. And all six learned to play the violin. Once, I calculated that I'd spent over eight thousand hours listening to, taking notes on, and helping my children master the violin."

"Uffda, that's a lot of hours." Miranda's Minnesota slang came out as she rocked back.

Mindy pointed at Miranda. "Yet, if you handed me a violin, I couldn't play a tune to save my life. Yes, I was physically present. I could explain to you logically how to finger each note. But I never engaged with the instrument. Engaging in the activity is the most crucial part. All the hours spent as a bystander won't train your fingers to play anything."

Miranda rubbed her chin. "That's a fascinating concept. You could apply it to different aspects of life. How many sermons at church motivate me to change my life, only to slip away as I get in the car, drive home, and resume business as usual?"

Mindy's smile widened. "Or we scroll through social media, moved by a video or an article, only to close the browser and not give it a second thought. We think we're engaging in this virtual world, but we're merely escaping."

Miranda brushed a lock of hair behind her ear to hide the note of alarm ringing in her brain.

Escape. That accurately described the way she used social media.

Escape from what?

"How do I know *what* to engage in?" She caught herself and backpedaled. "I mean, I know I need to engage in my children. But there are so many ways to do that. It seems like I'm overdoing it, and not doing enough, all at once." Coaching Little League teams, volunteering at church, and PTA work filled her time but failed to fill her soul.

"If we over-engage in the good, we miss out on engaging in the great."

Miranda considered that as she pushed that errant lock of hair behind her ear. She turned back to the woman. "How does someone tell the difference?"

"Let me tell you about my friend Harriet. Harriet Beecher Stowe." Mindy folded her arms.

"Wait, I know that name. Is she an author?" Miranda searched her memory of high school history but could only vaguely recall the name.

"Yes, but her story doesn't start there. Let me tell you the story of the book that started the Civil War."

The war didn't start over a book . . . did it?

Miranda searched the park. A line of children stemmed behind Olivia, waiting for her cartwheel lessons. Isabella fidgeted in her place of the line as she waited for her turn and waved at Miranda. Miranda waved back.

Miranda faced Mindy. "Where does her story start?"

"Harriet grew up as the daughter of a preacher in the northern states. Her family was against slavery. Still, like many Northerners, they were far removed from the problem of slavery, and Harriet didn't give it much thought, other than to read and believe the Southern propaganda about the great life they were providing for their slaves.

"Then, her family moved to Cincinnati, Ohio, one of the border states, and the hub of the Underground Railroad. Harriet met several runaway slaves and heard their harrowing stories."

Mindy shifted and leaned her shoulder against the bench. "Wanting to see firsthand, Harriet and her sister traveled to a Southern plantation, where she encountered working slaves for the first time and observed the details of their lives. She grew conflicted, as many Christian churches used the Bible to justify slavery."

Miranda bit her lip. Slavery being justified—in church? How could that be? She tuned back into Mindy's words. "Harriet struggled with the idea of slavery but told herself she was one woman. A white Northern woman. A mother of seven children. There was little she could do to combat the titanic of slavery in the United States."

When Mindy paused, Miranda wondered what one woman could do. Harriet's thoughts had often been her own. All around, Miranda witnessed injustices. But she was only one woman. A lowly mother with no worldly clout. How could she possibly make a difference?

Mindy interrupted her thoughts. "Two events occurred that moved Harriet from bystander to engagement. She lost a child to cholera. The agony in the eyes of the slave mothers mirrored her own internal pain. Seldom sold together, mothers and children were often ripped apart on the auction block never to be reunited. All done under the protection of constitutional slavery laws."

Miranda wrapped her arms around her unborn child. No way could she bear to have this child, or any of her other three, torn from her arms and taken who-knew-where to await who-knew-what fate, all in the name of the law.

She tried to shake the image of a sobbing, confused, and terrified Isabella being carted away by total strangers. "I can't believe that." Her voice was a whisper. "I can't believe our country allowed that to happen, and condoned it in the name of the Bible."

"It was a horrible reality." Mindy's face held no trace of the smile that had been there before they began this conversation. "The second event, the passing of the Fugitive Slave Act by Congress in 1850, made it a crime to aid any slave found in a Northern state. It required the person finding any slave to promptly return him or face severe penalties. Harriet couldn't abide by this law and felt called to do more than talk about the injustices." Mindy pointed into the air as she raised her voice. "She used her skill of writing. After research and interviews, a vision came to her one day in church. She received her story."

"That's a profound answer." To think she never gave Harriet Beecher Stowe a second thought after high school.

Mindy leaned forward. "She encountered many struggles, but *Uncle Tom's Cabin* changed the dialogue of the entire nation. In the middle of the Civil War, Abraham Lincoln invited Harriet to the White House and is said to have greeted her with the phrase, 'So, you're the little lady who wrote the book that started this great war.'"

Children squealed on the playground, birds chirped in the trees, but silence surrounded the bench. Miranda bit her lip. How had she not heard the details of this story before? "I can't believe one person could turn the tide of an entire nation. Stories like that are truly inspiring." But Miranda was no Harriet Beecher Stowe. She was just a Midwestern mom. She had few skills, no college degree, and almost zero experience.

Mindy's brows raised. "I sense a 'but.'"

Could she voice her inadequacies to a stranger? Though Mindy didn't seem like much of a stranger anymore. There was something . . . familiar . . . about her. Or perhaps it was the way Mindy made her feel. Not judged, not chided.

Understood.

She took a breath. "Inspiring but also overwhelming. I mean, I hear stories about great historical figures who overcame incredible odds to make their marks on the world." Her shoulders drooped. "It's hard to relate it to my life. Harriet knew her talent. She engaged with it." Miranda watched a black ant make its way over the ground at their feet. "What if you don't have any particular talents? I hear stories and want to make a difference. But *how* do I engage?" Miranda's gaze shot to Mindy. A sliver of hope pierced the emptiness inside her. Hope that it could somehow be filled. With what, she still had no idea.

Mindy patted Miranda's knee, her voice gentle. "Let's talk again next week. In the meantime, note activities that make you feel alive." She flashed that warm, familiar smile again. Mindy stood, bid Miranda a fond farewell, and strolled along the path toward a row of houses in the distance.

Miranda turned to find her girls.

Something about that smile . . . so familiar . . . so much like Mom's . . .

Stop it. As she waited for the girls to finish playing, Miranda eyed the space on the bench next to her. *Engage.*

In what? Why wouldn't Mindy answer a simple question? How presumptuous of her to expect Miranda to return the following week.

What was the deal with people making her wait for answers? First, her brothers. Now, this total stranger. As if she were still a twelve-year-old who couldn't process more than a spoonful of life at a time. And had Mindy just assigned her more homework?

Miranda rehashed their discussion, her fingers drumming her thighs. What made her come alive?

Olivia ran over, doing cartwheels and walkovers on the way. *It's easy to see what makes other people come alive.* Light radiated from her kids' eyes when they were fully immersed in something they loved. For Livy, any type of big body movement. Dance, gymnastics, sports. When she was outside, she was in her own world.

For Brendon, without a doubt, photography. His eyes had lit up when he'd opened the camera on his birthday. For months, she almost never saw him without the camera around his neck. Miranda grinned to herself. Landon said it best. "Who knew a camera could get him out of the house so early in the morning?" Brendon would sacrifice sleep for a picture of nature at sunrise. And the shots he got took her breath away. An innate gift.

She encouraged him to take this talent to the next level. But, like everything she suggested lately, he blew it off as her trying to control his life. Miranda frowned. How could she help him see his potential?

Isabella. Sweet, spunky Izzy. At four years old, she loved everything and anything. It would be interesting to watch her interests develop and see where she landed in this world.

Yes, Miranda could spot that spark so easily in her children, but what made *her* come alive? No idea. Running always grounded her and connected her with God and nature. Her love of building things by figuring out how parts came together had led her to major in mechanical engineering years ago. The degree she never finished. But even if she held an engineering degree, how would that translate to her coming alive?

Chapter Eight

"Hi everyone, I'm home." Landon's booming voice filled the house with energy. The girls dropped their activities and ran to greet him. He swooped each of them into the air, then plopped them down and bombarded them with tickles. It was a small tradition, but they loved it. Brendon stopped participating in the run-and-greet years ago and lately only joined the family when called for dinner.

Miranda welcomed Landon with a kiss, then turned to the kids. "Girls, could you run and tell Brendon dinner's ready?"

Olivia moved toward the stairs and hollered, "Brendon, dinner's ready!"

Miranda put her hands on her hips. "I didn't say to yell at him from here. I could've done that myself. Go upstairs." She chortled as she retreated to the kitchen to put the final touches on the meal.

The timer buzzed as her phone dinged. "Hey, honey, could you get the chicken out of the oven and set it on the table please?" She found her phone while Landon loped into the kitchen and grabbed the hot pads.

A number she didn't recognize preceded the text message. *Hey Miranda, Penelope here, from the playgroup. Alexa gave me your number. I wanted to check in with the Mom of the Year stuff. Are you still interested? You're a great candidate.*

Miranda stole a glance at Brendon. His attendance had improved through the last of the year. And he was so close to earning Eagle Scout. They could finish it this summer.

She tapped her response. *I'd love to be considered. Thanks for thinking of me. I think I still have the papers. I can start filling them out.*

A few seconds later the reply popped up. *Great. We're excited to work with you. I'll drop off a few more forms, and some committee members want to visit you this summer to start the portfolio. Would that work for you?*

Miranda typed. *You bet. When would you like to come?*

She'd need to plan it for a time when Brendon was gone to make sure he didn't make any snarky remarks while they were here.

Her phone dinged again. *Let me coordinate with the others and get back to you. Can't wait to see you again.*

Miranda typed a final reply then set her phone down and placed the last of the meal on the table. What was she doing? There's no way she'd win Mom of the Year.

After prayers, Landon plopped a pile of mashed potatoes on his plate. "What'd everyone do today?"

"We went to the slide park. It was fun." Isabella bounced in her seat.

Olivia speared some chicken. "And I learned how to do a left-handed—"

"Livy! You 'rupted me." Isabella glowered at Olivia, then turned back to Landon. "I went down the slide and played on the swings, and Livy taught me how to do a cartwheel, and Mommy talked to Gamma lady."

Landon's eyebrows raised in Miranda's direction. "Gamma lady?"

"There was a nice old woman at the park. We had a great conversation. She's been there twice—"

"Mooooom!" Isabella's lips scrunched together. "You're 'rupting me!" Without stopping to let Miranda finish, she continued her vast explanation, after which Olivia offered her own version.

Brendon ate quickly and stood to leave before Miranda could include him in the conversation.

Her gaze followed him as he grabbed his book and headed for the stairs. "Hey, Brendon, it's your turn for dishes."

He stopped and sighed, his shoulders slumping. He slowly turned around and trudged to the sink.

Miranda stood up to clear her plate. "Have you taken any new pictures lately?"

He shrugged as he loaded the dishwasher.

"I'd love to see them sometime."

"Okay, sure." He turned back to the sink and rinsed more plates.

Well, it was something at least. She cleared her throat. "Have you decided what you want to do for your Eagle Project?"

Silence.

She gathered a round of dishes from the table. Maybe he hadn't heard her. "Hey, Brendon. What would you like to do for your Eagle Project? This summer's the best window of time to get it done." And add it to the Mom of the Year portfolio.

Still nothing but the clinking of plates.

"We better get started on something soon. The scoutmaster said it could take up to a month to get everything lined up once you have a project picked out." She handed him the empty potato bowl. "Make sure you rinse this before putting it in the dishwasher, or it'll get potatoes all over the other dishes."

"Yeah, I know." He ran the bowl under the stream of water. He then set the bowl on the counter and reached up and wiped his cheek with the back of his hand. Was that a tear?

"Honey, what's wrong?" She put her hand on his shoulder.

His gaze met hers and, for a split second, his hardened shell cracked. Something about his look made her gut churn. "What is it?"

He shook his head. "I'm fine, Mom." He moved to get a cup, leaving her hand suspended in mid-air.

He wasn't fine. That much was clear. As he shut off the sink and headed toward the stairs, her mama bear instincts screamed to help. If only he'd let her in.

———

After tuck-ins, Miranda retreated to the bedroom where Landon sat propped against the headboard, his caseload of paperwork in his lap. He combed through one of the reports, pen in hand, marking it up. She grabbed a book and slipped into bed next to him.

Three pages in, she couldn't remember a thing she'd read. She faced Landon. "Honey, I'm worried about Brendon. He's going through something, but he won't talk about it."

Landon's gaze didn't leave the mound of papers. "He's a teenager. Teenage boys don't open up to their parents. It's a phase. He'll be fine."

He continued to mark up the report, but Miranda couldn't shake the pain she'd seen in Brendon's eyes earlier. "I don't know. I think it's deeper than the normal teen moodiness."

Landon's gaze lifted and met hers, a half smile on his lips. "Honey, he's fine. He may have a few things to work out but going through hard things builds character. We can't jump in and solve every problem. Your worry genes are working overtime again."

"You're probably right, but could you talk to him? He's always told you more than me. Maybe he'll open up to you?"

He'd already gone back to the papers. "Sure, yeah. As soon as I wrap up this case, I'll talk to him."

Well, it was better than nothing. Miranda backtracked a few pages in her book, *The Red Violinist*. Huh, violins. "You know how you've been wanting the kids to start music lessons?"

Landon set down his papers. "Yeah."

"I think we should revisit that and maybe sign them up for something."

"Are you sure?" Landon's voice conveyed his surprise. "Our last conversation didn't end well on this topic." When he'd brought it up before, Miranda had listed all the responsibilities on her plate. She wouldn't consider adding another dimension of activities to their life.

Miranda gave a sheepish shrug. Her previous response entailed a minor blow up. "Yeah, sorry I didn't handle it well. To be honest, the thought still scares me. But I think we should check into it. I talked with a lady today at the park—the one Izzy called Gamma lady. She has six kids, and all of them learned how to play the violin. If she can do it with six, I can at least try to make it work with three."

"That'd be great, honey, but only if you feel like it's doable."

"I think I'm ready to give it a try." The committee would probably like to see it on her resume. She should at least try.

She returned to her book, but thoughts of Brendon crowded out the words on the page. Maybe Landon was right. Teenage years were hard, and Brendon didn't need his mom jumping in to save the day at every turn. He'd be fine. Wouldn't he?

Chapter Nine

As they pulled into the parking lot, Miranda's gaze shot to the bench. As if reserved for them, Mindy sat at their usual meeting spot. Miranda blew out a breath. What made her come alive? Still no clue. How could she find the answer when she denied herself the indulgence of any activity not directly related to motherhood?

They exited the car and the girls ran off once again to various parts of the park.

"Girls, wait. We forgot sunscreen." Miranda retrieved it from the car. Olivia pivoted and sped back while Isabella screamed and ran in the opposite direction. Miranda squirted the white cream into Olivia's hand, then hurried toward Isabella. If she made it up the fort, she wouldn't come down until Miranda forgot about the lotion Isabella viewed as pure torture.

A few steps from the fort, Isabella veered away from it and ran straight to Mindy. Miranda was too far away to make out the conversation, but she could see Mindy reach into her blue purse and pull something out. Sunscreen. Miranda quickened her pace, trying to get there before Isabella yelled her typical, "I don't *want* any scum scream" chant.

After a few steps, she stopped short, and her mouth dropped open. Instead of a rant, Isabella stood perfectly still while Mindy slathered the protective layer over her face, neck, and arms. Then—Miranda gasped—Isabella reached up and enveloped Mindy in a hug before running off to play.

"I think I just witnessed a miracle." Miranda took her usual place on the bench. "Izzy hates sunscreen. It's a battle every time we go outdoors in the summer. You must be the sunscreen whisperer. What's your secret?"

Mindy chuckled. "No secret. Simple bargaining tools. I told her she could either have you do it or use some of my special kind. I think the pink container helped." She held up the bottle of sunscreen.

"Ah, yes. The power of pink. Izzy will do anything if it involves the color pink. Even more so if it sparkles. If you earned a hug out of her, you've officially made it to her inner circle."

Mindy nodded. "I consider it an honor."

"But it comes with a warning. She'll now attempt to talk your ear off anytime she sees you." Miranda tried, unsuccessfully, to cross her legs. Another downside of pregnancy.

"I can talk up a good storm myself." Mindy folded her arms and smiled. "I should challenge her to a contest sometime."

Isabella scampered up and down the slide. As Miranda studied her, she replayed the scene. Isabella hugged Mindy in such a natural and spontaneous way. Like she'd known Mindy her whole life. What would it be like to have a day at the park with her mother receiving hugs from the children? Miranda's chest tightened. So many moments had been ripped away with her mother's death.

"Is everything okay?" Miranda startled at Mindy's voice. She turned to find Mindy's deep blue eyes staring at her.

Miranda shook out of her daze.

"Sorry. Watching Izzy with you made me wonder what it would be like to have known my mother as a grandmother. She passed away almost eighteen years ago, before I got married or had children. Sometimes it's still hard."

Mindy placed a hand on Miranda's shoulder. Her soft eyes emanated understanding. "A loss like that never heals completely, regardless of how happy we are with our present life."

Miranda nodded. "Sometimes I ache to have one more conversation with her or show her something cute that the kids did. Or simply sit at the park together." Miranda stared at the slide, refusing permission for tears. This was not the time or place.

"I think your mother is closer than it seems. I bet she's stayed involved in your life from afar. I think she's proud of you. And of your children."

Something in those words pierced Miranda's shield of nonchalance. She glanced at Mindy, then quickly turned to face the playground again. She brushed away the rogue tear and readjusted her ponytail. "That's kind of you to say. Thank you." Her fingers fidgeted with her purse, and her voice lowered. "I keep trying to be the mother that she was to me, but I always come up short."

"That's because you aren't the mother she was," Mindy said.

Miranda's head snapped up. She gaped at Mindy.

"Don't misunderstand me." Mindy lifted a hand in the air, palm facing Miranda. "That doesn't mean you're a bad mother. It simply means you aren't the same type of mother as your mom. You were never meant to be. This is where we mothers get stuck. We compare ourselves to everyone around us and try to live in other people's armor."

"Other people's armor?" What was she talking about?

"Like David in Saul's armor."

"Are you talking about David, from the David and Goliath story?" Miranda shook her head. This Bible story taught people to pray and trust. She fought the urge to sigh. After years of doing both, her emptiness and confusion remained. A sinking feeling settled in her core. And a good dose of guilt and self-loathing. The story of a young man with God on his side wouldn't help.

"Yes, that's the one. I know on the surface it seems simple. But dig deeper." Mindy leaned in, her expression intensifying, as if willing Miranda to see something.

What did she want? "It's about a youth who stands up to a giant against all odds and miraculously wins." What more was there to the story?

"Indeed, there were big odds. But they were in David's favor, and he knew it."

"Say what?" Miranda turned toward Mindy.

"I don't *want* to play with another toy!" The unmistakable screech of a perturbed Isabella broke into the conversation.

"Just a minute." Miranda rushed to the sandbox.

Isabella was deep in an argument with a little girl over a toy.

"Izzy, stop that." Miranda grit her teeth. It didn't matter who played with what. For once, it would be nice to have Isabella give instead of dig her heels in at the first sign of confrontation.

Before Miranda unloaded, Olivia ran up. "Hey, Izzy, let's go to the grass, and I'll help you practice your cartwheel."

"Okay." Isabella's face lit up as she dropped the toy, jumped up, and trotted behind her sister.

Even at nine, Olivia's penchant for peacemaking and mediation came shining through, bringing a much better resolution than Miranda could have achieved on her own. She smiled to herself as she returned to the bench. "Sorry for the interruption." She plopped back down.

"That wasn't an interruption." Mindy winked. "That was an illustration of the story."

"Come again?" Miranda narrowed her eyes. Must she always talk in circles?

"Olivia's intuitive. She knew she couldn't beat Isabella at a battle of wills, so she used her passion for gymnastics and talent of mediation to end the confrontation. She could've used brute force, as most older siblings do. Instead, she utilized her specific skill set to improve the situation."

"I guess that makes sense," Miranda lied.

"Let's get back to the inside scoop of the story." Mindy didn't skip a beat. "David, a shepherd, arrived on the battlefield that fateful day to see the entire Israelite army paralyzed with fear. When he heard Goliath's taunts, he offered to fight.

"As expected, people scoffed at him. But the desperate king agreed to the plan. He prepared David in the best way possible, by putting his own armor on the shepherd."

Miranda shifted her weight and folded her arms. Nothing new here . . .

"But David's specialty was with a sling, not a sword. Not only would the king's armor not help him, trying to be something he wasn't would hinder him . . . most likely to the point of death and loss of the war."

Interesting. Miranda cocked her head to the side.

"What we don't hear in the Bible verses is the history of ancient warfare. The armies of those days were made up of three branches— the foot soldiers, cavalry, and artillery, which included slingers. Much like a game of rock, paper, scissors. Heavily shielded and armed foot soldiers could beat the cavalry. While the horses of the cavalry were oftentimes too fast to make good targets for the slingers, and could beat them. The slingers could penetrate the weak spots of the foot soldiers from great distances. In this case, Goliath was scissors, and David was . . . "

"Rock." Miranda's eyes widened. "David knew he could win, even before he stepped onto the field."

Mindy sat back and nodded.

The puzzle pieces shifted to formulate a new picture. "The miracle was as much in David knowing his own specialty as it was in the power of his throw."

"Precisely. He utilized his core." Another nod from Mindy.

They sat in silence for a moment.

"That's a layer of the story I've never considered. But I don't see how it relates to me. I don't see myself facing giants any time soon."

"My dear, any struggle you or your kids encounter is a giant. The internal voices that try to conquer your self-worth can be the most dangerous giants of all. Combine that debilitating self-talk with the restrictiveness of wearing someone else's armor, and you'll never defeat any giants in your life. You were never meant to wear another's armor. Not even your mom's."

A sliver of oxygen breathed air into her suffocating soul. Miranda gazed across the park and took a deep breath.

She blinked hard and chewed on the inside of her cheek. "But what if I don't know what my specialty is?" Or what if she didn't have one? She turned back to Mindy. "You asked me last week to find what makes me come alive." Miranda sighed. "All week, I noticed things in each of my children. Those were easy to spot. But every time I tried to focus on my own 'alive,' I hit roadblocks. I don't know what it is for me."

She shifted her gaze toward the green grass carpet on the side of the concrete path. Her voice dropped to a whisper. "I've focused on helping everyone else find their direction in life for so long, I think I've forgotten how to find my own."

Mindy dug through her purse. "Here's something that could help."

Olivia ran up, out of breath. "Mommy, I'm hungry. Did we bring any snacks?"

Miranda reached for the bag sitting next to her feet. "Grab what you want from here. Could you see if Izzy wants anything?"

"Sure." Olivia grabbed two cheese sticks. She ran toward Isabella, who was organizing the kids around her into a game in the sandbox. Miranda watched to make sure Isabella kept herself in check. Everyone seemed happy enough, so Miranda turned back to Mindy.

"Ah, this will work." Mindy pulled out a scrap of paper and a purple marker. "With grandkids around, I have an endless supply of markers at the ready, but pens can be harder to come by."

She drew two circles, slightly overlapping in the center, like a Venn diagram. In one, she wrote, "Talents/gifts/skills." In the other circle, she wrote, "Passions."

Miranda waited for an explanation.

"This helped me years ago when I struggled to find my purpose." She pointed to the talent circle. "In this circle, write down all your gifts and talents and skills you've developed. You won't show it to anyone, so be honest and list everything."

She tapped the other circle with the marker. "In this one, write all your passions. Again, be honest. Don't write what you *should* like, or things you do because other people like or expect them." She shot Miranda a knowing look. "These are activities that genuinely make *you* light up inside. Things that, when you engage in them, make you lose track of time.

"Don't overthink it, and don't take too much time. Listen to your gut and write whatever comes out. Then, when you have words written in both circles, study them. Notice patterns. Things that are the same in each circle, or complementary between the circles, move to the intersecting part, your core. They will help you live in your purpose."

Mindy replaced the cap on the marker. "Doing it once doesn't set it in stone. In fact, repeat this often, in different seasons of life. The lists will change with time and experience. That's okay. The key is to keep it true to you . . . your own passions and talents. And most importantly, keep yourself true to it."

"What do you mean by that?'"

"Engage." Mindy gave her a mischievous grin.

Miranda ran her fingers through her hair.

The woman handed the paper to Miranda and returned the marker to her purse. "This is a lot to chew on. Above all, give yourself grace to grow into your purpose. Seek it, but don't force it."

The girls staggered over, and Isabella flopped over Miranda's lap.

Miranda stroked Izzy's hair while speaking to Mindy. "My brain is going in a million directions. Thank you for helping me see an age-old story in a new light."

"Thank you for letting an old woman babble." Mindy turned to the girls. "My, you both worked up a sweat. Olivia, your cartwheels continue to shine."

Olivia beamed.

Isabella's head popped up. "What about mine? Did you see me do my cartwheel? Livy taught me."

"I did see you. And you, my dear, were marvelous."

Isabella smiled from head to toe.

"And remember"—Mindy got out her perfectly pink sunscreen and winked at Isabella— "you can use this anytime."

"Thank you again." Miranda resisted the urge to lean over and hug Mindy. She couldn't get all mushy now.

"Girls, can you say good-bye? It's time to head home." Before she'd finished the sentence, Isabella wrapped her little arms around Mindy. Following her lead, Olivia enveloped Mindy in one of her special Livy hugs.

"Oh my, your hug could tame a lion." Mindy pulled back and focused on Olivia's deep green eyes. "You have a special gift of looking inside people and helping them feel loved and seen. Don't ever let that go."

Olivia smiled, and tilted her head sideways with furrowed brows. Miranda bit back a grin. At least she wasn't the only one left confused by Mindy's messages.

Watching the interaction, Miranda's heart was simultaneously sad for missed moments like this with her mother and grateful for the strange woman who took the time to be a sweet fill-in for her daughters, if only for fleeting moments at the park.

She took Isabella's hand and followed Olivia. On impulse, she turned back to Mindy. "Will you still be in town next week? I'd love to visit again."

Mindy smiled. "I'd like that. Yes, I'll be here. I look forward to another meeting on our bench."

Chapter Ten

Throughout the week, Miranda busied herself with the usual summer activities. She took Olivia and Brendon to swim team and Izzy to swim lessons. She still hadn't worked through the circles. She had plenty of time while waiting to pick up kids from their activities, but she couldn't find the headspace to dive deep and go through the self-discovery steps. What if she found something she didn't want to see?

Or, worse, found nothing?

It didn't matter anyway. The Mom of the Year committee would be here next week, and it would take that long to get her house into any reasonable shape. Miranda gazed around, admiring the open floor plan on their main level. The only problem? No place to bulldoze the piles of clutter. Olivia's art supplies covered every inch of the beige carpet, Izzy's favorite blanket and pillow splayed across the couch, and DVDs littered the corner by the TV—remnants of last night's debate over a movie, which they'd ended up streaming.

She studied the main wall of their family room. Various pictures of the family members from past years surrounded their big family picture. *Shoot.* That picture was two years old. Maybe they could scramble and get an updated one? No, this would have to do. At least Brendon was smiling. Miranda stepped closer, her gaze locked on the younger Brendon. What happened to that smile? Would he ever find it again?

Miranda circled back to the room. Where to start? Cleaning the house during summer was like trying to shovel in the middle of a blizzard. With the kids home all day, she couldn't keep on top of the piles and projects. Wasn't pregnancy nesting supposed to kick in about now and give her an extra boost of energy? Maybe she'd exhausted the quota on that with her last pregnancy.

Lining up violin lessons was yet another thing on Miranda's to-do list. One less thing to do after the baby came.

So much to do. How could she etch out more time for focused introspection?

But something had awakened on that park bench. Something deep inside, calling her to give it voice.

A few nights later, too exhausted to sleep, the inner journey she'd pushed aside nagged her again.

Not now. Every limb screamed for rest. She could barely lift her head. She'd get up early and put pen to paper to fill in the circles.

Who was she kidding? Once the sun came up, she'd be buried in the busy-ness of running the house.

After tossing and turning a while longer, she sat up.

"Is everything okay, honey?" Landon reached for the lamp. Brendon's early delivery years ago had caught them both off guard. With the next two babies, Miranda's bags were packed by month six, and Landon jumped up, ready to get her to the hospital, with every twist and turn during the night.

"It's fine, hon. I'm uncomfortable is all." She wasn't lying. Miranda was seldom comfortable these days, and the heartburn grew worse with each passing night. "I'm gonna lie in the recliner to get my heartburn under control." She leaned over for a kiss then headed downstairs.

Wrapped in a blanket with the lamp highlighting a blank piece of paper, Miranda paused for a few moments.

Then she drew a circle.

What she thought would be a slow, methodical process became an open floodgate. She wrote as fast as the words popped into her head. Her inner yearnings erupted onto the paper.

The writing wasn't pretty, but the words were beautiful. The process pure and satisfying, as if God moved the pen, affirming talents He'd given to her in their initial meeting so long ago.

When she finished the first circle of talents, gifts, and skills, she examined it. "Fast diaper changer." A laugh erupted from within. When Olivia was in diapers, Miranda took her to the park with a friend, Erica, and Erica's baby. Olivia needed a diaper change. When Miranda thought she'd run out of diapers, Erica offered to give Miranda one of hers. In the time it took her friend to retrieve a diaper from her bag, Miranda found one hidden at the bottom of her bag, changed Olivia and sent her back to play.

"Whoa, girl, you're the fastest diaper changer I've ever seen."

Such a silly compliment. But to a young, overtired, and under-appreciated mother who was drowning in diapers, it was an emotional boost.

After that day, anytime Olivia, and later Isabella, needed a diaper change, Miranda rehearsed, *I've got this. I'm the fastest diaper changer Erica's ever seen.*

For some reason, that small compliment had impacted her in a significant way.

Miranda smiled now at the recollection. She peered back at the phrase. She may be good at it, but diaper changing would never make it to her passion circle, now or ever.

On the other half of the paper, Miranda drew another circle. Again, the words flowed.

When she studied the list, her heart smiled. Every word portrayed something she loved.

But some words in her passion circle wouldn't make it to her talent circle.

Like singing. That one brought a titter. If her kids read this word on her paper, they'd laugh out loud.

The children's only hope was to inherit Landon's musical abilities. After they'd met, he'd shown up at the end of one of her engineering classes, roses in hand, and presented a singing telegram to ask her out. Her friend, Sydney, the only other female in the class, squeezed her hand afterward and whispered, "If you don't nab him now, he's all mine."

Her heart still warmed thinking of Landon singing for her. A moment later, the smile faded. Landon would be so disappointed if he knew her inner struggles. He'd worked hard the first ten years of their marriage. He'd pushed through grueling years of law school and moved them around the country to support them. And then, there'd been the added effort to become a partner in his law firm.

He'd done all that to provide for the family so she could stay home with the kids. They both believed this was the best way to raise children.

Growing up, this had been Miranda's dream. How could she tell him it was no longer enough? He'd ask what more she wanted. She wasn't ready for that question. She still didn't know herself.

Would he view her as a failure because she couldn't cut it in the stay-at-home mom world?

Miranda shook her head. She'd figure this out on her own first, then think about how to talk to Landon.

She focused again on the circles, searching for patterns. She loved to build and fix things, and she was good at it. When the kids broke their toys, they brought them to Mom, not Dad. When Brendon wanted to concoct a new Lego creation, she was the go-to source for inspiration. Miranda paused and searched the two circles again. The words: *build* and *connect* jumped off the page.

I'm a connector.

Her eyes widened. What was that? Was it even a thing?

Something in Miranda awakened when she connected to nature while on a run, or helped connect people to something they needed. She felt alive. The very act of providing her children with what they needed to survive and thrive involved connection.

And machinery. Oh, how she loved building machines. Connecting parts together to form something magnificent. Her engineering classes hadn't been drudgery. Rather, they'd been the gateway into a world of discovery, of building and creating. Connecting.

"I am a connector." She said the words out loud. For the first time in a long time, something inside her settled.

She yawned and glanced at the clock. Two hours had slipped by. She made her way back up to her bed and slept better than she had in years.

Chapter Eleven

"Mom, check this out." Brendon walked into the kitchen with his camera.

Miranda pushed the toaster button down then wheeled around. "Did you get a good one?"

He held out his camera to reveal the sunrise shots he'd snapped moments before.

She gazed at the small screen. "These are incredible." Miranda scrolled through the images. They were good. More than good. And he'd shared them with her. Landon was right. His moodiness was only a phase. Hopefully one on its way out. "You have such a photographic eye. You see things with your lens that I'd never notice." She continued scrolling. "I love this close-up one with the dewdrop about to fall. Could we enlarge it and put it on the wall?"

Brendon's head dipped down as he shrugged. "I guess, if you wanna."

Miranda swiped through a few more. "I love all of these. You could start a website and sell them. Or stock photo sites might be interested. It'd be a great way to earn some money."

"Yeah, maybe." He took the camera back and turned to leave the room.

"We're heading to the park after breakfast and chores. Why don't you come with us? You could get some great pics there."

Brendon grabbed a piece of bacon. He shrugged. "Maybe."

"You could invite Christian to come." Best friends since preschool, she hardly had a picture of Brendon without Christian in it from their countless days together roaming the neighborhood. "I haven't seen him around for a while. Are they out of town?" Come to think of it, he hadn't been around since before the holidays.

His eyes darkened as his stance tensed. "I dunno. Maybe." He pivoted and headed toward the stairs.

What just happened? Did she say something wrong? This magical moment with Brendon slipped through her fingers as she fought to hold on. "I still want to enlarge that one picture. Send it to me, okay?"

He turned slightly. "Sure." Before she could say more, he bounded up the stairs.

It wasn't much, but she'd take it.

———

A brilliant blue sky greeted them at the park. Even Brendon's rejection of the park invitation couldn't dampen Miranda's excitement as she inhaled the scent of fresh cut grass. She smiled. Summer was in full swing. It transported her back to days on the farm, tinkering with the equipment in the shed while her brothers mowed the half acre of lawn. Tinkering . . . connecting . . . Miranda's pace increased as she made her way to the bench. Her talk with Mindy couldn't come fast enough.

Every time she'd tried to delve deeper into her circles, something pulled her away. She'd focused first on getting the house to potential-Mom-of-the-Year perfection for the meeting. Then the summer routine. Couple those with Olivia and Isabella begging her to help bust their boredom each day, and, if anything, Miranda had fallen backward in her personal journey.

Perhaps moments would open more when the kids returned to school in the fall. But then she'd have a new baby, and the cycle would begin all over again. How would she find the time or energy to work on her own development? Assigning a word to her core was one thing. Figuring out what that meant would be much more difficult.

Mindy sat on their bench adjusting her bright blue hat when Isabella ran up to her. As if they'd been doing the ritual for years,

Mindy reached into her purse and pulled out the pink bottle. Miranda laughed as Izzy tilted her face up, giving Mindy a better angle with which to rub in the sunscreen. Even though Miranda had slathered the girls before they left, she didn't say anything. A double layer wouldn't hurt. She slowed her pace a bit. Give Izzy a minute more with the Gamma Lady. Miranda's heart swelled to see this relationship build between her daughter and this sweet woman.

"Uffda." Miranda plopped onto the bench. "Pregnancy isn't the most comfortable state for the human body."

"Amen." Mindy finished rubbing Isabella's face and replaced the cap on the bottle. "It's funny how I forgot the pain of pregnancy. Until the next one started. Then it'd all come crashing back with my first bow to the porcelain king. I still remember that last pregnancy. We thought we were done at four children. We decided to go for one more. At the first doctor's appointment, we heard two heartbeats."

"No way. I'm a twin." Miranda patted her bulging belly. "Though now that I've gone through pregnancy, I have no idea how my mom did it with two. This womb is packed to the brim."

"I had no idea the human body could expand to such limits." Mindy raised and extended her arms as if blowing up a beach ball from her own belly. Then she folded her arms and leaned back. "We joked with our twins that when they heard we only planned one more pregnancy, neither wanted to be left alone up there, so they grabbed hands and jumped in together.

"To this day, they have a special bond. In hindsight, they were the perfect finish to our family. No one came last. They experienced life together from the beginning."

Miranda understood. Her life had been sweeter with Mark having her back. "Each pregnancy, Landon, my husband, hopes for twins." Miranda placed her hands on each side of her stomach. "But I'm afraid our little guy will have to settle for ending our family solo. This body's done with pregnancy."

Mindy peered at Miranda's bulge. "Pregnancy's an interesting obstacle opening."

"Obstacle opening?" What was she talking about? Miranda's shoulders drooped. She didn't have the energy to add new lessons right now. The last one still waited in the wings of her mind to work through.

Mindy leaned forward. "In many ways, pregnancy can be viewed as an obstacle. It brings body changes, the inability to enjoy activities you once loved. Not to mention pain and discomfort. Yet it's the pathway to the world of parenthood. It's the pathway to existence." She wagged a finger in the air. "My friend, Marcus Aurelius, once shared a statement that changed my life."

"Wasn't he a Roman Emperor?" *Not again.* Why did this nice old woman cling to the fantasy that she had friends who'd been dead for centuries?

If Mindy noticed Miranda's questioning glance, she made no acknowledgment. "Indeed. The last of the five great Roman Emperors. He once said, 'The impediment to action advances action. What stands in the way becomes the way.'"

Miranda sifted through the words. How could something blocking her become her path?

Mindy motioned toward the park. "Notice the stairs leading to that great slide. When a child is young, those stairs are a huge obstacle. They can't fathom climbing up one, let alone all of them. To a tiny toddler, they are one insurmountable wall stacked on top of another as high as the little one can see."

The image of Olivia making her way to these very stairs years ago filled Miranda's mind. Little Olivia would watch Brendon scurry up and follow him in a clunky crawl. She'd make it up one or two, only to back down.

"As the child grows," continued Mindy, "the stairs are no longer a hindrance to going up. They are the pathway to sliding down. A past wall becomes a future stair, making it possible to climb to new heights."

Miranda's gaze followed the steps up to the great slide. "I've never thought of them in that way before." How many other obstacles in life did this pertain to?

"As parents, the best way to help our kids learn and grow is not to clear the path, nor to overcome their obstacles, but to *utilize* them." Mindy crossed one leg over the other. "It's tempting to pray for obstacles to be removed, yet the Lord knows we need them to grow into what He needs us to be."

Miranda bit her lip. As hard as it was to admit, the woman was spot on.

A soccer ball rolled over. Mindy got up and, with one swift kick, sent it flying back to the group of kids in the open field.

"Nice kick."

Mindy bowed her head slightly on her way back to the bench. "I'm no Garrincha, but I coached a few Little League teams in my time."

"Who's that?" In all her years coaching Brendon's little league teams, Miranda heard the boys talk about Ronaldo, Messe, Beckham, and others, but this name wasn't familiar.

"Garrincha was his nickname. Manuel Francisco dos Santos was born in the 1930's with a crooked back, bowed legs, and one leg shorter than the other. He loved playing soccer, and the deformities many thought would hinder him instead helped him play at the highest level of soccer and become one of the best."

Olivia ran across the field, her moves graceful and rhythmic. How could someone with so many physical limitations move like that while commanding a soccer ball?

As if reading her mind, Mindy continued. "His knee deformities caused his legs to bend at awkward angles. This helped him cut and move in ways his defenders were unaccustomed to, enabling him to blow by them with ease." Mindy sat back and folded her arms.

Miranda rubbed her chin. "I love stories like this. Of people beating the odds and triumphing in life. It's amazing someone became better *because* of their limitations." She paused. Motherhood wasn't exactly an obstacle to be overcome. Should she voice her inner torment? She glanced at Mindy, who watched her through narrowed eyes as if she understood Miranda's conflicting thoughts. With a deep breath, she plunged in and let it all spill out.

"My life isn't much of a sports analogy. I've been in the role of wife and mother for so long, I don't know how to be anything else." Her voice grew soft. "To be honest, I struggle with the thought that I should try to be anything else, at least simultaneously. Shouldn't I dig into this role and save all my inner hopes and dreams—my core as you say—for another season? After attempting for half the week, I finally went through the circle exercise. Once I did, I loved what I uncovered. But how do I move forward when I'm so wrapped up in my role as a mother? I can't set my kids up with meals and move out to find myself."

Miranda paused. Had she said too much? Dare she utter the thoughts that leapt from the fringes to the forefront of her mind? She eyed Mindy, searched for any signs of judgment. How could she admit that she wanted more from life? Thoughts of a promise, made so long ago in a village on the other side of the world, begged to be voiced. If she mentioned it, she'd sound like a nutcase.

When Mindy's eyes met hers, full of acceptance and understanding, Miranda blurted before her brain could censor. "Before I married Landon, I lived in Niger with the Peace Corps and learned what real poverty is. So many issues to tackle . . . sickness, malnutrition, education . . . " The images of sick kids, hungry mothers, and endless walks to and from the rivers paraded through her mind. "The lack of water hit me the hardest. Women and children spent hours every day hauling buckets of water." The memory slowed her words. She shook from her daze and her lips opened once more. "When I left Niger, I vowed I would help solve at least one piece of that puzzle.

"Once I returned to school, I dreamed of building a drill that could dig deep enough to find water closer to the villages. I made sketches of a manual powered one and presented it to my class for our senior capstone project. They liked the idea . . . "

A smile played at Mindy's lips. "I sense a boy entering the scene."

Miranda nodded, unable to repress the smile that formed across her mouth. "I met Landon the summer before my junior year. We got engaged during Christmas break. Married the following summer. He started law school in Boston, so I turned my drawings over to my class and moved east. When children entered the picture, my promise became more of a pipe dream." She shrugged. "My one consolation came when I learned my classmates had run with the drill idea. They built a prototype, and it worked the way I envisioned."

Could Miranda tell Mindy the crazy part? Before she could command her lips to stop, they betrayed her. "I used to dream of returning to Niger with the drill, connecting the people I loved so dearly to precious water."

As the years passed, the vision had become softer and softer, until it faded to barely a whisper. A different life. A different path.

Mindy leaned over, her voice quiet. "Have you shared any of this with your husband?"

Miranda shook her head. She'd never told anyone, not even Landon. Why bring him into her crazy fantasy? "I thought about it a couple times, but I can't. We've always agreed that I'd be the stay-at-home mom."

"If you put him in a box, you deny him the opportunity to share your hopes and dreams."

"But I've always told him my hopes and dreams were to be a wife and mother. How can I tell him that now I feel suffocated by this role? That motherhood is blocking me?"

"Things may not be as they seem. Through motherhood, you'll become more than you ever could've been on your own." The response caught Miranda off guard. How could that be? Had this woman listened to anything she'd just said? No way was motherhood compatible with building drills.

Mindy pulled a red book from her purse and handed it to Miranda. The title read *Beneath a Scarlet Sky*. "Pino Lela found himself drafted into the enemy's army before he reached his full potential."

Miranda flipped the book over. This was about WWII? In Italy? WWII fascinated her. She'd read countless books on the topic, yet this title was new to her.

Mindy tapped the book. "I think you'll find this book a great study in turning obstacles into stepping-stones."

Another homework assignment? Miranda hadn't completed the last one. Or even the first one. As much as she loved books, couldn't Mindy give her the gist of the lesson now instead of making her fish for it on her own? "You know, I always read the last page of the book first. I don't mind spoilers."

Mindy sat back and wagged her finger. "This one you don't want to spoil. It's worth a good read. Or listen." Mindy motioned toward Miranda's purse with her head. Had she seen the earbuds that first day at the park?

"Listening's the only way I get books read anymore." Miranda handed the book back. "I'll write this one down." Like the dutiful student, she pulled out her phone and typed in the title. Right next to her unfinished assignment from weeks ago.

So much to do, so little time or energy to do it. Miranda stifled a sigh. She was right back at square one. How could she take care of the needs of her children and her own internal passions? "When I went through the circles you outlined last week, I discovered that I'm a connector." As the words left her mouth, they settled in her soul.

She shifted in her seat. The self-discovery didn't scare her, but her bold dream of implementing it was terrifying.

Mindy interrupted her thoughts. "The good news is there are no time limits. God knows how to help you progress. You don't need to fret or fuss about it. He will plant people and passions into your life to nudge you toward your role in God's plan. Some are fleeting, others linger longer."

Mindy caught Miranda's gaze with a piercing stare. "But your husband is a permanent part of you. Don't discount his ability to grow and adapt. Or his desire to help you on your journey, as you've helped him on his."

"Once again you've given me so much to chew on." Miranda didn't fully understand, but her soul soaked it in. "It's going to take a while to work through all these thoughts."

"And when you come to an understanding, perhaps you can explain it to me." Mindy patted Miranda's leg. "Because I'm still learning myself." She smiled that warm, unassuming smile that once again drew Miranda into a deep feeling of love and acceptance.

There was something in her face—in her whole countenance—that Miranda hadn't been able to name before. But now the word came to mind: contentment. Mindy sat at ease, shoulders straight, with an easy grin. Even admitting she didn't have it all figured out didn't faze her. Miranda longed to achieve that for herself one day.

"I better be on my way." Mindy stood and straightened her white shirt. "I'll see you next week?"

"You can count on it." Miranda's shoulders relaxed. Mindy would be here another week. As Miranda worked through these lessons in her mind, she would surely come up with more questions than answers.

Mindy walked down the path leading to the houses that shielded the park from the street. In which home was Mindy staying? It had to be one of the close ones. Why didn't she bring her grandchildren with her to the park? Perhaps they were older, like Brendon, and she needed a little outing to herself every so often.

"Mommy, watch this." Isabella's yell grabbed her attention.

Miranda turned toward the monkey bars where Isabella waited. Before she'd taken two steps to help Isabella, her daughter reached up to the first rung and, like a flash, moved from one rung to the next, all the way to the other end.

Her face beamed as she ran to Miranda for their traditional double high five. "I did it, Mommy! I made it all the way, all by myself."

"That's awesome, honey. I knew you could do it. You practiced and didn't give up. Great job." Her girl had grit.

"Are you hungry? Would you like to head home for lunch?"

"Nooo! I wanna stay." Isabella zoomed back to the monkey bars. Miranda couldn't blame her. Izzy would want to make sure her new skill stuck.

"Okay, five more minutes, then we need to go."

Isabella nodded, then grabbed the bars for another go.

Miranda found Olivia making a grass nest with one of her new friends. They talked and giggled as they pulled the plush blades of grass and arranged them into an elaborate nest fit for a king bird, or squirrel, or whatever animal they imagined would take residence.

"Hey, Livy," Miranda hollered when she got within earshot of the pair. "We're leaving in five minutes."

"Okay, Mom." Olivia waved to Miranda, then turned back to the task at hand with her friend.

Miranda returned to the bench and combed through the conversation. Obstacles. Armor. Soccer players with bent knees. Everything swirled around her head. Knowing the concepts was easy. Figuring out how they pertained to her life was not.

One thought overtook all others. She needed to talk to Landon. But how? Would he laugh at her? Be angry with her? As scared as she was to face that conversation, it was time.

Chapter Twelve

Running at the crack of dawn had its advantages, especially in the hot, humid Midwest summer. This morning, as they started on their usual route, Miranda surveyed Landon out of the corner of her eye. Their pace, slowed by the pregnancy, produced the perfect platform for talking. Time to bring him into the loop.

For the first mile she tried and failed to formulate the words. As they rounded out mile two, Landon cleared his throat. "Honey, is everything okay? You've been quiet lately."

Miranda jogged a few more steps in silence, then the floodgates burst open. "I want to tell you something, but I don't want you to freak out."

"Okay . . ."

"I hate motherhood."

This time Landon stopped.

"Wait, that didn't come out right." With Miranda's slower pace, it didn't take long for her to stop and return to her immobile running partner. "I don't hate being a mother. I love being a mother to our children. They're my world. I hate trying to squeeze myself into society's views of motherhood. I keep trying to lose myself in this role, but instead of happiness and joy, I feel emptiness and guilt."

Without speaking, Landon started running again. Miranda struggled to keep up with his increased pace. After many silent steps,

Miranda, between labored breaths, said, "I'm not saying this right. I don't want to drop everything and leave. I don't want to get a job and forge a career of my own. I just want . . . no, I *need* something in my life that's mine. Does that make sense?" She paused, gulping in three breaths of air. "I need to grow myself, even as I work to grow the kids. I'm losing my identity. I know being a mom should be enough. But I don't feel like I'm me." More labored breaths. "Does that make any sense?"

She turned her head, searching for his reaction. Where before his responses were quick and resolute, not giving space for her wavering, silence now lingered. A silence she both appreciated and feared.

The pounding of their feet against the pavement thumped in her ears. Had she said too much? Did she freak him out?

A deep breath from Landon. "What is it you need? How can I help?"

The wind escaped her lungs. Had she heard him right? Now Miranda stopped. "Let's walk back. I can't keep up this pace any longer." In all their years together, any talk of personal development came in the form of Landon and his career goals. The moves. School. The extra projects and promotions all centered around his fulfillment. His growth.

Hers was assumed.

Now, with the question lingering between them, with the opportunity to give voice to her years of yearnings—she drew a complete blank.

"That's just it." She might as well let him in on the whole mess of her guilt-induced thoughts. "I don't know what I want. I feel guilty that I want something more. I have no right . . . I wish I could be content with where I am here and now."

She paused and considered the absurdity of what fought to come out. He knew about her Peace Corps experiences and her frustration with the extreme unfairness of life in various parts of the world.

When Miranda opened her lips again, the words tumbled out. "When I was in Niger, I had enthusiasm and energy, and I worked hard at any task they gave me. But, at that point in my life, I didn't have a skill set to make any real difference. I promised myself I would dive into my classes to learn how to design and build a pump that would get them water, right in their village. Years later, when Sydney told me they had made a working prototype of my pump, I dreamed of moving it forward more, refining it, and taking it to Niger. To my village."

As they walked home, Miranda stole a glance toward Landon. Would he laugh right alongside her inner critic? The lawyer in him produced the perfect poker face.

She turned her head. There it was, almost imperceptible, but there. The tiny tilt of his head . . . his tell. He was processing her words. Listening to understand, not to form a rebuttal or a cross examination.

How could Mindy have known he was ready?

Miranda plunged ahead. "Since then, life moved into fast forward. Now, here I am, almost twenty years down the road, feeling guilty."

He tilted his head toward her, his eyebrows raised. "Why guilt?"

"Because I made an empty promise. I haven't done a thing to help. And now, with my role as a mom, I'm stuck. Trying to make good on the promise now would steal my focus from the kids. If I zero in on the kids, then I'll never get to the promise. Either way I turn, I find guilt." The building tension within spurred her feet to walk faster.

His response again surprised her. "Honey, guilt won't help you achieve anything. You need to let it go and decide what you want. I'm here. I can watch the kids to give you chunks of time. I didn't know this was so important to you. Would finishing your degree help?"

Now Miranda's stride faltered as her eyes grew wide. "Are you serious?" She hadn't mentioned that since their talk months ago. "Do you think that could be an option?" Her pulse quickened, as did her pace. "I mean, yeah, I'd love to do that . . . But I'm not sure now is the right—"

"No *buts*. If it's something you want to do, then go for it. We'll figure things out. The kids will be fine. I'm sure programs have online options now. You can work out a schedule that'll let you go at your own pace. If you don't start now, the time will pass. At the end of it, you can either have a degree or still be wishing you did."

Her heart threatened to burst from her chest. Once on board with an idea, Landon became a bulldozer, not letting anything get in the way. He surveyed the path to any dream in the same way—set a goal, list the steps to get there, and make it happen. That quality had helped him rise to the top of his class and then to become one of the best lawyers in the Midwest. Perhaps she could channel some of that drive to move into her next steps.

As they rounded the corner to their house, the sun rays poked over the horizon, shedding a new light on the day ahead. Miranda soaked in the beauty of the brilliant blues, reds, and oranges as her mind moved through the possibilities. "The more I think about it, the more I like that plan. I could still do a type of the drill as my project. I'll check into programs this week."

By the time they walked in the back door, an excited energy surged through Miranda. A spring filled her steps as she climbed up the stairs to the shower. She got ready for the day without one glance at the clock to mentally count the hours until she could crawl back into bed.

She made a list for the day. Drop off dry cleaning. Sign the girls up for the next session of swim lessons. Search for mechanical engineering programs. A warmth surged through her along with a smile she couldn't contain. She'd check with her alma mater to see if any of her credits were still viable. Perhaps they could help her finish what she'd started there so many years ago.

She surveyed the room. Vacuuming . . . done, room clutter . . . cleaned. The house stood poised to welcome the Mom of the Year committee today. Perhaps she'd even tell them her newly formed plans. Surely there were bonus points in the portfolio for education.

Miranda greeted her children with newfound enthusiasm. No fake "happy mom" smile today. She basked in the moment, genuinely interested in their lives, their dreams from the previous night, and their talk of the day's activities to come. Somehow, regaining a sliver of her personal identity helped her embrace her role as mother.

Miranda poured pancake batter on the griddle for Olivia and Isabella and reveled in their early morning chatter. She wouldn't pester Brendon yet. He could sleep in today.

While giving a detailed narrative of her dream, Olivia stopped and rubbed her forehead. "Mom, I have a headache."

Olivia rarely complained of pain. Miranda touched the back of her hand to Livvy's head. It felt a little warm, but nothing alarming.

"Let's see if eating helps. If not, I'll get some medicine for you. How does that sound?" Miranda touched her daughter's forehead once more. She had to stave off anything that could be hitting Olivia. It would be sad for her to miss out on a day of summer fun.

Some of her concern rose for a different reason, however. If she stayed home with a sick Olivia, she'd miss her bench time with Mindy tomorrow. She grimaced. So many things to tell the woman . . . her talk with Landon, the prospect of going back to school and, most of all, her internal drive reviving.

Go get the medicine now.

The thought came so clearly, Miranda turned to Olivia. "What did you say, honey?"

Olivia, sprinkling chocolate chips on the cooking pancakes, didn't respond.

"Livy, did you say something?" Miranda asked a little louder.

Olivia turned toward her. "What, Mommy?"

"Nothing. Those chocolate chip pancakes look delicious." She brushed the thought aside.

Go get the medicine now.

Again it came with such force that she searched to see who spoke. She turned back to the girls, but they were occupied. They hadn't said anything.

Get it now.

Miranda handed the spatula to Olivia. "Do you want to flip the pancakes? I'm going to get some medicine for you, in case your head-ache doesn't go away."

"I wanna do one!" Isabella climbed onto the counter, not about to be left out of any kitchen action, no matter how tricky the maneuver.

"Okay, Izzy, you can flip two, then let Livy flip the last three." Miranda headed up the stairs.

Her unplanned urgency confused her as she opened the medicine cabinet in her bathroom. She shifted through the various bottles of medicine, hunting for the pain reliever.

When she lifted the bottle of Tylenol, the familiar shake of the pills was gone. *That's weird. I just bought this last week, why would it be emp—*

In one gasp, Miranda's world stopped spinning.

Her hand trembled as the empty bottle dropped to the floor with a dull, echoing thud. Her heart fell to her feet as she raced into Brendon's bedroom and flipped on the light.

There, face down, vomit dripping off the side of the bed, lay her pale, listless son.

A sound pierced the air, a primal horrified screaming as she rushed to Brendon and tried to revive him. Olivia and Isabella both came running to the room. The horrific sound was coming from her own internal pain and disbelief, exploding out her throat.

"No, no, no! Not this! Not you!" Miranda shook her limp boy. "Brendon, wake up. Wake up honey. Please wake up!" She flipped him onto his back, shaking him more.

No response.

"Mommy!" Olivia cried as she entered the doorway. "What's happening? Mommy? What's wrong with Brendon?"

The question snapped Miranda back to her senses. "Brendon is really sick. I need you to please get my phone and dial 911. Can you do that for me, baby? Bring my phone to me as fast as you can." Miranda couldn't keep the shaking terror out of her voice. Olivia pivoted and disappeared.

"Mommy, what's wrong with Brendon?" Terror filled Isabella's wide eyes.

"He's sick." She had to get Isabella away from the room. "Could you go brush your teeth and get dressed? Could you do that for me please?"

Isabella cocked her head. "But we didn't eat breakfast yet."

Breakfast. The pancakes.

"I have a special job for you. Could you please go to the kitchen and unplug the griddle? Then take the pancakes off and start eating, okay, honey? Run fast."

As Isabella scurried out, Olivia returned with the phone. Miranda took it and heard the operator. "What's your emergency?"

"It's my son." Miranda couldn't finish before the tears and cries made her voice incoherent. Between sobs, she said, "I think he overdosed. Please send someone now. I can't get him to wake up. There's vomit. He won't open his eyes."

The dispatcher calmly said, "The ambulance is on its way. We have a GPS lock on your phone, but could you confirm the address for me?"

As if speaking through a fog, Miranda's lips somehow formulated their address.

"That's great, thank you. What's your name?"

Still shaking Brendon to wake him up, she mumbled her name.

"Okay, Miranda. I need you to do something for me. I want you to put the phone on speaker and set it down. Then I want you to get in close to your son and look, listen, and feel for any sign of breathing."

At this prompting, Miranda's CPR training from years ago kicked in. She moved into the preliminary actions. As she got close to Brendon, she could see his chest rise and fall. Shallow, but there, the slow movement allowed precious oxygen into his body. *Praise God. Please, God!*

"Yes, he's breathing. I can see his chest moving."

"That's a great sign, Miranda. Would you like me to stay on the line with you until the ambulance gets there? They're two minutes away."

The question wouldn't process. Then, somehow, her brain kicked into gear. She spied her daughter standing in Brendon's doorway. "Olivia, I need you to go downstairs and open the front door. When the ambulance pulls up, bring the people straight up here. Then get Isabella and go next door. Ask Mrs. Jones if you two can stay at her house for a little while. Tell her Brendon's sick and needs to go to the hospital right now. Can you do that for me, sweetheart?"

Olivia nodded and headed downstairs while Miranda turned back to the phone. "I'm okay, I need to call my husband."

She hung up and dialed Landon's number. When he answered, her sobs overtook her words.

"Miranda, what's wrong?"

"It's Brendon . . . pills . . . overd—" Her throat strangled the rest of the word. After a couple ragged breaths, she managed to add, "Please meet us at the hospital." She couldn't control her sobs again.

"I'm on my way. I'll meet you there."

She dropped the phone and shook her son again, willing him to open his eyes.

The paramedics flew in like a whirlwind. They scooped up Brendon and placed him on the gurney in seconds. As they rushed him to the back of the ambulance, one of them turned to Miranda. "Would you like to ride with your son or drive and meet us there?"

She turned to climb in. "I'm not leaving my son."

Olivia ran back from next door. "Mommy, Mrs. Jones isn't home. What should we do?"

Miranda's stomach dropped. Before she could process her options, the new neighbor, Elizabeth, appeared around the open ambulance door. "I thought you might need some help." Without waiting for a con-firmation from Miranda, she turned to Olivia and Isabella. "Hey girls, would you like to come and play at my house for a while? I got some new toys for my grandkids, but I need someone to test them out first."

Olivia looked from Elizabeth to Miranda.

Sometimes angels wore jeans and T-shirts. "You have no idea how heaven-sent you are right now. Thank you."

She turned back to the girls. "You two go with Miss Elizabeth, okay? You know the house—the one Jess used to live in."

At Olivia's still-panicked expression, Miranda pulled her in for a hug. "Things will be fine, honey. Don't worry, everything will be fine." She hoped she sounded more convincing to Olivia than her shaky voice sounded to herself.

She mouthed one last *thank you* to Elizabeth and jumped into the ambulance. The doors slammed shut, and they sped toward the hospital.

Chapter Thirteen

"How many pills were in the bottle?" Though the nurse stood no more than two feet away from Miranda, her voice sounded distant and muffled.

Miranda shook her head, numb. "I'm n-not sure, it was almost new." The barrage of questions highlighted Miranda's inadequacies. No, she didn't know if there were other pills involved. She hadn't checked any other pill bottles. No, she didn't know what time it happened. They'd all gone to bed around nine-thirty the night before, and, no, nothing seemed out of the ordinary. It had been a quiet night. There was no telling what time Brendon might've opened the medicine cabinet. Yes, he'd been having some rough times lately, but nothing that should've made him want to end his life. Each answer wrapped around her lungs like a crushing python, stealing her breath.

The hospital staff ushered Miranda back to the waiting room while they worked to revive Brendon. She was nearly there when Landon burst through the doors and ran toward her. When he reached her, she collapsed into his arms. Despair clenched her chest prohibiting the release of the screams that clogged her throat.

He held her tight. "Everything's going to be okay. We'll get through this, no matter what happens. We'll handle it together."

Miranda's torrent of emotions boiled over. "How could I not know? How could I be so out of tune with my own son, that I couldn't see—" Her sobs forbade her to continue.

"You can't let yourself go there. I didn't see it coming either. We can't beat ourselves up, or we'll be in no shape to help him."

"What if he doesn't survive?" Miranda's deepest fear bubbled to the surface. "Please tell me he'll make it."

As if on cue, the doctor rounded the corner to the waiting room. "Are you Brendon's parents?"

They rushed to him, Miranda's heart beating out of her chest.

"We've stabilized him. Physically, he'll be okay. We're giving him activated charcoal to absorb any of the drug still in the GI tract. He's also receiving N-acetylcysteine, called NAC, for short." He put his hands in the pocket of his white lab coat. "It's the antidote to the poisoning effect of the acetaminophen overdose on the liver. He shouldn't sustain any prolonged liver damage, but we'll monitor his enzymes to be sure."

His words were a jumbled, far off warble. Her heart pulsed in her eardrums and drowned out his voice. "How is he? Is he awake?" Many more questions fought for attention, but only those emerged.

"He's coming in and out of consciousness. We've given him the NAC through his IV. When he wakes up, we can discontinue that and give the remaining doses by mouth. If he isn't willing, we can discuss other options."

"How long will he need to stay here? How long does the medication take?" Miranda found a voice for the multitude of questions swirling around in her head.

"The dosing lasts from twenty-four to forty-eight hours. Then we'll do some follow up tests to confirm his body systems are returning to normal. He'll need to stay at least three days for observation. After some evaluations, we'll have a family meeting and take it from there. He may need more time either here, or in the adjoining mental health facility."

He met Miranda's eyes, then Landon's. "Don't worry. We'll take good care of Brendon and equip you with what you need to help him at home once he's ready to leave."

"Thank you so much, Doctor," she said. "Thank you for—" The lump returned to her throat.

Landon put his arm around her. "Thank you for saving our son's life. He, and we, owe you everything." His voice cracked and his arm pulled Miranda closer.

"You're welcome." The doctor shook Landon's hand and turned to Miranda. "You're the one who got him here in time. I applaud your ability to act quickly."

Praise. The last thing Miranda deserved at this moment. She smiled anyway.

"If you'll excuse me, I'll go check on him. He should be more alert within the next half hour or so. It'd be good for you to be with him when he wakes up." He patted Landon's shoulder and squeezed Miranda's hand, then pivoted and disappeared around the corner.

Miranda and Landon were perched at Brendon's side when he opened his eyes. He blinked and scanned the room, eyes wide.

Miranda lurched forward. "Brendon, you're in the hospital. We're here, honey. We love you."

He squinted at her, then Landon. His gaze spanned the room again, and his forehead wrinkled.

"You're alive," she said. "You're in the hospital."

He rotated toward them and opened his mouth, then clamped it shut.

She grabbed his hand. "What is it, honey?"

He flopped his head back onto the pillow and stared at the ceiling.

If she left the room, perhaps Landon could get through to him. "I'm going to step out for a bit."

She wandered the halls in a daze and ended up at the cafeteria, where she sunk into a corner chair. The aroma of cooking meat and the pungent metallic tang of the antiseptic hospital smell swirled together, making Miranda's empty stomach lurch. She closed her eyes against the nausea, taking deep breaths in an effort to calm her stomach . . . and her soul.

The minutes ticked by and the hospital staff went about their day, so normal and happy. She fought the urge to stand up and scream at them.

For what? For doing their job? For living their lives as if hers hadn't been flipped upside down?

In a heartbeat, everything was different. How could her family move forward from this?

How was she supposed to act toward Brendon? Normal? As if nothing had happened?

The last thing he'd want would be to be treated with kid gloves.

But how could she not? She'd almost lost him. Nausea washed over her again.

She almost lost her little boy.

Wasn't it only yesterday that the nurse had laid that precious baby boy in her arms? His first steps, first lost tooth, and his carefree swinging in their backyard. These images played through her mind. Flying kites with Landon. Welcoming his two baby sisters with wonder in his eyes, so protective of them both.

What had she done to make his life go off course? How out of touch had she become to not even realize the depth of his depression?

Maybe she pushed him too hard. Did she say or do something to make him feel as if his life wasn't worth living, or that he'd never measure up? She had to keep this from happening again in the future. But how?

The park visits flashed before her. The talks with Mindy on the bench. Reaching for something more and starting to move in that direction.

How dare she.

This was her fault.

She'd taken her focus off her kids and put it on herself. She'd given in to this selfish idea that she should pursue her own life. Reality check 101: she was a mom. And failing miserably at her one job. If she couldn't help her own children master the hard times in life, how could she help anybody?

"Miranda?" Barbara, a woman from their congregation walked toward her carrying a lunch tray, dressed in a nurse's uniform. She cocked her head to the side as concern clouded her eyes.

Miranda clicked into Sunday smile mode. "Hey, Barb. Good to see you. I forgot you worked here." She commanded her voice to stay even. No need to rouse suspicion.

"Mind if I join you?" Not waiting for an answer, Barbara plopped her tray onto the table and dropped into the chair opposite Miranda. "What brings you here? Is everything okay?"

If Miranda stayed, she'd give something away. She had to get out. Fast. "Brendon had something he couldn't kick, so we brought him in for some tests is all. It looks like everything'll be fine." She scooted her chair back. "I should get back to him. It was great to see you. Say hi to your family for us." Before her cracking voice could give anything more away, Miranda stood, forced another smile, and scooted out of the cafeteria. The last thing they needed was to provide fodder for the church gossip train.

Later that day, Landon still at Brendon's side, Miranda slipped out to gather the girls and try to maintain some sort of normalcy for them.

She climbed Elizabeth's front steps, breathing in the aroma of the colorful flowers hanging from baskets on the porch. What a refreshing change from the harsh chemicals that had saturated the hospital. The bright blooms offered a ray of hope that had been absent in the dull gray corridors today. Jess had never grown flowers when she lived here. They added a nice pop to the porch. As Miranda reached for the doorbell, Elizabeth opened the door.

"I don't know how I can ever thank you enough for coming to our rescue today." What would she have done if Elizabeth hadn't shown up at that exact moment?

"Think nothing of it. I've loved having them here. How's your son?"

"He's doing okay."

Then, the pause.

For the explanation. Initial symptoms, what the doctors did for him, and the projected outcome.

Here, standing face to face with the lack of information lingering in the air, Miranda couldn't bring herself to admit the ugly truth.

On the outside, they projected a happy, upstanding family. A model family. Good citizens. Regular church attenders. Believers.

A structure ingrained in her from her earliest memories. Growing up, her own family projected the same perfection, even to one another.

Her mouth opened, ready to release the full story, but she clamped it shut. She couldn't admit the dark truth of what had happened within the walls of her own home.

"Brendon got very sick last night. We still don't know what caused it." A true statement. She honestly didn't know what had caused *it*. "Fortunately, he's stable now. The doctors said he'll make a full recovery."

"I'm so glad to hear that." If Elizabeth knew there was more to the issue—and how could she not, considering how Miranda had stammered through the carefully-crafted explanation—she made no hint of it. "I'm glad he'll be okay. The girls have been great. They both gave the thumbs-up on our toy stash for the grandkids."

Miranda smiled. *Thank you for changing the subject.* "If you have their approval, you're good to go. They can be tough toy critics."

Isabella popped around the corner. "Mommy!" She turned her head toward the hall. "Livy, Mommy's here." Then she ran into Miranda's outstretched arms. "Mommy, I like it here. They have fun toys. Funner than Auntie Jess's."

"Oh, really? They must be super toys." She set Isabella down. At least she could be easily distracted from the trauma. With one hand holding her bulging middle, Miranda started to lean down.

"Please, let me." Elizabeth gathered Isabella's shoes and bent to help her put them on. "I learned all about Auntie Jess and the fun games they played in this house. Izzy gave me a tour, and Livy provided a perfect description of the layout when they lived here. It sounds like they were well-loved by your family."

"They were pretty much an extension of us." Miranda scanned the interior of what had once been her second home. Her throat constricted. "The girls spent almost as much time roaming these halls as they did ours. I'm sorry if they acted like they owned the place."

Elizabeth patted Isabella's curls. "Oh, no, they've been wonderful." She eyed Miranda. "In fact, I'm trying a new recipe tonight, and I'd love to get their seal of approval before my grandkids come next month. Would it be possible for them to stay for dinner? I'm sure you want to get back to the hospital for a while yet today. I can get them fed and settled in with a movie. They're welcome to stay as late as you'd like."

Olivia came around the corner as Elizabeth finished. "Oooh, a late-over? Can we please stay for a late-over mom?"

Perfect. Keep Olivia focused on this. Maybe she won't ask about Brendon. She nodded to Olivia, then faced Elizabeth. "Thank you so much. That would be a huge help." She hugged each of the girls, then turned to go as they ran back down the hallway. She needed to get away before Olivia asked the real questions . . . the ones she wasn't ready to answer.

She took a few steps out the door, then stopped and slowly spun. "I . . . I'm sorry I haven't been very welcoming—"

"What are you talking about? You're a busy mom with an over-flowing plate. You don't have to be the president of the welcoming committee on top of that. Please don't give it another thought."

"I . . . it's been a bit of a struggle having my dear friend move away. This house holds so many memories for me. I guess it's hard to accept change." The hurt of losing Jess was still raw, and the words sounded shallow.

Elizabeth stepped onto the porch and put an arm around Miranda. "Losing someone you care about takes time to get over. You don't have to force anything. If you ever need a friend, I'm here."

Something in her tone, or touch, brought warmth and calmness to Miranda. "Thank you."

Miranda descended the porch steps, but Elizabeth called her back. "Oh, I almost forgot. Some women stopped by your house earlier."

The committee. Miranda closed her eyes and scrunched her lips. How would she ever explain this? She'd blown her chance before the process even started. What a fake.

She turned around. "I can't believe I forgot to call them. I was supposed to meet with some friends today."

Elizabeth smiled. "When they pulled up, I went over and explained that your son came down with something, and you needed to go get him checked out. They understood and said to have you call them to reschedule."

This woman had been way too kind to Miranda. "Thank you. That was so thoughtful of you. With everything that happened this morning, their visit completely slipped my mind. I'll call them right away."

Elizabeth nodded. "They said they were from the Mom of the Year committee. I told them they wouldn't find a better candidate than you. I wish you all the best with that."

"I . . . thank you . . . That was kind of you to say." The knot in Miranda's stomach tightened. *You would never have said that if you knew what went down today.*

Elizabeth waved her off. "I'm sure you want to get back to Brendon. The girls will be fine here. Don't worry about them. See you later tonight."

Miranda waved, then scurried to her house and grabbed a change of clothes and toothbrush for Brendon.

Before heading back, she pulled out her phone and dialed Penelope's number.

Voicemail. Phew. A minor miracle. She couldn't take any more prodding questions today. At the beep, she said, "It's Miranda. I'm so sorry about today. It's been pretty crazy around here. My son, Brendon . . . " *Keep it together. Do not let your voice shake.* She swallowed past the lump in her throat.

A small cough to cover the stammer.

"He . . . he wasn't feeling well this morning." Best to keep to the script Elizabeth told them. "We took him to the hospital, and they're still running tests. We hope he'll be home in a couple of days. I'd love to re-schedule something for next week. It might be easiest to coordinate via text." Yes, get this to text, so she wouldn't have to answer extra questions. "I'm so sorry again for today. Talk to you soon."

Sobs erupted as she clicked off the call. What was she doing? She was no Mom of the Year. She was the fraud of the year. And now she was lying to cover it up.

As she drove to the hospital, her temples throbbed. The girls would have more questions, especially when Brendon came home. How much should she tell them?

Izzy would be simple. Mercifully, *Brendon got really sick,* would satisfy her.

Olivia was more complicated. How much should Miranda divulge?

The foggy memory pulled Miranda back to her childhood. How old had she been? Seven? Ten? She couldn't remember. Unable to place a full time line of events, only bits and pieces flashed before her now. Her second-oldest brother, Samuel, got sick. Mom said he contracted a mysterious illness they couldn't figure out, so they rushed him to the hospital.

Once he got home, Mom seemed withdrawn and hollow. One night as Miranda wandered by her parents' bedroom, hushed tones filtered through their closed door. Chewing the inside of her cheek, Miranda crept closer to listen. She couldn't decipher much, but Dad said a word she didn't know, and she told herself she'd ask Mom about it later.

The following day, when Mom smiled again and the family resumed their regular routine, Miranda never asked what the word meant.

Now, decades later, the word shot through time and attacked her skull like a knife.

Suicide.

Miranda's return to Brendon's bedside was met with an icy stare. "How are you feeling?"

"Like I could use some more pills." His green eyes, harsh and unyielding, cut her to the core.

"Are you hungry at all? I could get someth—"

"No." He turned his gaze toward the window.

A knock on the door came to her rescue. A woman entered. "Hi, I'm Marie. I'm one of the social workers. Is now a good time?"

Miranda's phone binged. Another saving grace. "Please come in. I'm Miranda, Brendon's mom." She moved toward the door. *Please let this woman get through to Brendon.* "I'll step out and let you two talk."

She stepped into the hallway and checked the text. Penelope. *Phew.* The conversation was moving to text. *Got your message. No worries. I hope Brendon feels better. I leave for vacation tomorrow. Back in 2 weeks. Let's meet then.*

Good. That would give her time to get their family out of crisis mode.

Who was she kidding? She couldn't go through with this contest. They'd see right through her.

Miranda stayed outside the room but glued her ear to the cracked doorway. One glorious, beautiful sound reverberated through their muffled voices.

Brendon's laugh.

A short burst that left almost as fast as it came. But it had come. How long had it been since she'd heard that sound? If she couldn't get through to Brendon, at least someone could. *Thank you, Lord. Thank you for sending Marie. And thank you for letting me hear his laugh.* A spark of light on this dark day.

A few minutes later, Marie walked out as Landon rounded the corner holding a bag with dinner. The three of them found chairs at the end of the hallway.

"Mr. and Mrs. Williams, you have a great son." Marie shuffled some papers on her lap. "He's going through some deep struggles right now. We'll do more evaluations over the next two days, which will help us develop a plan of action."

She explained the options and recommended a counselor named Sarah Roberts. "Brendon said he's willing to see her when he's discharged. That's a positive sign. It'd be a good idea for you two to see Sarah as well. She can be a valuable resource."

"Thank you so much. You've been an angel sent for us today. Especially Brendon." Miranda shook her hand as they stood.

Landon extended one arm as he placed the other around Miranda. "Yes, thank you for all your help."

As they neared the room, Miranda examined Landon. Behind his smile, his eyes told the truth. He shared her fear.

Please, let the counseling help.

Chapter Fourteen

Would dinner conversation ever return to normal? Would any conversation be normal again? The clanks of the forks against the white glass plates covered the silence in the breaks of Olivia and Isabella's banter. Thank goodness for chatty girls. They carried the family through Brendon's first night home.

Brendon finished before anyone and scooted his chair back.

Miranda's stomach dropped. He couldn't go upstairs. Not yet. She couldn't let him be alone. Not in that room. "Hey, how about we play a game together? How about some Uno?" He used to love that game. At their family meeting during his stay in the hospital, the therapist had counseled them to find activities to keep Brendon occupied. "Come on, it'll be fun." Her forced cheeriness did little to calm the raging waves within.

He eyed her, probably seeing right through her poor acting abilities, and shrugged. "Yeah, okay, I guess."

The knot in Miranda's stomach loosened. Uno for the win.

Olivia scurried to the basement and retrieved the cards while the others cleaned up the kitchen. They then gathered around the coffee table in the family room. Olivia grabbed each card as it was dealt. "Are we doing uno or dos this round?" A couple years ago, Brendon randomly started saying "Dos" when someone was down to two cards, instead of waiting for the traditional one card call. They'd fought him on it at first, but somehow it stuck, and they'd played the "dos" version occasionally since.

Miranda shot a glance in Brendon's direction. Not even a smile. She coughed, trying to dislodge the lump in her throat while getting his attention.

Brendon didn't look up from organizing the cards in his hand.

Maybe forcing him to stay was a mistake. Miranda forced the smile back to her mouth. "Let's just do it the normal way tonight."

As the round unfolded, the girls laughed as Landon joked with them. Brendon slumped on the couch flicking cards toward the pile without a word.

The pit returned to Miranda's stomach. At least he was here. But he wasn't . . . not fully. This was not how she envisioned their first night home together. She was trying too hard, and pushing him away. She should let him go. Clearly, he was miserable in the middle of this coerced family time.

Green six. Miranda laid it down, calculating the route to a possible victory as she studied the wild card and yellow three remaining in her hand.

"Dos."

"Huh?" It took a beat for the word to register. Miranda gaped at Brendon. Nothing had changed in his body position. But the corner of his lip lifted as he half laughed. Then he put on an overtly serious face. "I'm sorry, miss, but you're gonna have to draw two cards."

Miranda's breath hitched before she joined in the girls' giggles. Humor. Small, but there. Maybe they could walk through this after all.

Brendon only lasted one more round, then excused himself and made his way up the stairs. Every mother instinct in her screamed to chase him down and force him to stay with the pack, where she could keep a watchful eye on him. She paused as the cards for the next round were passed out. Should she follow him upstairs? Dig deeper to get him to talk? In the hospital conferences he hadn't given much by way of answers as to what was behind his despair. The counselor told her not to push, but to remain open and let him know she was willing to listen when he was willing to talk.

So easy to say. Much harder to carry out.

A swoosh of warmth blew past Miranda's face filling her nose with the essence of chocolate as she closed the oven door and set two more minutes on the timer. Mom's voice echoed in her memory. "If important guests are coming, bake a cake. The aroma creates a cozy and inviting atmosphere." Today's guests could help her reclaim some semblance of self-worth. The timing of the rescheduled visit worked out perfectly. With Brendon at a counseling session and the girls playing at a friend's house, nobody would expose Miranda's great failure.

Miranda surveyed the rooms. The clutter cleaned, the corners dusted, and the kids' artwork displayed on the craft room wall. She stopped in front of the two-year-old family picture—back when they were all so . . . normal. It'd been three weeks since the *event.* A week since Brendon returned home, and she found herself checking on him multiple times during the nights. Would the fear ever go away?

Her shoulders slumped. How could she go through with this? After the epic failure of mothering, how could she hope to portray herself as any sort of Mom of the Year?

Wait. If she remembered right, if her brother Samuel had attempted suicide so long ago, that would've been before Mom won Mom of the Year. Maybe she had a chance after all. Mom did it. So could she.

The doorbell jolted her to attention. *Here goes nothing.* She took a deep breath, squared her shoulders, and opened the door.

"Hello, Miranda." Penelope stepped into the freshly mopped foyer, followed by two other women. "What a beautiful house."

Penelope pointed to the red-haired woman who wore a knee-length linen dress the same color green as the specks in her eyes. "This is Gabriella, and I think you already know Sheila." Seriously? Sheila was on the committee? And they were still considering Miranda? She must not have noticed the eye roll when Izzy and Zack duked it out at playgroup. *Please, let that be true.*

Miranda pasted on her best smile. "Sheila. Hi." Why did her voice lift an octave? She extended her hand to the other girl. "Hi, Gabriella. It's so nice to meet you."

Gabriella extended her perfectly manicured hand. "It's so great to meet you. Penelope and Sheila told me you're a great candidate. I'm excited to talk with you."

Great candidate? Sheila said that? *Smile. Act natural.* "That's so kind of you to say." Too kind. If only they knew, they'd . . . well, they wouldn't be having this conversation. "Thank you so much for rescheduling this meeting. I'm sorry about being gone last time." *Please don't ask anything.*

"No problem at all. How's your son—Brendon, right? How's he feeling? Did they ever figure out what was wrong?" Penelope smoothed her long chestnut hair.

"He's much better, thank you for asking." *Keep smiling.* "They're still working on a few things, but we're confident he'll make a full recovery." Why did she sound so much like her mother?

Miranda hurried them to the family room. "Please, have a seat. Would you like anything to drink? We have water, various juices, and Izzy's favorite, strawberry milk." Oh no, should she have admitted that she gives her daughter milk with all that sugar?

Amid murmured *no thank you*'s, Penelope smiled. "We won't take too much of your time." She handed Miranda some papers. "I know we gave you some of last year's requirements, but these have recently been updated, so we can spend a few minutes getting on the same page."

As they worked through the list of requirements, Miranda smiled and answered the questions. Oh, she knew the right answers. They were the same ones her mother gave throughout the years to so many people. It was easy . . . too easy . . . to let her mother's fictitious answers flow through her own lips.

They reached requirement ten. *The mother should show her success through the characteristics and achievements of her child/children.* Miranda's heart jumped to her throat. The words indicted Miranda, refusing to release her attention. A heaviness descended and threatened to extinguish her smile.

Characteristics and achievements of her children? She could never complete this form without either lying or disqualifying herself.

When the visit ended, Miranda commanded her leaden feet to move as she escorted the ladies to the door. Every step seemed slow and cumbersome. Surely one of them would notice.

Keep smiling.

Miranda forced herself to focus on Gabriella's words. "It's been so lovely to visit with you." Gabriella leaned in for a hug. *Don't let her sense anything.*

Sheila also leaned in for a hug. "We look forward to the nomination process. Once you've filled out the forms, we'll go through them to make any necessary additions." She waved away Miranda's questioning face. "People are normally bashful about tooting their own horn. That's where we come in. We can help make you look better than you ever thought possible." She flipped her chestnut hair and winked.

Oh, I'm sure you'd find your match trying to put a positive spin on me. Miranda laughed and smiled back. "I need all the help I can get."

Penelope pointed to the stack of papers in Miranda's hand as she stepped out the door. "All of our phone numbers are on the first page. Please call us with questions. Thanks again for letting us visit your beautiful home."

Miranda sloped into the door as she waved good-bye. The weight crushing her threatened to buckle her legs. As they drove away, she heaved a sigh and closed the door with a thud. Pressing her back against it, Miranda sank to the floor. What just happened? Her chest constricted. An ache settled in her shoulders. The pit in her stomach would rival the Grand Canyon.

Was this the cost of hiding the ugly truth from the world and wearing the happy face mask? Mom did it so flawlessly. Flowing conversations. Ever-present smile.

In a flash, the image of David putting on the king's armor took center stage in her mind. Was this how it felt to wear someone else's armor?

She shook her head, clearing away the haze. *That's it. I'm trying to be someone I'm not.* She replayed the conversation she'd just had. So fake. All of it.

Papers in hand, Miranda wandered to the kitchen table and slumped in a chair. She reviewed the list of requirements. Should she go through with it?

The door opened, and Landon strolled in with Brendon. "Hey, honey. How was your day?" He kissed her on the cheek.

She smiled at him. "It was good. The girls should be home any minute now. They're playing at Emily's house."

"Both of them?"

"Izzy wanted to tag along, and Olivia said it was fine, so I let them both go." She studied Brendon. "How was your session?"

He made his way to the fridge and opened it. "It was okay. What's for dinner? I'm starving."

She took the hint and swallowed the rest of her questions. At least he stayed downstairs. Baby steps.

He grabbed a handful of grapes and meandered to the table. "What's that?" He motioned toward the portfolio papers.

"Nothing . . . a popularity contest for moms. Some women wanted me to do it, but it's not me." As she said the words out loud, the weight lifted from her shoulders.

He shifted the papers and read some of the requirements. *Please don't notice number ten.* "Mom, you should do this. You do all of these things."

Miranda blinked. Did he just give her a compliment? *Keep it together. Don't turn into a bumbling idiot in front of your son. Act cool.* She shrugged. "I'm not sure . . . I don't have the time, and it doesn't matter that much." She'd won something greater than any committee could give her. Her son had complimented her.

Brendon returned to the fridge for more grapes.

Miranda stood, papers in hand. "Is there anything you two are craving for dinner? I haven't started anything yet. We have stuff to make—"

"Let's go out for dinner," Landon said. "A new Mexican place opened. The guys at work said it's a total dive, but the food's amazing."

A half smile played on Brendon's lips. "That sounds good. Can we do that, Mom?"

Oh, how she'd missed that smile. Small, but there. And to have him willingly sit with the family in a place where he couldn't gulp down his food and escape to his room? She'd take that any day.

"Hmm, let me see. No cooking and no dishes. I suppose that would be okay. As soon as the girls get back, we can head out."

Miranda glanced at the application. She'd think about that later. She shoved it into the junk drawer. She was going to dinner with her family. And her son was excited about it. Validation that really mattered.

The girls burst through the door, dripping wet. "Mommy! We played water fight." Isabella always raised the decibel level a couple octaves when she returned from a play date.

Olivia charged in, filling in the details. "It was so much fun. We filled up water balloons and got into teams—Daddy!" She ran to Landon, arms open for a hug.

He did a quick catch and release. "Easy there, my wet one. We're going out to eat. Run and change clothes so we can leave."

She turned to Miranda. "Do we get to go out?" Upon Miranda's nod, Olivia fist pumped the air. "Water fight and dinner at a restaurant? Best. Day. Ever." She scurried up the stairs.

Miranda followed to help Izzy get cleaned up.

Her youngest chatted as they picked out an outfit. "We splashed in the water, and played and threw balloons. I got so wet. Then we saw a butterfly. Like that one at the park. Do you remember that one, Mommy? That big, big one?"

Miranda stopped short while putting Isabella's shirt over her head. The park. The bench.

The visits with Mindy had come to an abrupt end. How long had it been?

No. No more of those selfish indulgences. If Brendon's attempt had taught her anything, it was that now was not the time for her to try to *find herself.* Besides, Mindy would be long gone by now. Miranda had put the talks out of her mind completely.

Almost.

A spark inside had ignited, and try as she might, she couldn't douse the flame. The embers smoldered, begging to be brought to life.

But those dark days in the hospital loomed over her like a storm, threatening to extinguish any flicker that dared approach the surface.

———

July 21st brought a heat wave to Bridgetown—and Brendon's fifteenth birthday. A stray tear slipped down Miranda's cheek as he blew out his candles. This could've been a very different day.

After she and Landon settled into bed that night, Brendon's head poked into the doorway.

"Mom? Dad? Are you still awake?"

Miranda and Landon shot up, and she flipped on the lamp. "Absolutely, honey, what do you need?"

He dropped his gaze as he shifted between his feet. When he lifted his head again, his watery eyes danced in the lamplight. "I wanted to say thank you. You know, for not giving up on me. And sorry for causing so much stress in the family over the past few months."

Miranda's heart simultaneously leaped and broke. "Honey, don't apologize. I'm the one who's sorry. I failed you when you needed support the most."

"You didn't fail me. I failed myself. And I failed you both."

"Brendon." Landon leaned forward. "You didn't fail anybody." He gripped Miranda's arm and met her eyes just long enough for her to see the love there. "Nobody's failed here. As long as we keep trying each day, we won't fail, not in the long run. We'll never give up on you. Not ever. You don't have to do anything to prove your worth. We love you the way you are here and now. I want you to understand that, deep inside your soul."

"Yeah. Okay. That's . . . Well, I'd better . . . " His head disappeared from the doorway.

Miranda's mouth dropped open as Landon slid his hand down her arm and threaded their fingers together.

"Well, that was big." Landon broke the silence between them.

"There were so many things I wanted to say. But I didn't want to overwhelm him. I'm not sure how to handle this." Miranda shifted to face Landon. Should she bring it up? She had to. "Did I ever tell you about a time when Samuel was in the hospital with a mysterious illness?"

Landon paused for a moment. "Not that I remember."

She pieced through the jumbled bits in her mind, including the word she'd heard—and forgotten for so long—from her parents' room.

"I think Samuel tried to end his life. I mean, I don't have any proof, and my family hasn't said a word about it since it happened."

Landon smirked, eyes rolling. "That's a shocker. Heaven forbid anyone in your family communicate about tough issues."

"Honey." Miranda's voice lowered. "I know my family hasn't been the best at communicating, especially around—"

"Your family has so many skeletons in the closet they could outfit an entire haunted house." Landon dropped her hand and pushed back against the headboard. "All in the name of protecting the great Johnson legacy."

Miranda shot him a warning look. "Okay, I get it. Not the best at being open. But that's not the focus here."

"I know, I'm sorry." Landon's shoulders drooped. "But . . . suicide? They'd brush that under the rug and not at least talk to you about it?"

"I was so young, not much older than Izzy. And we haven't exactly told the girls everything, either. Outside the counselor's office, we haven't even talked with Brendon about it." She motioned toward the doorway where their son had stood moments ago. "I walk on eggshells around him, not sure what to say or how to say it. Do I tell other people about it?"

Landon shifted in his spot. "Will Brendon feel like we're belaboring the situation if we keep talking about it?"

"I don't know. If I bring it up with anyone, will he feel betrayed? It's such a weird position to be in. If Samuel did try to end his life, I understand why Mom would hesitate to discuss it."

"Have you ever talked to Samuel about it?"

Miranda rocked back. "Are you kidding? Don't get me wrong, I'd love to call and ask him what happened. Ask if it was a suicide attempt, and, if so, how he moved on. But how do you broach that subject? We never get past talking about the weather and the kids when we're at reunions." Heat crept up Miranda's neck. "That type of conversation would rock our family dynamics for sure. Jeremy won't even hint about what they want to discuss in August."

"How about in August you get some answers? In the meantime, like Sarah said in the last session, we walk forward with Brendon and the girls. Be here for whatever step Brendon's ready to take."

Her heart warmed at Landon's "march forward" attitude. He was her life raft, keeping her afloat. Now more than ever. Miranda turned out the light, and they settled into bed. They had a long road with Brendon ahead of them, but tonight's conversation was nothing short of miraculous. Small though it was, she'd witnessed a breakthrough.

Breakthrough. Obstacles turned into stepping-stones. Miranda combed through her last visit with Mindy. Could this experience possibly lift Brendon, and their entire family, to a higher plane?

Chapter Fifteen

The first of August dawned hot and sunny and introduced the newest member of the Williams family to the world. Healthy and happy from the start, baby Ashton brought a much-needed light into their lives. Even Brendon surfaced from his room often to hold his little brother, bringing warmth and hope to Miranda's heart.

Of course, no one offered to hold Ashton in the wee hours of the morning. Had night feedings been this draining before, or was she getting too old to function on so little sleep?

But those moments also held a precious gift. Miranda had dismissed the warnings of the older women from church before, but each night she held Ashton a little longer, trying to etch this phase of his life into her forever memory bank . . . the season when he depended completely upon her for everything.

Miranda sat in the rocking chair next to his crib, holding this small miracle in her arms. Once he finished eating, she snuggled him and watched him drift to sleep, safe in her arms. She was his person. His protector. Right now, she was his everything. What a privilege and honor God had given her, to be the earthly guardian of this precious soul.

Maybe that's what Rose from church had been trying to communicate. Wasn't it just yesterday Miranda had rocked Brendon like this? Time melted away so quickly.

She studied her son, a finger outlining the arc of his eyebrows. A tear trailed down her cheek. What was she thinking searching for fulfillment outside her role as a mom? How selfish she'd been. There was no need to reach beyond what was already in front of her. She should—would—find it right here, in her role as a full-time mom.

———

The days blurred together as Ashton's midnight appetite continued. Her resolve to savor every second crumbled into craving one night of sweet, uninterrupted sleep. Until then, she searched for something, anything, to keep her brain occupied and her eyes open.

Something that could feed her soul while she fed Ashton. Perhaps a book.

As Miranda responded to her son's cries again, she grabbed her phone and searched through her audiobook library.

Beneath a Scarlet Sky. When had she downloaded that? It didn't matter. It was there, and it was new.

Ashton settled into his nursing position and Miranda put in her earbuds.

The book began with a peek into the life of the author. Less than five minutes into the preface, goose bumps erupted on Miranda's arm and a chill swept down her neck. She pressed the pause button to catch her breath. The man had come a hair's-breadth away from crashing his car . . . on purpose?

Suicide. There it was again. Was it that common? Or was she now hypersensitive to it? And he spoke about it so casually, in the same way one would talk about a dinner party. Would she, or Brendon, ever get to the point where they could discuss his . . . issue . . . as casually?

Listening to the preface, learning how great things turned out for the author, Mark Sullivan, Miranda's heaviness lightened ever so slightly. Perhaps this road with Brendon could take him to a new avenue.

The voice continued to describe Mark Sullivan's transformation. It hadn't been an overnight change. Writing the book had taken a decade filled with obstacles. In the end, however, he succeeded in bringing to light one of the world's greatest unsung heroes of World War II: Pino Lella.

Miranda pressed pause again and sat back, her mouth gaping. Mindy hadn't said anything about this part of the story. And yet, this tiny blurb from the author answered questions she hadn't even formulated the words to ask. Questions regarding Brendon's future. Would he ever be able to get through the dark clouds and move forward? Would they all be permanently wounded by this event in their lives?

She listened to the introduction again. With a heavy sigh, tension melted as hope seeped into the fissures of Miranda's soul. She closed her eyes and relished the moment. The author desired to be part of a story bigger than himself. In essence, he wanted a purpose—a vision for his life.

Mindy had once told her the number one correlation to youth having a vision for their life was close association with an adult who had a connection to their own purpose.

Had Miranda gone about this all wrong? Perhaps in hovering over Brendon and putting her own purpose aside, she'd sent him the wrong message. Could her best gift to him, as well as her other children, instead of being a martyr, be a model of living her own purpose? Such a small switch. Yet, at that moment, in the middle of the night, it seemed so right.

Miranda dove into the book. The life's work of Mark Sullivan had started at the lowest point of his life. The book transported her back in time where she could almost hear the bombs falling from the sky over Milan, Italy.

She triumphed with Pino as his purpose came alive while helping Jews over the vicious Alps to freedom in a new country. She despaired with him when the German army drafted him, at which point he thought his purpose had been thwarted.

When she got to the part where he was recruited as a spy for the allied forces, she grabbed her phone and shot a text to Jess. One of the few benefits of the time difference—she could text Jess in the middle of the night.

Jess, new book to read. Beneath a Scarlet Sky. Only partway in and I'm hooked.

The return from Jess came quickly. *You're the third person to recommend it. Gotta get a copy. It'll be a good break when we head to the field next week.*

Miranda's shoulders slumped. *You're leaving again?*

She should've taken Jess's offer to fly out when Miranda called her from the hospital with Brendon. Some Jess-time would have been the perfect medicine right now. *I was hoping you could come visit. Pictures of Ashton don't do him justice. You have to come see for yourself :)*

The return text popped up. *I wish I could. Steve got a field assignment to establish a refugee settlement in southern Greece. Everything's set for the book launch, so I'm going to help.*

Miranda typed, *Congrats again. I can't wait to see this one on the shelves.* Good thing text messages don't show body language. Jess would surely have seen the green surging through her.

Thanks again for your last review. Feels good to have the final edits finished. Now we wait for the launch date so I can head to the field.

Miranda couldn't give up quite yet. *Or you could make a quick jump across the pond? Maybe stay a couple of days, then be back in time to head out with Steve?*

Jess's reply popped up. *We have so much to get ready. More children than normal, so need to stock up on extra supplies and keep some semblance of childhood in their lives. So many are forced to grow up too fast.*

Miranda's thumbs typed before her brain could censor. *Spare me the lecture on childhood woes. I might be a lowly mom, but I do have experience with children, and even some on childhood trauma.* The last part she threw in to hit Jess with a pang of guilt, a reminder their own family could use some added support from their trusted friend.

The response from Jess was slow in coming. *I think you're tired and cranky. Maybe you should head to bed and get some rest.*

She was right, of course. Miranda's head throbbed from exhaustion. Which only served to loosen her carefully guarded gate of emotions.

Her fury flew through her fingertips. *Yes, sleep WOULD be nice. But I don't have that luxury. You wake from a full night's sleep every morning, skip around the world playing with kids, and then clock out. I stay up night after night, caring for one, taking care of his every need. There's no 'next shift' staff to come in and take over. In the morning, I dive into three other lives, helping them do more than just play games and draw pictures. I have to be there for them 24/7. No fancy title or pat on the back from some big organization. No clocking out. No breaks. Sleep is a luxury for me, not a given like it is for you.*

She paused. She couldn't send it. It was unfair and mean. She started backspacing.

Then again, who did Jess think she was? As if sleep would cure everything. Hot tears sprang to her eyes. Her thumb clicked the green arrow.

Even as she heard the swoosh, regret gnawed her stomach. She'd crossed a line.

The response was swift. *That's not fair, and you know it. You, more than anybody else, know our fertility struggles.*

Again, Miranda's fingers typed before her brain gained control. *You hardly tried. You stopped treatments.*

The reply scrolled onto the screen. *And you moved forward. We both chose our paths. I'm at peace with mine. It doesn't seem like you've come to terms with yours.*

Ugh. Jess always cut through Miranda's facades and got straight to the guts of the matter.

And she was right.

Again.

Steve and Jess had gone wide, caring for children all over the world. Miranda and Landon dove deep, caring for children within the walls of their home. Both were fulfilling a purpose in vastly different areas. Was one nobler than the other? Even through her midnight fog, she knew. She'd been horribly unfair to Jess.

She should apologize. She should step up and accept the too-close-to-home observation of her dear friend. Her thumbs hovered over the keyboard.

Ashton pulled back and cried. Miranda set the phone down and stood to burp and calm his cries with the mother sway. She yawned, exhaustion overtaking her. She craved sleep like an addict craves a needle. Jess would never get it.

Chapter Sixteen

Brendon fumbled with his seat belt as he sat next to Miranda on the plane. In the adjacent row, Isabella and Olivia fiddled with the cool gadgets and buttons around them. Miranda glanced at Landon, seated next to them, and smiled in response to his wink. She nursed Ashton to help his ears acclimate to the abrupt change in pressure during takeoff.

The plane lifted and turned its nose west. In a few short hours, they'd be in Idaho. Her home. Her farm. Jeremy and his family had moved in ten years ago to take care of Dad and, in the process, returned the farm to its former glory.

They'd pushed this visit off for too long. Miranda gazed out the window of the plane at the vast expanse of land between them and their destination. The seventeen hundred miles from Minnesota to Idaho prevented Miranda and Landon from regular visits.

More than a trip home, this offered a chance to reconnect with her roots. To feel her mom again. To get in touch with who she was, and to fully commit herself to who she needed to be—for her husband, for her girls, for her new baby. And especially for Brendon.

When the kids discovered the free movies on the monitor in front of them, they morphed into plane zombies and hardly made a peep for the three-hour flight. Miranda peeked at Brendon's movie choices. When he started his second Avengers movie, she also clicked on one.

Landon's mouth turned up at the corner. She turned to him, and he tilted his head toward her monitor.

"What?" she mouthed. He shrugged and smiled. It was no secret she wasn't a fan of fictitious superhero movies. But to have a conversation with her son, she would gladly sit through every boring movie ever made.

"Grandpa!" Olivia and Isabella burst from the car and ran to Miranda's dad, who rocked on the porch in his favorite chair. Though he could no longer stand on his own, he beamed and lifted his arms to receive them.

Brendon also ran to give his Grandpa a hug. "Hi, Grandpa. How's life on the farm?" Brendon's broad smile matched his upbeat tone. Miranda raised an eyebrow and exchanged a questioning glance with Landon. He shrugged.

Maybe this is what Brendon needs. What they all need.

Miranda allowed her feet to soak in the softness of the fresh cut grass. The giant oak tree in the back still towered over the two-story white brick home. The faded blue shutters on the windows now seemed sad and lonely, but they transported her back three decades to when the shutters were new and bright, matching her childlike outlook on life. To her right, she spied the shed, her second home. Hours spent there next to Dad, tinkering with any machine that needed fixing. Lilies in full bloom lined the front porch, beckoning her with their brilliant sprays of color. Miranda took a slow breath in. The scents of fresh dirt, growing potatoes, and aging wheat blended into a beautiful perfume—the essence of earth.

So good to be home.

"Hi, Dad." Miranda leaned down and hugged her frail father, careful not to squeeze too tight. The kids found their cousins and ran around the corner to the large backyard.

"The farm looks fantastic. You must still crack the whip behind the scenes." Miranda made an Indiana Jones whipping motion with her arm. Her dad had always run the farm with perfect precision, a trait Jeremy inherited. It was as beautiful as ever.

"Oh, you know me, a tyrannical master." His weak voice still rang with playful joy. Dad's reputation for being the kindest farm owner in all southern Idaho had also made him one of the most popular bosses for those searching for work in the grueling summer months. The work was hard, and he expected excellence. But he motivated his workforce, children and hired hands alike, through love and kindness rather than fear and anger. As Miranda studied his chocolate brown eyes, that same love and compassion shone through. She smiled at the memory.

He patted her hand. "You have your mother's smile. I've missed that smile . . . " Clouds appeared over the clarity, and he shook his head.

"Ah, daughter of mine. It's so good to see you. Thanks for coming all this way from . . . " His stare blanked, and he dropped his head into a shaky hand. "My mind's not so good anymore. I can't finish a sentence without losing the words I need."

"Dad." Miranda launched her forced cheerleader mode. "You look great. And the forgetting stuff? I say, embrace it. Now you have an excuse to forget things you always wanted to. By the time Easter comes around, you can hide your own Easter eggs." As the words came out, even to her, they sounded awkward and unnatural.

Despite her clumsy attempt at humor, he laughed. The laugh that filled Miranda's earliest memories. She smiled, then held out his grandchild. "I don't believe you've met our newest addition, Ashton Brent Williams."

Miranda's father teared as he held out his arms.

She placed the wide-eyed baby into them. "Landon and I want him to always remember his heritage. If he grows to be even half the man you are, his life will be a roaring success." Would this be the last time Dad's namesake would feel his touch? Her chest warmed with confirmation that all the coordination she and Landon had done to make this trip happen was worth it.

Tears flowed down his cheeks as she leaned in for a hug. "Oh, Miranda. You certainly know how to make an old man proud, even if I don't deserve it. I love you so much. I hope you always remember that."

"I'll never lose the roots you gave me, and I'll never forget the love you showered on everyone around you, including me." She held on for a moment longer, then backed up to take a picture.

"What's all the ruckus?" Jeremy bounded out the front door and scooped Miranda into a huge bear hug. "Hello, little sis," he whispered into her ear.

Then he shifted and hugged Landon. "It's been too long. We were beginning to think the crazy Midwest winter did you all in this time around. It looked like this year was brutal."

"More than you know." Miranda glanced at Landon, who agreed with a slight nod.

She pivoted toward the farm. "Jer, you and Rebecca have done an amazing job with this place. It's more beautiful than ever. How have you kept it up?"

"Technology's not just for gaming and social media. Did you know moving pipes is now done by an app?"

"What?" Miranda's eyes opened wide. Moving pipes, her most hated chore, involved manually hauling the heavy steel irrigation pipes up and down the long rows of crops. A dirty, massive job performed at the oddest hours of the day. "There's an app for that? How will this generation ever learn about the crippling labor it takes to get water to the crops?"

Jeremy laughed. He had Dad's laugh. "But it makes my job easier, and saves water too."

"You're the perfect choice to carry on Dad's legacy." Miranda hugged her big brother again.

Rebecca appeared in the doorway, wiping a wisp of chestnut hair away from her brown eyes. "Hello and welcome. Dinner's about ready. Come in, come in. It's way too hot to be standing around out here." She leaned in to hug both Miranda and Landon. "How was your flight? And drive? Did everything go okay?"

"Great. No issues at all." Miranda pulled back from the hug with a smile.

Landon gave Miranda a little squeeze. "You head on in, I'll help your dad."

"Oh man, Bec, here I thought your cooking couldn't get any better, yet you once again upped the bar." Landon patted his stomach as he leaned back in his chair.

"Rebecca's cooking might be the one thing keeping me alive at this point." Miranda's dad wore a satisfied smile as he surveyed the full table.

Miranda wagged a finger at him. "Dad, you have to stop all this talk about dying."

"When you get to be my age and most of your friends have already kicked the bucket, it becomes the main topic of conversation. Who's died, who's next, and who surprised us all by hanging on so long."

Miranda leaned back. He seemed to be waiting for the end to come.

Dad leaned in and patted her hand. "It's okay, honey. It's not as doom and gloom as it seems. I'll get to see your mom again." He paused, his gaze finding a picture of her on the wall. "I miss her."

Her chest constricted. "So do I, Dad. So do I."

As she got up and gave him a hug, Jeremy and Rebecca exchanged a glance.

"Who wants dessert?" Rebecca popped up and disappeared into the kitchen.

"I do!"

"Me too!"

"I want some!"

The kids, who'd been having their own conversation, flipped to attention.

"Did someone say dessert?" A lone figure appeared in the dining room. "If my nose is right, Mom's apple pie's on the menu."

Miranda simultaneously jumped and shrieked at the familiar voice. "Mark!" She rushed to hug him. "What . . . ? How . . . ?" She hugged him again.

The kids crowded in as she backed away. "Uncle Mark!" Mass chaos ensued as each child vied to receive a hug and tickle from fun Uncle Mark. They clamored around him until Rebecca returned with a golden-brown apple pie, steam swirling from the top, and started dishing it up. The kids scampered back to their places, abandoning their awesome uncle.

Miranda scooted her chair closer to Landon to make room for Mark. "What happened to Mexico?"

"You bought that excuse?" Mark plunked into a chair and slid into the space. "As if I would miss a chance to see my baby sis and meet the newest nephew of the clan. Where is the little guy?"

"You're never going to let go of that three-minute gap, are you?" She nudged his shoulder. "He fell asleep about twenty minutes ago after a little scream fest. Don't you dare wake him." She jokingly poked his arm. "I'm sure you have a Tootsie Roll with his name on it."

"It worked on Brendon, didn't it?" His mischievous smile made his hazel eyes sparkle. "One lick of the Tootsie Roll, and my role as favorite uncle was set for life."

That smile, along with his flawless baby face, had landed him several modeling jobs when he dropped out of college and left their religion and the family two decades ago. He'd found his way back to the family. He hadn't made any moves toward the others.

"So, the big shoot was bogus?" She wagged a finger at him.

"Not the shoot. The timing. We did it last month. And let me say, doing a photoshoot in Cancun in July is torture. I've never been hotter and sweatier in my life."

Miranda's hand instinctively shot up, her index finger stroking the inside of her thumb. "You know what this is?"

He didn't need to answer. Even her kids knew that one.

Olivia pointed her fork toward Miranda's hand. "It's the world's smallest violin playing 'My Heart Bleeds for You.'" She stabbed another chunk of the pie. "It means she's not sad for you." She swallowed. "Did you know I get to start playing the violin? Mommy said I could—"

"Me too! Me too!" Isabella cut in. "I get to play it, too."

"Is that so?" Mark angled toward the girls. "I can't wait to hear your first concert."

"The first song's gonna be 'My Heart Bleeds for You.' It'll be dedicated to our Uncle Mark." Brendon kept a straight face even as everyone laughed.

"Then I'll finally know what it sounds like." Mark winked. "How was your summer? You've grown at least a foot since I last saw you."

Brendon sat a little taller in his seat and opened up his shoulders. "I caught up to Mom a while back. I'll probably pass Dad this year."

Miranda warmed. How she'd missed these regular, everyday conversations with him.

Mark leaned back. "What're they feeding you in Minnesota? I thought it was all a vast sea of snow and ice. Does it melt enough to scavenge for food around there?" Mark frequently sent photos of himself on the beach in California throughout the winter, often accompanied by a screenshot of their own weather report.

Miranda laughed. "You'll have to visit sometime . . . see for yourself."

Brendon's lips curled at the corner. "Come this February. It's great beach weather."

"I may not be a brainiac like your mom, but I know when *not* to come for a visit, and that would be in February." Mark shoved a forkful of apple pie into his mouth.

Miranda turned to Rebecca. The smell of cinnamon and hot apples overtook her senses. "You've outdone yourself once again. This pie is amazing." She sank her teeth into the warm gooey goodness surrounded by perfectly tender layers of pastry.

"A Johnson family classic. Mom's pie lives on." Jeremy lifted his forkful in the air.

"Your mother." Dad put down his fork and scanned their faces. "She could bake a lot of things well. But this pie. Her apple pie . . . " He shook his head slowly.

"Mom knew how to bake a good pie." Miranda savored another bite. She closed her eyes and let the flavors transport her back in time. Sitting at this same table, in this same house, though the memories were now bits and pieces of fractured reality. Long ago this space brought her comfort and confidence, but now she sat with questions and cover-ups.

She opened her eyes and turned to Jeremy. "Speaking of Mom, can you please tell me what the se—"

Jeremy's sharp glare and discreet shake of the head cut her off. He quickly flicked his gaze toward Dad, then back to Miranda.

". . . the secret is to this amazing pie?" She shifted her gaze to her sister-in-law. "I've made it over a hundred times, but have yet to replicate it this well, Becca." She turned to her dad, who didn't seem to have noticed her near-slip. Whatever was going on, it wasn't just a secret from her. "Dad, no wonder you're sticking around for this. I would too."

She smiled, even as the pit in her stomach grew. What could be so bad they wouldn't discuss it with Dad? Then again, their family wasn't one to touch on anything sensitive . . . with anyone.

With his mental decline, it could be detrimental to stir up old issues. Especially those surrounding Mom's death. What good could that do him now?

What good would it do anyone now?

Landon's tap on her leg brought her back to the conversation. "Honey, should we get the kids ready for bed?"

Yes, the kids. The sooner they got them down, the sooner she could confront her brothers. It must be something big for Mark to tear himself away from his cushy life and make a pilgrimage to the rural Idaho farm. "Okay, kids, you've got five minutes to finish up, then it's time to brush teeth and meet for scripture share."

"But Mo-om." Olivia threw her head back. "We just got here. I'm not tired, and we barely got any time to play."

"You'll have all day tomorrow to do whatever you want." She had to get to the conversation with Jeremy.

"Can we sleep on the trampoline?" Olivia rested her chin on her hands, which were pressed together in a begging position.

How could Miranda resist? "Sure. But get extra blankets. Even though it's summer, nights get cold here."

The squeals erupting from the cousin entourage overpowered anything else she tried to say. She shooed them off to gather what they needed for their trampoline-camping adventure.

Dad placed his napkin on the table and edged his chair back. "I think it's past my bedtime."

"Here, let me help you." Landon jumped up and moved toward Brent.

The doorbell rang, and the front door swung open. "Hey, everyone, it's me." A young woman in scrubs appeared in the entryway. "You must be Miranda and Landon." She approached Miranda, hand extended. "I'm Janean, Brent's nighttime nurse. He's anticipated your visit all summer."

Miranda stood and shook her hand. "We're excited to be here. Thank you for all your help. Jeremy told me you've been wonderful with Dad."

"Thank you. I love working with him." She reached out to Brent, and Landon released him.

The minute Janean and Dad rounded the corner to his bedroom, Miranda snapped around to face Jeremy. "Start talking."

Chapter Seventeen

"Mom, can we go outside now?" Olivia trudged into the room, pajamas on, carting an armful of blankets. Isabella followed, dragging a sleeping bag behind her.

Miranda's gaze lingered a second more on Jeremy before she turned to Olivia.

"Yes, go ahead." The two girls ran outside.

"Oh wait, we need to do scripture share," Miranda said "Whose turn is it tonight?"

Landon retrieved his bag. "It's mine." He motioned toward Olivia. "Go grab Brendon and tell him to come in." He faced Jeremy and Rebecca. "You and the kids are welcome to join as well. We take turns sharing a scripture each night."

Once everyone gathered, Landon opened the Bible app on his phone. "I'll share one of my favorites. Roman 8:28: *And we know that all things work together for good to them that love God, to them who are the called according to his purpose.*" He paused for a moment. "The best, and worst, word in this scripture is the word *all.* No matter what happens in life, God can use it for our good." He locked eyes with Miranda, then glanced around the room.

Miranda held her breath. Was he going to go on? Dive into their *all* from the summer? *Please don't choose this moment to force my family into a hard discussion. We already have one to go through. Don't make it more.*

He smiled at Isabella. "Izzy, I believe it's your turn for prayer."

Miranda's shoulders lowered as she let out her breath.

After prayer, they got the kids settled outside, then regrouped on the couches in the family room. Miranda's gaze wandered around the room. Not much had changed in the twenty-plus years since she'd lived there. The wood paneling spoke to the western cabin motif that flowed throughout the house. Family pictures adorned the walls, as did each of the children's senior year photos. A cross stitch she'd given to her mom was surrounded by old family pictures. It was a Christmas gift. Mom's crystal blue eyes had shone soft when she opened it. She'd spent the better part of an hour finding the perfect position, beaming when it nestled securely on its hook.

Mom's last Christmas.

"I forgot how chilly it gets here at night." Miranda reached for the blanket by the couch and wrapped herself in it. The rustic scent of the family home lived in its fibers. "Okay, you two." Miranda pointed to Jeremy and Mark. "Spill it. What's going on?"

The door to Dad's room opened, and the nurse appeared in the hallway.

Would the distractions never end? Miranda clenched her teeth but forced a smile. "Did he get settled in okay?"

"He's drifting off to sleep now. His vitals are good tonight." She motioned toward Miranda. "I think having you here boosted his spirit, as well as his cognition. He's tracked better tonight than I've seen in a while."

Miranda's heart ached. Could she make the visits any more frequent? With the distance, the kids' ages, and a new school year starting, the likelihood was . . . well, not likely. "Thanks for taking such great care of him."

"It's been my pleasure." Janean nodded and excused herself.

When the door clicked shut, Miranda's gaze shot back to Jeremy. No more interruptions. It was time for the truth.

Jeremy's eyes darted from Mark to Rebecca.

Heat crawled through Miranda's cheeks. "After waiting months, you have to get permission from each other?" The sharpness in her voice rang in her ears. "I'm sorry, but I can't take any more. We've been through so much. What more could possibly be hidden in the Johnson family archives?"

Miranda's voice grew louder, prompting a pat on the leg from Landon. "Honey, the kids are right outside, and your dad might not be asleep yet."

She dropped her volume but kept the tone. "How could this be any bigger than Mark leaving college and the church when he moved to New York and shacked up with, what was her name? Chandra?" Miranda gestured to Mark. "Or Samuel's divorce? We managed to make it through those crazy sagas."

The news of Mark seeped out two decades ago, through hushed tones with shaking heads. Mark told Miranda, then took off. His communication with the rest of the family had been limited for years. Though he'd kept in contact with Miranda, he'd only re-appeared at family reunions and started reconnecting within the past few years.

Jeremy cleared his throat again. "That situation pales in comparison." He glanced once more toward Mark, then slowly continued. "When Rebecca and I first moved here, we did some deep cleaning. You know how Dad didn't want to get rid of any of Mom's stuff?"

Of course she knew. After the funeral, they'd discussed going through her stuff but waited. With the pain too fresh, especially for Dad, they boxed everything and put it in the attic. Told themselves they'd go through it later. The years slipped by. No meeting called, no mention of going through her belongings.

"When we moved in, the attic was too crammed for our things. In an effort to clear space, we sorted through some boxes and Becca found a sealed envelope without a name on the outside. We opened it." Jeremy rubbed the back of his neck, his shoulders deflating. "And . . . I wish we hadn't." He paused.

"What did it say? Was it from Mom?" To hear from her mother one last time. Hadn't she begged for that? But his last comment penetrated. Did she want to know?

Jeremy slowly nodded. "It wasn't addressed to anyone. It read like a journal entry of sorts. She wrote it shortly after Mark declared he was done with religion, and the 'rat race of conformism.' Right around the time Samuel and Noel were going through the divorce."

Another family skeleton buried deep in the archives. When Miranda's second oldest brother, Samuel, divorced, it had rocked the family, especially Miranda. The first to get married, Samuel and Noel portrayed the epitome of Johnson perfection. Miranda welcomed Noel as the sister she'd never had. She adored Noel. The divorce severed the bond between them and left Miranda not only hurting for her brother, but grieving for the sisterhood she'd lost.

Mark's declaration. Samuel's divorce. Mom's death. The darkest year of Miranda's life. Until now.

Jeremy continued. "This letter was dated a couple weeks before she died. As far as we can tell, it's the last thing she wrote." He shot a pained glance at Rebecca again. "It declared her failure in everything important in life. She believed she'd failed as a mother. One son chose an alternate lifestyle. Another broke the holiest of sacred bonds. She'd devoted her entire life to her kids, but it wasn't enough. She'd failed and couldn't fix it. If she couldn't help her own kids succeed, then she—"

"No. No. No." The room started spinning. Miranda's hands flew to her head. She couldn't stop the dizziness. She needed to collect her thoughts. To purge the words. "Stop. This can't be right. You don't think the car accident . . . " She couldn't finish the sentence.

Landon took her hand.

Jeremy shrugged.

Rebecca leaned forward. "There's no way to know for sure. That's why we didn't tell anyone. The police never found evidence to suggest anything other than an accident."

Miranda reeled as the raw footage, clips from the past, charged through her mind. "The police knew Mom and Dad. The whole community did. This would've rocked the entire county. They could easily have ruled it an accident, especially given the road conditions."

Jeremy said, "She didn't direct the note to anyone. Never placed it anywhere for anyone to find. She definitely struggled, but I don't think she deliberately tried to end her life."

Of course, that would be his explanation. Sum it up nice and tidy. Too tidy.

"Such a Johnson thing to do." Heat exploded up Miranda's spine, encasing her skull. "Distort the truth and hide it in a dark box, and then wrap it up all nice and proper, strangling the real story with a nice little bow on top. What are we afraid of? After all these years, can't we just be honest with each other?"

"What are you talking about?" Jeremy shifted on the couch.

"I'm sick of the secrets, of following the unwritten rules. Anything to keep the façade of the perfect little family. You know where that has gotten this family?"

Landon squeezed her hand. She let go and sat upright, fire surging through her veins and erupting out of her mouth. "Messed up with no way to let anyone in. No way to share what we *really* feel, what we *really* think. Who we *really* are."

Miranda faced Mark. "Honestly, I don't blame you for pulling away. Once, when Mom talked to me about you running to the world's ways, she said how ungrateful you were for all she had done for you. Talked as if you were doing it purely to spite her, not something you had given a lot of thought to on your own."

"Well I was pretty selfish in how I went about leaving. Shutting everyone out didn't help, either." Mark shifted in his seat.

They weren't going to explain it all away this time. "Oh, come on. We've all been there with Mom. If any of us showed the slightest flaw, she'd have none of it. There was never any freedom to not have it all together. There was no messing up."

Miranda dropped her head. "It's suffocating to pretend to be the perfect family." She raised her head, her cheeks warming. "We're all facing struggles, but we won't talk about them openly enough to support each other. We're the ones who should have each other's backs, but instead, we're the first to pick up the stones."

Landon reached again for her hand. "Mirand—"

She shrugged it away and shot him a warning glance. He'd told her to get things out in the open. Why stop now? She turned her fiery gaze back on her siblings.

"And what do we do when we get together? We put on our happy faces and pretend everything's perfect. And who put on the most perfect face of all?" Miranda's voice rose to a shrill. "Mom!"

She stopped and exhaled. Every ounce of fight left her. Her trembling body collapsed into the couch.

The others sat motionless.

The ticking of the old grandfather clock presided in its corner, ever marching time forward, the only sound filling the silence.

Landon cleared his throat. "To think I ever wondered where Isabella got her fiery spirit."

Miranda smiled at him, grateful for his effort to ease the awkwardness.

Jeremy stared at her, eyes wide. "I don't think I've ever heard you talk like that before. You've always been the one to soothe any disagreement between us guys."

"That's what scares me." Miranda's voice quieted. "I've taken on the role of making things appear fine. Just like Mom."

She cast her gaze to the floor. Tears fought their way out. Who cares? Let them deal with her tears. "Make everything run smoothly. Just like Mom. Put on the perfect, happy face. Just like Mom. Will all that pressure make me snap?"

Just like . . . Mom?

Her eyes burned.

She clenched her jaw. Every muscle in her body tightened until she sat rigid on the couch. "Where's the note? I want to read it."

Jeremy clasped his hands as his shoulders slumped. He cleared his throat again. "We, um . . . " He peeked over his shoulder at Rebecca, as if begging protection. "We shredded it."

"You *what?*" Miranda sprang to her feet.

Jeremy leaned back and waved his arms in defense.

"You *shredded* it? The last bit of information we could use to determine what went on inside her head, and you destroyed it?"

She stepped toward him. To do what? Hit him? Strangle him?

Before she could act, Landon's hands encased her shoulders, pulling her back. "Honey. Let's all take a deep breath."

Miranda whirled around, her chest heaving. The softness in his eyes made her pause. Her shoulders relaxed as the storm within her drained, taking with it her energy. She slumped back onto the couch. Where did she go from there?

Landon gently continued. "This isn't easy for anyone. But at least we're talking about it. That alone is a big step forward."

"When did you destroy it?" As the anger retreated, her thirst for answers advanced.

"Right after we found it." Jeremy rubbed his chin. "Honestly, we were so shocked, we didn't know what to do. It felt like incriminating evidence, and our knee jerk reaction was to get rid of it."

"What did Dad say? Did you show it to him?" Miranda wasn't about to let him off the hook.

Another pleading look toward Rebecca answered her question.

"You didn't show it to him."

He gave a single shake.

"Why?"

"Believe me, we debated over whether to tell anyone or to let it die with the rest of the family secrets. In—"

"Can't you see? Secrets don't make things go away. They're like cancer. They decay and corrode from the inside out. We can't go on like this."

Even as the words spilled, they echoed through her soul. The secrets she'd kept, and still held, ate through her consciousness, threatening to engulf her.

Miranda pressed her hands against her burning cheeks. If only she could douse the flames from the outside. Her chin trembled. She opened her mouth to confess. To tell of that phone call with Mom so long ago. But she clamped it closed again. Years of covering the inner torment with a pretty façade forbade her. Hypocrisy at its finest.

She peered at Mark, the only person to whom she'd made any mention of her secret regarding Mom's death. Even to him, she hadn't told the whole story. Now, with the evidence that her death may not have been an accident, the weight of her own shame was burying her alive.

She angled back to Jeremy. "Why now? Why the sudden change of heart to let it out now?"

Mark jumped in. "Do you remember when I did a shoot in New York this past spring?"

Miranda nodded, keeping her eyes on him. Where was this going?

"On one of the breaks, I went with some guys to grab a bite to eat, and as we rounded a corner, I almost ran right into Noel. As in Samuel's Noel—er, ex-Noel."

Miranda's jaw dropped. "That's crazy. Did she see you? Did you guys talk?"

"She and her new husband were on their way to a show, but we hugged and chatted for a couple minutes. Her new husband seemed like a great guy. They're living in Colorado but traveled to New York for an anniversary trip."

"I can't believe you randomly ran into her," Miranda said. "Their split broke my heart. I loved having her in the family." She looked from Jeremy to Mark again. "But what does this have to do with the letter?"

Mark laced his fingers around his knee, rocking back. "Right after that trip, I stopped here to check in. When I told Jeremy about running into Noel, we relived that crazy year with Samuel, and me, and then Mom . . ."

His gaze shot to Jeremy, who picked up the story. "It seemed like the right time to bring up the letter. Mark couldn't believe it either."

Mark sat forward in his chair. "I still don't know if I believe it. I don't think she'd . . . I don't think it was on purpose. Not Mom."

He tilted his head toward Jeremy but kept his gaze on Miranda. "I asked if he'd talked to anyone else about it. When he said no, I told him to at least tell you."

Mark made no mention of her confession about the wreck being her fault, and Miranda didn't ask. The pain of the letter was too new. She couldn't process it.

Secrets. Cancer. Sitting in the silence that followed, her secret continued to consume her.

Chapter Eighteen

"Rough night. How are you doing?" Landon lay on his back next to her in their bedroom. Her bedroom. The one she'd grown up in. The one where she'd spent countless nights safe inside the harbor of their house.

Often on nights like this, she'd open her window to collect the fresh breeze and fall asleep to the sound of the sprinklers, happy and content with their seemingly storybook life—the life that was now light-years away.

She rolled onto her back and stared at the ceiling, one arm cocked over her forehead. Mouth open, she attempted to respond but couldn't formulate any words.

"I never met your mom, but, from what I've learned through the years, it seems out of character for her. She was the glue that held the family together."

Miranda stayed silent for a moment longer, the recounted pieces from the letter ping-ponging through her mind.

"I can't believe they shredded it." Miranda's hands balled into fists as her body tensed once again. "I could've found something they missed. Now, all we have to go on is the ten-year-old memory of Jeremy and Bec." She huffed, but part of her understood their rash actions. What would she have done if she'd been the one to find it? Probably the same thing.

Miranda continued. "As bad as things got for a while, I can't see her doing it. She always ran toward a problem, not away." There had to be something more. Something they'd missed.

It couldn't be true.

"Without the letter, we can't jump to any conclusions." He reached out and squeezed her hand. "There's too much unknown to think the worst."

"You're right." But what if her mom did struggle with some deep-seated feelings of failure? Strangely, that held some comfort. For the first time, her mom had shed her super-woman cloak. She'd become human.

Landon kissed Miranda. "Let's get some sleep. We can talk about it more tomorrow."

Sleep. As if.

Minutes later, she listened as his breath deepened. How was he able to do that? Have the world turn upside down, then climb into bed and turn it all off?

As the minutes ticked into hours, Miranda fed Ashton and replayed the evening's events. How could her mother reach such a low point? Miranda struggled through her own battles. What if she never got over them? Had she passed that on to Brendon, cursing him to a lifetime of similar trials?

Miranda glanced at the clock. Two-thirty. Nine-thirty Jess's time. She grabbed her phone. If anyone could help her process this craziness, it'd be Jess.

When she opened their text conversation, the remains of their previous encounter glared back at her, piercing the dark room—and her conscience. Jess's last reply. *And you moved forward. We both chose our paths. I'm at peace with mine. It doesn't seem like you've come to terms with yours.* Her honesty was brutal, and accurate in exposing Miranda's gaping void.

She tossed the phone, flopped back on the bed, and stared at the ceiling. How could she be at peace with her path when it was crumbling before her eyes? It was all too much. How was she supposed to process this?

Miranda woke from a fitful sleep to the smell of bacon. As she fed and rocked Ashton, squeals of laughter pierced the second-story window and she stole a peek outside. The kids jumped on the tramp around their mass of sleeping bags, Brendon leading the way with tricks. She smiled. At least the cousins could reconnect on this trip. And this was a much-needed break for Brendon.

She made her way to the kitchen as the kids spilled through the door, led by Olivia . . . or rather by Olivia's nose. "I knew I smelled bacon. Is it ready yet? I'm starving."

The kids swarmed the table, their chatter filling the awkward silence lingering from the previous evening. Mark jumped into the mix, followed by Jeremy. Soon the conversation revolved around Jedi forces and superhero unicorns.

Over the course of the next four days, the adults slipped back into their roles. Smiling, chatting about kids' activities, sharing recipes. Safe topics. The Johnson Modus Operandi, smile and stay polite. Don't let any more secrets bubble to the surface.

Yet, each night as Miranda rocked and nursed Ashton, she conjured up the ideal conversation. One in which they spoke openly and honestly. Sharing their loads and growing together. She opened up about Brendon and spilled her secret in at least ten mental scenarios.

Each morning brought more smiles and status quo. Talk of the farm, upcoming plans, fun stories of years gone by. No more drudging up the deep issues. No one waded into that arena again, and Miranda didn't push. What more could be said? Hashing through decades-old memories would get them nowhere.

The evening before they left, Miranda's dad felt good enough for a farm walk, so she took his arm and they meandered around the expansive yard.

She soaked in the scent of each plant they passed. Irises, daisies, and ripening apples all mingled together. She mentally captured the scene rolling before her gaze. The mountains on the horizon. The fields of golden wheat. The lilac bushes, past their blooming season, conjured memories of exploding purple blossoms each spring.

They stopped by one of the apple trees. "Looks like you'll be getting a bumper crop of apples this season, Dad."

He raised his free arm and examined the ripening fruit. "I think you're right. Give 'em a few weeks, and they'll be ready to drop. Like me."

Not again. "Dad. You hold on. Think about how many pies you can eat from this harvest." If only he'd look forward to something.

He patted her hand. "Oh, Miranda. You've been such a joy to parent." His face grew serious, his eyes crystal clear. "Do you remember when you were little and first learned how to move pipes?"

"How could I forget? I think they weighed twice as much as I did. That first time, I wore more mud than skin by the time we finished." She laughed at the memory, but at the time, it was anything but funny.

"Remember what I told you when you complained that this work was too dirty for a girl?"

She smiled. In all her youthful arrogance, she'd put her hands on her hips to drive home the point. "You told me to forget myself and get to work. I was so mad at you, but you were right." All these years later, the rebuke still rang in her ears.

He faced her, his brown eyes holding a penetrating stare. "I was only half right. What I should have told you was to forget yourself, but never forget who you are." His thick, weather-beaten hand squeezed hers. "Don't forget who you are."

Miranda rocked back. Just as she was on the verge to discovering this a few months before, life had abruptly reminded her that she had no business focusing on herself. She couldn't go there now. She smiled. "Okay, let's make a deal. How about let's both not forget who I am." She gently nudged him as he let out a chuckle. "Oh, and another part of the deal is that you stick around long enough to enjoy the pies from this apple harvest."

He smiled. "It's a deal."

Standing on the front porch of Dad's house, Miranda's throat caught. Would this be the last time she hugged him? Though smiling, his eyes conveyed a different message than joy. He was trapped and ready to shed this mortal body. As they hugged, she held on a beat longer, imprinting his earthy scent into her soul.

Hollow hugs and smiles accompanied the farewell with the others. Still unsure of how to broach the sensitive subject matter, Miranda played the game along with the rest, pretending no meeting had occurred, nor any harsh words exchanged.

On the plane ride back, moments from the week replayed in her mind. The letter. The outburst. The string of questions in her late-night thoughts. Mostly, though, her last walk with her dad lingered in her mind. "Don't forget who you are." But who was she, really . . . A connector? What did that mean? What about the drill. Her drill . . . ?

The answers would have to wait. She had too many motherly responsibilities right now. She stole a glance at Brendon, asleep next to her. What could she do to help him on his path forward? What did the future hold for him?

Cool air coaxed the green from the leaves to highlight the deep hues of autumn. Miranda soaked in the brilliant yellows, oranges, and reds as she took the long route home from dropping the kids off at school one October morning. She meandered through various neighborhoods, admiring the bright colors filling the tree-lined avenues. As winter gathered strength for its assault, Miranda tried to bask in these kaleidoscope days while they lasted.

She pointed out the pretty colors to Ashton, even though he didn't understand a thing. She talked nonstop anyway, explaining the variety of trees surrounding them.

Her chatter ceased as the car rounded the next corner. The slide park. In a flash, all the talks with Mindy, Miranda's sparks of hope, and the beginning of her personal journey flooded her mind.

As if on autopilot, she turned into the park's parking lot.

Somehow, she knew what she would find. And she wasn't disappointed. On the same bench sat the familiar old woman. Not looking anxious, or lost, or lonely.

Simply sitting there.

Waiting.

Chapter Nineteen

Her stomach fluttered. It couldn't be. Could it? She unclasped her buckle, eager to run to Mindy. Then flopped back in her seat.

She gritted her teeth as her body tensed. A warm surge worked its way up her back into her neck. Wasn't this what distracted her from Brendon's struggle? How dare Mindy think she knew what was best for Miranda. How dare she waltz into Miranda's life and fill her head with naive and selfish ideas. Well, she'd tell that woman exactly what she thought. As Miranda grabbed the door handle, Ashton fussed.

She glanced at the clock. Way past feeding time.

If she nursed him in the car, she could avoid Mindy all together. Or maybe she should hurry home instead. She peered again at Mindy. The air surrounding her danced. The woman's aura lured Miranda to the bench.

How should she approach? She couldn't put on a happy face. She couldn't pretend like her life hadn't been turned upside down. It would be easy to blame her turmoil on Mindy. But it wasn't her fault. How could that lonely old woman possibly have known what was going on behind the scenes, what would happen with Brendon? How could she have known the unanswerable questions she would uncover about her mother?

Ashton's cries grew louder. Miranda sighed. She may as well face the woman now. She turned off the car and pulled open the side door of the minivan. Ashton calmed when he saw her face, a signal food would soon follow.

She unstrapped him, grabbed the quilted diaper bag, and headed toward the bench.

She dragged her feet but when she arrived, Mindy patted the bench next to her as if no more than a week had passed. "Isn't fall the most miraculous time of year?"

The storm inside her calmed. "It's my favorite. I can't get enough of the beauty." She motioned toward the trees, with their brilliant hues of reds, oranges, and yellows, surrounding the park. "I'm surprised to see you here. I thought you'd be long gone by now."

"Nope, still here." Mindy flashed her all-encompassing smile. "Turns out, my family needed me a bit longer, so I'm hanging around."

"I hope they're okay." Miranda paused her search for the nursing blanket.

"They've undergone some hard times, but they'll come out stronger. I only wanted to be here as added support."

"They're lucky to have you." Miranda's throat caught. What she would give to have had her mother here to help her walk through the past few months. The void she'd left was now filled with impossible questions. Her ribs tightened. She'd never have a family like Mindy's. A mom to help them through hard times. To share daily wisdom.

"They don't need me," Mindy said. "Not really. I merely help them see what's already inside them." She leaned over Ashton's car seat. "I see your little guy's made his world debut. Congratulations."

"Thank you. He's the perfect caboose for our family. He may be the youngest, but he's already learned how to make himself heard." His feet kicked in time with his cries, his indication that he was at the end of his patience. "Do you mind if I nurse him here? I need to get him some food, stat."

"You feed that little boy anytime, anywhere."

Miranda put her cover on and positioned Ashton to nurse. His fussing quickly turned to small sighs and big gulps as he kicked in contentment. "I thought my teenager could pack away the food, but this little guy's appetite is endless."

Mindy touched his toes. "My, you forget how small they start."

"And how fast they grow." Miranda pulled the cover out to check on him. "I can't believe how big he's gotten already. He outgrew the three-month clothes before he hit the eight-week mark."

"A great start to a strong and healthy life. With that growth pattern, he may turn out to be the tallest one of the family." Mindy touched his foot and chuckled.

"Wouldn't that be funny? To have the youngest end up the biggest of all the kids." Miranda gazed down at him again. Hard to imagine this tiny one growing to be taller than Brendon.

Brendon. Miranda's smile faltered.

"How are the kids settling into school?" If Mindy noticed the change, she made no mention of it.

"They're doing okay. Back-to-school time's always crazy, and, with a new baby this year, we reached a new level of chaos."

"Sometimes embracing the chaos is the best way to get through it."

"I'm afraid I don't have much choice. Everything's a bit off-kilter, and the more I try to gain control, the more I lose it."

Mindy touched his small foot again. "You have your circles confused is all."

No. Not today.

She couldn't take another life lesson about soccer, or butterflies, or anything else this lady had to offer. "Look." The edge in her voice came out sharper than she intended. "Today I can't smile and be cordial. Our family experienced some serious trauma over the summer, and I've been barely coping ever since." Miranda tried to soften her voice. "I've enjoyed our visits, but I'm not ready to implement any lessons right now. I don't have the emotional capacity."

Showing no sign of hurt or anger, Mindy nodded. "I get it—"

"No, you don't," Miranda stopped and stared at the ground, the trees, the kids playing. Anything but at Mindy and those deep, examining eyes. "I can't take it anymore. I'm so drained, I can't receive anything with grace right now, regardless of how well-intentioned it is."

Deep breath in, slow exhale. Mindy didn't deserve her anger, but Miranda couldn't hold it in any longer. "I came here week after week, thinking maybe there was something to all of your talk and advice. Things started to come alive in me, or seemed to. Then my world crashed." The lump in her throat forbade her from continuing. The ever-familiar sting of tears welled in her eyes.

She bit her lip. *Not here. Not now.*

She'd worked hard for so long to keep everything in and be the anchor for her children.

For Brendon. She continuously ignored the clench in her stomach and pasted on a smile whenever Brendon was in the room. Old habits passed down from her family.

But here, in the presence of this woman, a virtual stranger, Miranda's defenses crumbled.

A tear reached the edge and silently slipped down the bridge of her nose. No use dancing around the obvious. Surely Mindy could sense she held something heavy in her heart.

She waited a few more seconds, then blew out a puff of air. "My son, Brendon . . . He tried to"—she swallowed hard—"to end his life." She didn't even look at Mindy to gauge a reaction, just plowed on as the tears poured freely. "He's doing much better now. But it rocked our family." She sniffled. "I try to hold it together and help us move forward. But I can't get past the fact that I failed."

"What do you mean, failed?" Mindy showed no signs of judgment or pity.

Something about her kind manner invited Miranda to continue. "Brendon surprised us and was born two months early. When we brought him home from the hospital, he was so tiny, Landon and I were almost afraid to hold him. When we made it through the first night at home, we gave each other a high five for keeping him alive. Each day we marveled that we were actually doing this parenthood thing."

Miranda ran a hand through her hair and smiled through her tears. "It was surreal. This tiny human, completely dependent on us. In all my years of babysitting, I thought I knew all the ins and outs of child-care. But having someone rely wholly on you brings it to a new level."

Miranda changed Ashton to the other side to nurse. "As the girls, and now Ashton, joined the family, I find myself still filled with wonder and awe. But I also feel the gravity of my responsibility." The lump grew larger in her throat. "Then, this summer, Brendon tried to end his life, the life I worked so hard to preserve. I failed him. Sure, I kept him fed and clothed. I taught him the basic physical functions. But I didn't protect him. I let his emotional health spiral downward to the point that he'd try to take the most precious gift of all."

She shifted and stared into Mindy's eyes, which portrayed a pain that matched her own. "You do know this pain, don't you?" It wasn't a question.

Mindy nodded. "I'm well acquainted with the grief of a child's darkest moments. Thanks to my grief, my life spun out of control for a long time."

Mindy laced her hands over one knee and slowly rocked back, lifting her face toward the sun. "I put on a strong front and moved forward. But inside, it was dark for so long. Too long. It impeded my ability to be a light." Mindy focused on Miranda. "My son turned his darkest moment into a turning point. I can say this with clarity now that we've been on the other side for so long. He became a much better person for having gone through his harrowing experience. We all became better because of it. Looking back, I wish I'd released sooner the baggage I carried for too long."

"How did you move forward?" What was the secret? Could there be a secret to release the clamp around her chest?

"A dear friend taught me a lesson she learned walking through her own dark season on the parenting path." Mindy's eyes glazed into a faraway look.

Oh no. Not another "friend" from hundreds of years ago.

"Liz moved in a few houses away from us and became an extension of our family. The kids still call her Grandma Liz and bring their own kids to visit her when they come home.

"She often came over in the winter months while the kids were at school for 'hot chocolate chats.'" Mindy smiled. "On one of those days, she told me of a dark season in her life filled with deep sorrow. Her story shocked me. She seemed light and self-confident, not like someone carrying the heavy burden of grief. She taught me one of my life's greatest lessons. The circles of control, influence, and concern."

Mindy reached for her purse. "It's better if I show you, as she showed me." Once again, she pulled out the purple marker and chuckled. "You'd think I'd remember to put some pens in here."

"You and me both." Miranda smiled. "I always end up writing with the girls' crayons."

Mindy found a piece of paper and drew three circles, one small, then two around it, each bigger than the last, resembling a bull's-eye design. She labeled the smallest circle, *Control*. On the next one, she wrote, *Influence*. And on the outer ring, *Concern*.

"We live our lives between each of these circles. There are things we directly control, those we influence, and others we're concerned about but don't have any direct ability to control or influence."

She tapped the innermost circle, the control circle. "The only thing over which we have complete control is something that Viktor Frankl called the last of human freedoms. The freedom to choose how we'll react to any given set of circumstances."

"Viktor Frankl? Who's that?"

"Who he was makes his statement even more powerful. A psychiatrist from Austria, Viktor was also a Jew who spent over three years in Auschwitz. He lost his parents, his brother, and his beloved wife during those three years."

Mindy commanded Miranda's complete attention. "His captors stripped everything away from him. His family. His home. His belongings. Even his clothes. He lived at the whim of the guards in the camps. He had no control over anything. Anything, that is, except the power to choose his response to what happened to him."

Control. The irony of that statement coming from within the walls of a concentration camp made it all the more powerful.

Mindy's voice reeled her back. "When we realize the only true control we have is over ourselves, everything else falls to its rightful place." Mindy looked up from the paper and met Miranda's gaze. "That includes the actions of our children."

Miranda backed up. "Now wait a minute. Are you saying I have no control over my four-year-old and her actions? That sounds like a dangerous parenting pattern. Have you ever read *Lord of the Flies*, a book about giving children complete control? It didn't end well."

Mindy nodded. "Ah, yes. Kids marooned alone on an island. Their taking control brought out the darkest of human nature, resulting in murder and anarchy. It's a stark check of what could happen if we don't utilize all three circles together, especially in parenting." She tapped the marker on the paper. "Parenting is one of the trickiest areas to navigate these three circles. When our kids first enter the world, we exercise complete control over them. When they eat, where they go . . . everything.

"The art of parenting comes in transitioning out of the control circle. The physical realm is simple to see. As our children learn to crawl, then walk, we relinquish control over their mobility.

"The emotional realm is tougher." Mindy folded her arms and leaned back. "It's hard to know when to step back versus when to lean in as our children navigate the many nuances of life. Especially when they make choices that veer from the path of life we envision for them."

Ashton gurgled and burped. Miranda brought him up to her shoulder and gently patted his back.

Mindy reached out and stroked his fingers, which instinctively wrapped around her finger. "We snuggle them as newborns and, though it's hard to admit, we map out their entire lives. Graduating, meeting someone, getting married, finding a successful career. Living a life of happiness."

Miranda chuckled. She could give a play by play of Ashton's perfect future already.

The wise woman continued. "When they make decisions that veer from the path *we* conceived for them, it's tempting to step in and try to pull them back—to our path." She nodded toward the circles. "As they grow and develop, our circle of control only contains our own actions and reactions to life. Though our children still fall into our circle of influence"—Mindy tapped the second layer of circles— "we don't control them. You may be a mother of many, but you are a master of one."

Miranda stopped patting Ashton's back and turned toward Mindy. "Wait, say that one more time."

"You are the mother of many, but the master of one."

Miranda let the phrase settle. It soothed her soul like aloe over a burn. The guilt, still lingering, loosened its deep sting.

Mindy continued. "If we forget our own core and instead place motherhood at the center, we base our entire self-worth, perhaps even our entire existence, on what happens to our children. If my kids become great successes, that means I was a good mother. But if they struggle or go down paths I wouldn't choose for them, what does that mean for me? Does it mean I failed in motherhood, rendering my entire life worthless? It's dangerous to wrap our self-worth in the results of someone else's life, regardless of how close they are to us. Regardless of how much we love them."

Miranda thought of the conversations on the farm. The letter. Her mother's confession of failure—all directly tied to the decisions and paths of her children. "My mother . . . I think she may have been suffering from a deeper anxiety than mine." She paused. Was she going to go there? Divulge the Johnson family secret to a woman she barely knew?

Her lips didn't wait for permission. "She died in a car accident. In winter. The roads were bad. She hit a sheet of black ice, lost control, and crashed."Miranda took a breath. "At least that's what the police report said."

She paused and peeked at Mindy, pleading with her to hear what she wasn't saying.

Mindy leaned in. "Is there something that leads you to believe the police report wasn't correct?"

"Nothing official." Miranda bit the inside of her cheek. She could share the obvious part, but she wouldn't go *there*. "A decade ago, a letter surfaced in which she wrote about being a failure. A couple of my siblings pursued paths in opposition to our upbringing. According to the letter, she took it personally and internalized their actions as a reflection on her." Miranda wrapped her arms tighter around Ashton, in part to stop her own trembling. "Why would she absorb their decisions like that? I mean, they were grown adults. They weren't even living under her roof. How could she feel like she'd failed them?"

Even as the words came out, they held a mirror to her own life. She avoided Mindy's penetrating gaze, shifting once again to see the ground in front of her. Her eyes burned.

The silence lingered between the women for a moment. Then Mindy softly spoke. "Mothers have an influence on their children. Perhaps stronger than anything else in the world. As do children on their mothers. But as a mother, you don't control your children, nor their fate."

Miranda raised her head and took the tissue Mindy held in front of her.

As she wiped her eyes, Mindy spoke again, her words quiet, but direct. "Release control of your children and understand your over-arching job is to help them find their own path."

She wanted to believe the counsel. "How do I do that?"

Mindy smiled. "You take a lesson from God's parenting style. He sent us here to learn how to choose for ourselves. I'm sure there are times He aches to step in and stop us from making choices that could harm ourselves or others. He influences us through His Spirit, but He doesn't take control."

"Sometimes I wish he would." Miranda shrugged. "It'd be nice to have someone to blame for my poor choices."

Mindy pointed her finger in the air. "When we make a poor choice, God doesn't wring His hands and say what a horrible God He is. He helps us up, wipes the dust off, and sends us on our way again."

Good point. The constraining clamp around Miranda's chest loosened more.

The alarm rang on Miranda's phone. She jumped, then glanced at Ashton and smiled. Sound asleep. As the youngest of four, he could sleep through a tornado. "Oh goodness, it's time to pick up Isabella from preschool." She snoozed the alarm. What she wouldn't give to sit and talk for hours with this life mentor.

"You don't want to be late for that little one. She'll never let you forget it." Mindy winked.

"You know her well." Miranda nodded. "She definitely adds spice to our family."

"Every family should be so lucky to enjoy her flavor of spice." Mindy folded the paper and returned it to her purse. "It'll take her far in life."

Miranda gathered the diaper bag then turned toward Mindy. "I can't tell you how much today meant to me." There was more to say, but words seemed inadequate. "Thank you. And I'm sorry for drop-ping off the face of the earth after our last visit."

"No need to apologize. I'm glad you returned. It was nice to visit and meet Ashton." Mindy tucked her finger into his tiny fist. "Next week, I'll need to snuggle him."

"Will you be here next week?" Miranda shouldn't even ask after her disappearing act last time.

"Yes, indeed. Right here." She patted the bench as if to claim it as her own. "I'll see you then."

As Miranda walked to the car, her phone pinged.

Penelope.

The committee. She meant to text Penelope, but, in the swirl of activity in the previous months, which included welcoming a new life into the world, she'd completely forgotten.

She tapped the message. *Hey Miranda, checking in to see how the application's going. Do you need any help?*

She could still fill out the application. Where was it? Somewhere in her paper piles no doubt. Maybe she could still do it. Her mom did it, even after everything with Samuel. It could be a way to connect with her.

Chapter Twenty

Mom of the Year. Miranda considered it as she drove to pick up Isabella. Should she go through with it? There was still time. Brendon seemed to improve each week. True, he wouldn't have his Eagle completed, and his presence in church had been sporadic since the incident. But she could come up with something for that one question.

As she put her car into park in front of the preschool building, Miranda let out a long, slow breath. No. She wasn't her mother. She didn't have anything to prove to anyone. She stared at her phone. Then, as if her fingers already knew what to say, they flew across the keyboard.

Thank you for thinking about me for this award. I'm honored that you considered me. However, I'm not going to move forward with it. Thanks again for your efforts with this.

As she hit send, a calm settled in, unraveling the knots in her stomach.

Later that night, as Miranda and Landon were settling into bed, Isabella stumbled into their room, rubbing her eyes against their lamp light. "Mommy, I'm thirsty."

Miranda got Isabella a drink and sent her back to bed. She kissed Isabella's forehead. "Night-night, sleep tight, don't let the bedbugs bite. See you in the morning. Love you."

Isabella wrapped her arms around Miranda's neck. "Night-night Mommy. You're the best mom in the whole world!"

Miranda smiled as she hugged Isabella back. "And you're the best Izzy in the whole world."

Miranda turned out the lights, then peeked into Brendon's room. His lamp glowed, but he was asleep. She crept into the room to turn it off. He'd fallen asleep writing something, the pen still perched in his hand. A book lay open beneath his face. His journal.

Her arm instinctively reached to slide it out. What she wouldn't give for a glimpse of his thoughts.

As her hand grazed the notebook, she pulled back.

Circle of control.

Why did she want to read it? This was not within her realm of control. It was Brendon's story to record and share at his discretion, not hers. He would share his thoughts and feelings with her if and when he was ready.

She reached instead to flip off the lamp and kissed him gently on his head, then retreated from the room.

Landon glanced up from his book. Miranda crawled into bed beside him.

He took off his glasses and turned toward her. "Okay, what gives?"

"What're you talking about?"

"Something's different. You seem . . . I don't know. Like you've found some sort of light in all of this craziness. Whatever you're taking, I want some." He closed his book.

Now was her chance. "It's simple. I let go of the control."

He lifted an eyebrow.

"Let me grab some paper. It's easier to show you than explain." Miranda opened the drawer of her nightstand, hunting for a pen and paper. She found a half sheet of paper, but no pen. She searched around her nightstand. Nothing. She slipped onto the floor and scanned underneath. There, in the back corner, sat a purple marker, probably left from one of Isabella's art projects.

She laughed as she grabbed it. "How fitting that I would be writing this with a marker." She ignored Landon's quizzical gaze as she drew three circles and explained each one. When she finished, the same light flickered in his eyes that had warmed her soul upon hearing the idea.

He slowly shook his head, a grin emerging on his lips. "It's such a simple concept, but it makes perfect sense."

"That's what I thought when Mindy explained it." She tapped the control circle. "The only thing we can control is us. With Brendon, our main focus is to love him where he is, how he is."

Landon nodded. "Not belittle him for who we think he should be."

Miranda's shoulders relaxed. It was good to be on the same page.

As they turned out the light, Miranda shifted to a comfortable position. Something still nagged at her.

Master of one. So much time and energy focused on forcing Brendon into *her* path. Trying to get *his* actions to prove *her* worth. However, releasing that control also left a void. Without leaning into her children's accomplishments for validation, she now had to search inside herself.

To her core.

Chapter Twenty-One

Sunday morning began with the usual scramble. As Miranda made her last calls to the kids, a pouting Isabella rounded the corner in stocking feet. "I can't find my princess shoes."

"You'll have to find something else to wear. We need to go now." Could they make it on time, just once?

"Nooooo!" Isabella punched her fisted hands toward the floor as she stomped. "I wanna wear my princess shoes. I don't like the other shoes."

Landon walked down the stairs. "You can find them after church and wear them next week, but right now, we need to go."

"I want my princess shoes. I can find them." She scurried up the stairs, darting past both Miranda's and Landon's grasp.

Miranda laid Ashton in his car seat as Landon loped up the stairs after Isabella. He stopped short at the delighted squeal coming from above.

"You found them. Thank you, Bwendon."

Then, as if he'd never flinched at going to church, Brendon followed Isabella down the stairs, dressed and ready to go, his sandy blond curls freshly washed and styled.

Miranda took it in stride. Still, she and Landon exchanged a *who is this kid?* glance as they loaded their family—their entire family—into the car.

As they drove, the kids chattered in the back. Brendon joined in the conversation, laughing and joking with Olivia. He even allowed Isabella to interject herself into the conversation.

Miranda reached for Landon's hand. Perhaps they'd finally turn a corner.

———

As they gathered the children after the services, Rose shuffled by and touched Miranda's shoulder. "What a beautiful family. Cherish these moments with them."

Miranda hugged her girls with one arm, patted Rose's arm with the other, and smiled. A genuine smile. "Thank you Rose. I'll do that." And she meant it.

As Brendon rounded the corner at the end of the hall, Miranda's smile faded. A shadow had eclipsed the light he'd carried into the meeting, and brought a pit to Miranda's stomach.

No. Please no. The therapist, Sarah, had warned of setbacks. She told them the road forward wouldn't be a straight course. There would most likely be many bumps and bruises along the way.

But things had been going so well. *Please, have this feeling be a mistake. Please help him keep moving forward. Hasn't he suffered enough?*

The closer he got, the bigger the pit in her stomach grew. The darkness in his eyes made the hair on the back of her neck stand up.

Landon strode up from the other side carrying Ashton. "There are my beautiful girls. Now we need . . . " His voice trailed off as his gaze found Brendon. His glance back to Miranda told her she wasn't mistaken in her assessment.

Miranda set her jaw and smiled. As they walked to the car together, Brendon's shoulders slumped lower and lower as if each step weighed him down more than the last.

What had happened over the past two hours? In church of all places?

The girls laughed and talked on the way home, but stony silence replaced Brendon's previous banter. The minute they pulled into the garage, he leapt out the door and into the house before Miranda could blink.

The girls ran inside shortly after, leaving Landon and Miranda staring at each other, unspoken questions between them.

Landon pierced the silence. "Did you see the same thing I did?"

"I know Sarah said this could happen. I hoped we'd be the exception. How could things change so quickly? He was so happy this morning."

"Should we talk to him or give him space?"

Miranda combed through the therapy sessions in her mind. What were they advised to do in this situation? She'd been so sure it wouldn't happen to them, she hadn't paid close attention. "Let's see if it'll work itself out. Maybe some alone time will help him reset."

They unstrapped Ashton and entered the house, greeted by the aroma of baking ribs from the slow cooker. Oh good. Brendon's favorite meal. If anything could bring him out of his funk, it would be the ribs and potatoes she'd started in the slow cooker that morning.

As they made the final preparations for lunch, Miranda scouted the stairs every few minutes, willing him to make an appearance. No such luck.

That was okay. They could give him some space.

But, the last time she gave him time alone . . .

Miranda set a plate on the table then leaned close to Landon. "I'm going to check on him."

He nodded, concern evident in his clouded eyes.

Miranda lurched up the stairs. She pushed away the flashes of that awful morning. It couldn't happen again. She paused halfway down the hall. She couldn't do this. What if she found something worse than last time? She shuddered. Should she go get Landon? She started to back up. To run away from the possibility of . . .

No. She could do this. Had to do this. She steadied her shoulders and pushed forward. Holding her breath, she softly knocked on the door.

"Come in."

She blew out the breath—*thank you, God*—and pushed the door open.

Brendon sat on the edge of his bed, his head in his hands. He didn't look up when she entered.

"Hey, honey." What she wouldn't give to have his therapist here. She crept to the chair by his desk and sat. "Would you like to talk about anything?"

Silence.

Don't be afraid of silence. Sarah's words from a session now echoed in the quiet. Give him time to formulate his own answer. Don't fill the void with prodding.

How long was she supposed to wait? She counted to herself. Ten . . . fifteen . . .

He lifted his head. His face twisted in agony, eyes brimming with tears. Her heart ached to wipe away his pain. She'd take on ten times his pain if it would free him from the torment.

He took a deep breath. "Why do they have to be so mean?"

"Who?" Mama bear roared inside her chest. She'd find out who he was talking about and march straight to—

"I thought they were my friends. Why do they do this?" He blinked. A trail of tears zigzagged down his face.

Miranda stood and perched next to him on the bed. She lightly touched his back. He didn't flinch or pull away. She wrapped her arm around him, and he melted into her shoulder as his body shuttered with sobs.

She swallowed past the lump in her throat. "What happened?" Was this connected to his suicide attempt?

Brendon unfolded himself from her embrace and fixed his gaze toward the floor. Silence again enveloped the room.

Wait for it. Don't force it.

When he started to speak, it was barely a whisper. Miranda leaned in closer.

"Do you remember when I went to Christian's birthday party last year?"

"Yes, I remember." Brendon had called to leave the slumber party shortly after midnight, saying he wasn't feeling well. She'd driven the few blocks to pick him up. He'd entered the car quiet and closed off, but she'd brushed it off. He'd been sick, after all.

Wasn't that when the bitterness toward the family began? Yes. That time marked a distinct change. What had happened?

"Well . . . at the party . . ." His gaze shifted toward her, then quickly back to the ground. Was he scared she'd be mad about something?

Miranda patted his back. "It's okay, honey. What happened?"

He pulled a loose thread from his pants and became laser focused on it. She fought the urge to grab it out of his hand and demand that he explain.

Wait. Let it come from him.

The words crept out. "Alice, and some other girls, snuck into the house." He stopped again, as if waiting for a reaction from her. Miranda knew Alice, a darling girl whose family attended the same church. The year before, Miranda had thought a little crush was building between Brendon and Alice. In fact, she and Landon once talked about how sweet it would be for the two to start dating in high school.

"Well . . . Alice went into one of the bedrooms. A few minutes later, Christian told me to go in. When I did, she was sitting on the bed without her shirt on." He quickly shot a glance at Miranda.

Her stomach dropped. *Stay calm. Don't show any reaction.* "What happened then?"

"She told me to come over."

A million scenarios rushed through Miranda's head. None of them good. She waited.

Landon's voice found its way up the stairs. "Hey, honey, lunch is ready. Can you guys come down?"

Miranda touched Brendon's shoulder. "Hold that thought." She shot to the door and stuck her head out. "Start without us. We'll be down in a little while."

She darted back to the bed. "What did you do?" *Please don't let him hear the panic in my voice.*

"I told her she was gonna get cold without a shirt. Then I walked out."

In a snap, her son appeared in a whole new light. Her teenage son had stood up to peer pressure—from a girl he had a crush on. Without batting an eye.

He coughed. "Anyway, when I came back out, Christian made fun of me. He told me I'd have to be gay not to want some action with Alice. Then, a couple of the other guys asked if I'd turned gay on them. Then they started making fun of gay people." He paused and clasped his hands together, his eyes hardening. "I yelled at them to stop, that being gay didn't make a person bad." He threw a glance her way. "You know, like Kevin, from Dad's firm."

Oh no. That couldn't have ended well. "They assumed you were talking about yourself and used that as more evidence against you?"

He nodded, fresh tears welling up. "After that, it didn't matter what I said, they mocked me and said they'd better warn all the other boys in school. I told Christian to knock it off, that he knew I wasn't gay. He said he wouldn't believe it unless I went back in the bedroom and 'proved it' with Alice." Brendon let out a deep sigh, his chest deflating along with it. "That's when I called you to come pick me up."

Miranda rocked back. That night in the car, he hadn't said a word. With all of that welling up inside, he'd stayed silent. "Why didn't you say anything to me then?"

A corner of his mouth raised. "I knew you would turn the car around and freak out on all of them."

"Of course I would've." Waves of anger washed over her. "In fact, I'm going to go have a talk with Christian right after we finish."

Brendon grabbed her arm. "No, Mom. That's why I didn't say anything then. It would just add more fuel to the fire. Your stepping in would've made it worse. I would've gotten pegged as a mamma's boy on top of everything else."

He was right, of course. Yelling at those kids would've fed her primal protective instinct to defend her son. But it wouldn't have solved anything. Deep breaths. She forced the anger back down. "What happened after that?"

He stared out the window. "It got pretty bad. The rumor mill at school spread like crazy, and soon complete strangers taunted me in the hallways and at lunch. More than being gay, rumors started about all sorts of things. Alice told people I'd tried to force her . . . that I took off her shirt."

That little tramp.

"We had third hour together, and the class started passing notes around about me."

Third hour. The one he'd started skipping.

He turned toward her, the pain in his eyes reaching out to her. "But you know what the hardest part has been?"

Could her heart take knowing more? "What's that?"

He stared back at the ground. "Church."

Miranda sat back. How could church be the—

Then it hit her. Alice. And Christian. Both regular members of their congregation. Both attended Brendon's Sunday School. Week after week, Miranda and Landon had dragged him to the one place they thought could be his refuge.

They'd sent him into the fire.

Guilt pounded her chest like a drum. "Oh, honey." She wrapped her arms around him again. "I had no idea. I'm so, so sorry. That must've been excruciating for you."

Brendon swallowed hard and nodded. Then he smirked. "You know what's ironic? One week we studied the lesson on Joseph from the Bible. You know, the one who ran away from Potiphar's wife?"

Miranda nodded.

"I thought I was doing the right thing." He gave a little laugh. "As I came home that night, I even thought about that story, about how I'd been like Joseph." Then his smile dropped. "Turns out, there was no pharaoh waiting to save me and turn me into a hero."

A light sparked in Miranda. "But you skipped the whole middle. Joseph didn't go right from Potiphar's house to the Pharaoh's court. He went to prison. For years."

Brendon cocked his head. "I guess I forgot about that part."

"When you read that story, it's easy to skip from the beginning to the end and see the happily ever after. When Joseph was trudging through the mucky years in prison, he didn't know that he would be a future ruler. He probably thought he would be executed. I bet Joseph wondered why he was being punished for making the right choice. But prison turned out to be exactly where he needed to be. That's where Pharaoh found him."

Mindy's words leapt into her mind. "You know, I met a woman a while back who taught me a great lesson. Often, the obstacles in our lives turn out to be the step to get us where we need to be."

Brendon sat up a little straighter.

She took the cue and proceeded. "I'm sure that, if you were to ask Joseph while he was stationed in Potiphar's house, what he would need to get a position in pharaoh's court, he wouldn't have said, 'Well, I think a number of years in prison would be the perfect preparation.' Yet, his imprisonment opened the doorway to a whole new life. One that saved not only his family, but also the entire nation of Israel."

The corners of Brendon's mouth lifted slightly. "Yeah, I guess you're right. I hadn't thought of it that way before."

There it was. Light settling back into his emerald eyes.

But what had chased it away today? They were in a good place now. Should she bring it up? Maybe she should wait until later.

She couldn't wait. "So . . . what happened today?"

A cloud appeared where the light had flickered moments before. Uh-oh. She'd pushed too far.

He slumped again. He eyed her, then stared back at the floor. He swallowed hard and rubbed his lips together.

Please tell me. Please trust me enough.

His voice again turned to a whisper. "As class was ending, Christian leaned over and said, 'Next time, you should try a gun.'"

"What? How did he—?" Miranda jumped to her feet. "That's it. There's no way this is going to be swept away. He's gone way too far this time. It needs to stop. *Now.*" Someone needed to know. That had to be some sort of crime. She turned to march out the door and straight to Christian's house.

"Mom, stop." She wheeled around and stared into his eyes. Those sea green eyes. Eyes that had carried the burden of pain alone for too long. So much needless pain.

"It won't do any good. It would only make it worse if he knew I told you." He sat up. "I'm stronger now. I have another session with Sarah tomorrow. I have you and Dad. I have a support network. I'll get through this."

She hesitated at the door, and he smiled. "Christian's words don't have power over me. They got to me a little today, but in the end, I controlled my response."

Again, her teenage son transformed before her eyes. Had he listened in on Mindy's lessons at the bench?

Yes. He was stronger now. He'd make it through this. And she'd walk with him. Not bulldozing the path for him. She'd let him build the strength by working through it in his way.

Chapter Twenty-Two

Miranda pulled up to the park on another dazzling fall day. The plush, tree-canopied streets now splashed the brilliant blue background with vibrant hues of the season. The air provided just enough cool to combat the sunny skies without making a jacket necessary. She'd counted down the days until this visit. She couldn't wait to tell Mindy about the breakthroughs at home.

As Miranda approached the bench, Mindy turned toward her sporting the craziest pair of sunglasses she'd ever seen. Oversize pearlescent pink hearts covered her eyes. Brilliant white pearls lined the frame of each heart. On the sides, slender rows of shimmering beads hung like tiny curtains, as if shielding her from distractions. The bling on the rows danced in the sunlight, highlighting the luminescent pink shade of the glasses.

Mindy smiled, her straight white teeth sparkling in the sun. "Hello, my friend."

Ashton squirmed as soon as Miranda sat, and she shifted to get a better hold on him. When Mindy held her arms to take him, he lunged toward her.

Huh. He'd never done that before. "I think he loves your sunglasses as much as I do. I've never seen anything like them."

Ashton snuggled into Mindy's arms.

"Oh, these old things?" Mindy tipped them down toward the bridge of her nose, revealing her playful eyes over the rims. "I only wear them when I need an eternal perspective on life."

Miranda chuckled. "Well, those do give a different view." Would she be brave enough to sport such a spectacle in public? Mindy paid no attention to the stares from strangers.

"Yes, they do." Mindy nodded. "They're the perfect antidote to getting lost in the here and now. These are my eternal eyewear." She pushed them back up into position.

"Please share—what's eternal eyewear?"

"It's seeing how everything around you fits into the eternal scheme of things."

"Okay." Miranda twisted her lips. This was no different than what they learned in Sunday School each week. "You mean, seeing others as Christ sees them."

"In one sense, yes. But it's also seeing yourself as Christ sees you. As a chosen vessel, like Paul."

Where was she going with this? "Christ called him a chosen vessel. He was one of the greatest missionaries of all time."

When Mindy nodded, dangling beads clinked together as they shimmered in the sun. "Indeed, he was. But Christ called him a chosen vessel *before* he became that great missionary. Before he even converted."

"Wait, what?" Miranda siphoned through the catalogue of Bible stories tucked in her brain.

"After Christ stopped him on the road to Damascus and covered his eyes with scales, He appeared to Ananias and commanded Ananias to go take care of him. When Ananias balked at helping one of the persecutors, Christ told him, *'Go thy way, for he is a chosen vessel unto me . . .'*"

Miranda ran her fingers through her hair. "Huh, I guess I hadn't thought much about the timing of that statement."

"The timing makes all the difference." Mindy kissed Ashton's head. "We don't have to do anything to prove our worth to God. He sees us as part of His masterpiece, even when we're in the middle of making mistakes. As with Paul, God sees beyond our mistakes. He sees what we can become. As burdensome as our mistakes are to us,

He offers to lift them from our shoulders. We don't have to carry the shame of our past." Mindy tipped the glasses forward again, and Miranda could see her eyes. Something about those eyes.

Miranda flicked her gaze toward the ground and focused on the grass in front of her feet. Her past again attacked her present, highlighting the shame she'd carted around for so many years. The car wreck . . . the phone call. Could God look beyond her mistake?

No. Her actions hadn't been a mistake. She'd been willful in her treatment of her mother. Willful and . . .

Selfish.

She stole a glance toward Mindy. Could she see the shame Miranda had carried all these years, strapped to her with unbreakable cords? Could Miranda let go of the burden? She opened her mouth. Nothing came out. She couldn't do it. She couldn't put a voice to her guilt and condemn herself all these years later. She looked again at Mindy. Those soft, blue eyes. Not forcing. Inviting.

"Do you remember me telling you about my mom? About the letter she wrote before she died, saying she failed?"

Mindy slowly nodded.

Miranda's chest contracted, threatening to strangle the secret within. Slowly, the words bubbled to the surface. "If she was teetering on the edge of a cliff . . . " One deep breath, and her confession spilled over. "Then I'm the one who pushed her."

"Why do you say that?"

"The night before her accident . . . " Miranda tried to swallow the lump in her throat. "We got into a fight. She'd given me a trip to Niger for my birthday months before, just the two of us. But she needed to renew her passport before we could book plane tickets. A few months passed, and she hadn't gotten around to doing it. I pushed and pushed, but she always had some excuse."

Miranda stopped. The pieces slid together. That dark family year. Her mom had been dealing with so much, in multiple areas. Of course she kept forgetting about the passport. A wave of guilt-induced nausea stabbed Miranda's gut. How had she not seen that before?

"That night, the last time we talked, I asked her again. I accused her of not wanting to go on the trip with me, of stalling until it would be too late. I told her to do it the next day so we could get the tickets.

She said there was a big storm coming, and the roads would be bad. I've never told anyone this. Not even Landon." The lump grew in Miranda's throat. She couldn't say it. How could she have said it then? Heat rose in her cheeks. The darkness inside threatened to swallow her whole.

If only it would.

Slowly, like a robot, she released the words. "I accused her of making more excuses. She'd grown up driving those roads all winter long. Why was she scared of one measly snowstorm? The passport office was only two miles from our house. I told her if she loved me, she would brave the roads like a true Idahoan." Miranda's voice cracked. "The next morning, when I learned how bad the storm was, I called to tell her to not go . . . to apologize for my selfishness. But she didn't answer."

Hearing the words out loud brought the memory crashing down. The endless ringing. The rising panic.

Then . . . the phone call that changed her life. And solidified her condemnation.

Miranda buried her face in her hands as her body rocked with sobs.

The slight breeze blowing dried leaves along the cement path provided the only sound between them. The pressure of Mindy's hand on her back supported her more than any hollow words could've. Despite the grief that moved through her, the grip of guilt slowly loosened in the wake of her spoken secret.

Mindy broke the silence. "That's a heavy burden to bury. You've kept it hidden a long time. But shame breeds in darkness. The deeper you bury it, the more it grows. You now have a choice to make. You can allow your shame to imprison you in the past. Or"—Mindy released one hand from holding Ashton and lifted it toward the beautiful blue sky—"you can release the past and allow the future to flow."

"But how?" Miranda uncrossed one leg and crossed the other. "I don't know how to let it go." A flicker of hope warred against the emotional captivity that had plagued her for so long.

"You follow God's invitation to cast your burden on Him." A playful smile formed on her mouth. "Don't worry, He's a good catch. He won't miss." She grew serious once again. "He invites. He doesn't compel."

CHAPTER TWENTY-TWO

Miranda's head snapped up. "What do you mean He—?"

"We have to voluntarily hand our load to him. It's only when we release our grip on our pain, our grudges, and our struggles that He can carry them for us. The first step is letting go."

"And the next step is walking away?"

"The next step is walking forward. With Christ." Ashton stirred, and Mindy swayed side to side, lulling him to sleep. Her gaze once again found Miranda's. "But as long as you hold onto your burdens, you remain a prisoner of the past. You can't fully embrace the present. Like the Jewish artist who blamed himself for the holocaust."

"Huh?"

"In the early 1900's, he traveled to Vienna to study at a prestigious art academy. Because he was Jewish, they said he couldn't be admitted. But he begged the university to at least let him take the exam. Because of his talent, the school admitted him. The person sitting next to him, a young Adolf Hitler, got rejected. For years after the war, the Jewish man thought that, if he hadn't pushed, if his spot had been given to Hitler, then the Holocaust may not have happened."

Miranda rocked back. "But he had no control over Hitler's actions. There were so many other factors involved." Like the first rays of sunrise, understanding brightened a dark spot in Miranda's heart.

Mindy leaned in. "Nor did you have power over your mother's actions. You don't have the control to change what you said then. But you do have the option to give yourself grace now. To forgive oneself, according to an Auschwitz survivor, Dr. Edith Egert, is to give up the need for a different past."

Could it be that simple? To hand her burden to Christ? She'd cried countless nights for God to forgive her. It never occurred to her that she needed to forgive herself. And her mother.

A draft of cool air brushed against Miranda's warm cheeks as leaves swirled softly in circles around their feet. She recounted the conversation she'd tried to rewind and reword thousands of times throughout the years . . . trying to give herself a different past. Even the recent conversation with her brothers in August on the farm. She'd replayed that visit since returning home, willing herself to go back and resolve the unspoken tension and do something to change the family dynamic when she'd had the chance.

Could it be that simple? To release the need for the past to change, and instead move forward with the knowledge gleaned?

"When you release the need for a different past, and only focus on that which you can control, you also release the need for every situation to happen as planned." Mindy's words, though spoken softly, hit Miranda like a trumpet. The arguments with Mom. The visit with her brothers. Resolutions she craved, yet hadn't been able to bring about.

Miranda's phone alarm broke the momentary silence. She snoozed it with a sigh. "I wish we had more time. I'm learning so much from you."

"You're merely discovering what's already inside, waiting to surface. I'm just an old woman who likes to babble." Mindy grinned, then gently shifted Ashton back into Miranda's arms. "And thank you for letting me relive the joy of snuggling a new baby." She took one last look at Ashton and stroked his head.

Something glistened in Mindy's eyes. Was she crying?

Miranda leaned toward her, but the alarm rang again, which startled both her and Ashton. She was about to be late picking up Isabella.

Mindy pulled a tissue from her purse and blew her nose. "You better be on your way." She winked, no sign of tears.

Miranda shrugged off the thought of Mindy crying as she rose. "Goodbye. Thanks again for your advice and wisdom."

Let the past go. Embrace the present. Welcome the future.

Could it be that simple?

Chapter Twenty-Three

That night, Miranda fed Ashton with her eyes half closed. Landon entered the room as she finished. She sighed as she stood. "If I don't get at least a few hours of uninterrupted sleep, my head will explode." Miranda laid the baby in his crib. He'd spent the last week turning the night hours into party time.

Landon leaned over the crib and stroked Ashton's head. "Maybe he's teething."

"It's early for that. The others didn't get theirs until about six months. He's barely two-and-a-half." Miranda flopped into the recliner.

Olivia burst into the room with Isabella tight on her heels. "Mom! Dad! I have my Halloween costume figured out."

"Whoa, wait a minute. Didn't you already decide on your costume last month?" Miranda had sighed with relief when Livy had declared she wanted to be a dancer and wear last year's dance costume. Miranda's circle of talents did not include costume design. She cringed when the kids came home with grand illusions of what she could conjure up for them. Change direction two weeks before the big night? While adjusting to a new baby? She barely had time to breathe.

"I thought of something even *better*." Ever the dreamer, Olivia wasn't swayed in the least by Miranda's hesitation. "Let's all go as

Moana characters. I'll be Moana, Dad can be the chief, Brendon can be Maui, and—"

"No!" Isabella cut in. "I wanna be Moana." Her mouth puckered into her signature pout as she folded her arms in a huff.

Miranda could've called this a mile away. With *Moana* topping Isabella's current movie preference, she'd never consent to go as anyone other than the Island Princess. Miranda sensed a meltdown on the horizon, and she was in no mood to play referee at this point in the day—on zero hours of sleep.

As Miranda geared up to put her foot down on the call for costume changes, Brendon slid through the doorway. "I see what's happening here."

Before Miranda could get a word out, he continued. "You're face to face with greatness." And there, right before their eyes, he sang Maui's signature song from the movie.

Unfortunately for all involved, Brendon inherited Miranda's lack-of singing ability, but that didn't stop him from stomping, flexing, and portraying the lovable character in his own classic Brendon style. Landon jumped in partway through, and they finished the song as a satirical father and son duet. By the time they rounded out the last line, everyone was laughing so hard no one could hear them. Miranda's cheeks throbbed from the laughter.

After the song, they each held an extended muscle flexing pose, which made everyone howl even more because they were both in their pajamas. It took a while before anyone could speak. Every few seconds, Izzy or Olivia cracked up and sent the rest of them into hysterics again. How long had it been since they'd laughed like that, all together? Especially with Brendon in the spotlight. This moment of laughing together was healing for them all.

"I'm perfect for Maui." Brendon continued to flex his long, skinny pasty arms, sending the girls into another giggle fit.

"Well, you certainly have the height for it," Landon said. It was the only positive correlation between the slender, blond, green-eyed boy and the muscular, tanned, Polynesian demi-god. And it was true. Brendon had grown at least six inches the past year, surpassing Miranda by his birthday and closing in on Landon's six-foot-three frame.

"I think it's a perfect fit." Olivia could hardly speak through her bout of laughter.

Isabella stomped the ground. "I wanna be Moana!"

"Hey." Olivia turned toward Isabella. "How about we both be Moana? You can be her when she's little, and I'll be her when she is bigger."

Isabella clapped. "Yes! I want to be her when she put the flower in her hair."

"Dad can be the chief." Brendon folded his arms in the manner of Moana's father in the movie, which also happened to be the stance Landon was holding right then. The coincidence threw them all into peals of laughter again.

Caught up in the moment, Miranda quit thinking about how she would pull off getting costumes for everyone in time. "Who would I be?"

She'd opened her mouth to suggest she could be Moana's mom, the wife of the chief, when Brendon jumped in again. "Oh, that's obvious, Mom. You're the village crazy lady."

She started to object when they all started laughing again. "That's truer than you know. Although, I met someone recently at the park who would also fit that role perfectly."

Olivia paused her giggles. "I know who you mean, Mom. It's that funny lady who was at the park this summer. The one who got Izzy to put on sunscreen, right?"

Miranda nodded. If Olivia had seen Mindy's unique sunglasses, that would've solidified it in her mind.

Olivia broke her thought process. "She'd be perfect. Can you ask her if she can come with us on Halloween? Please, Mom? Please?"

"She's visiting her own family, and I'm sure that, if she's still here on Halloween, she'll want to spend time with them and see all their fun costumes on Halloween night."

They talked more about how they could make this idea come alive. For the first Halloween in years, Miranda let herself dream with them instead of discouraging the plans due to her lack of costuming confidence. For Ashton, it was a toss-up between having him be the funny chicken, the friendly pig, or the shiny crab.

"Okay, everyone, it's way past bedtime. We'll finalize costumes in the morning." Miranda walked the kids back to their rooms to re-tuck them in.

After finishing the good-nights, Miranda flipped their light switches and headed back to her room. She paused as she passed the pictures of the kids on the wall.

Her kids.

Her family.

She needed to let go of the past and focus on the future. It was time to lay her past at His feet and walk forward.

Oh, Mom. How I love you. Thank you for raising me. Whatever happened that day doesn't matter anymore. I still miss you deeply. I'm forever sorry that the last words I said to you were selfish and caustic. I'd give anything to have a real good-bye. To tell you that I love you. But I need to release the guilt and let go of my shame. You were the best mother I could have asked for. I'll take the lessons you taught me, let go of the rest, and move forward with my own family now.

Let go of the rest . . . One issue still prodded her, prevented her from moving forward. Her struggle to force her siblings into a different family dynamic. Maybe she needed to accept her brothers as they were. If the occasion came, she resolved to be more open. But she didn't need to force anything with them, or with anyone. She could view them as Christ saw them, as fellow travelers on this eternal journey.

As she flipped the hall light switch, something changed within. The heaviness that had weighed on her for so long—too long—dislodged. In its place, a lightness took root. Along with a question. What did walking forward entail? How did she walk forward with her family and still find her own purpose?

Ashton whimpered from his crib. She scooped him up and settled in to nurse him again. With any luck, he would soon be sleeping longer hours, allowing her more moments of precious sleep as well. As she settled in to nurse, she turned to Landon, who was working on his computer. "Honey, are we actually going to do a family theme for Halloween? It's only two weeks away. I don't think I can pull off six costumes by then."

"Two weeks is plenty of time for the almighty Amazon." Landon turned his computer to show her some samples of Moana costumes. "I'll take care of it. You won't have to do a thing. We'll get them ordered and call it good. No stress on your part." He clicked on one. "See how easy this is? Costume one is done."

———

A week later, the aroma of chili bubbling in the crockpot rounded out the fall season. Miranda lifted the lid and inhaled the spicy scent as she stirred the blend of beans, hamburger, and tomatoes. Her stomach growled. She'd better get started on the corn bread.

The air danced with anticipation as the girls hovered around the front window. Costumes were scheduled to arrive today.

"How many more minutes, Mommy?" Izzy ran from the doorway to the kitchen.

"Honey, I already told you, I have no idea when it will come. And staring at the road won't bring the truck any sooner." Miranda stirred the cornmeal into the eggs, sugar, and oil.

Olivia kept her vigil at the window. "But what if it doesn't come tonight?"

"We still have a week before Halloween. There's plenty of time for the package to come. If it doesn't come tonight, it'll come tomorrow. Help set the table while you wait."

The grumbling girls trudged into the kitchen and grabbed plates and silverware. A knock at the door brought squeals and clinks as they threw the utensils and plates on the table in their dash to the front door. Olivia reached it first and threw it open. A moment later, she returned with a box. "I was getting scared that they wouldn't make it. I can't believe they're here." She dragged in the box and ripped it open.

Even Brendon, who Miranda was sure would lose interest after his one-hit-wonder performance, laughed as he held up the Maui costume.

"Are you still up for this?" Miranda bit her bottom lip. If he wasn't ready, she'd let him off the hook. His health was more important.

He stuck his arms into the sleeves of the costume. "How else am I going to get any muscles?"

She chuckled. "Yep, that oughta bring all the girls running." When was the last time they'd bantered like this? "It's a good thing the village crazy lady will be with you. I can fight off the girls as they come in droves." She crouched into a defensive stance.

"That'll scare them away." His laugh was like an old friend who had just returned from a long journey.

The girls ripped into their costume boxes and squealed at the results. "Mom! This is perfect." Olivia hadn't even removed the plastic. "I love it."

"Where's mine?" Isabella searched through the box.

"Here it is, Izzy." Olivia handed her a smaller version of the Moana costume. Luckily, Landon had found one with long sleeves, perfect for their Midwest Halloween. In any given year, it was a toss-up whether they would be trick-or-treating in shorts or full winter gear. The long sleeves would save Isabella, who refused to cover any sort of costume, no matter how big the goose bumps on her arms got.

Izzy squealed as she grabbed the perfect pink flower and attached it haphazardly into her hair. Miranda had better put it away, or it would get lost by the end of the week.

"Can we try them on, to make sure they fit? Please, Mom? Please?" The girls both clung to their costumes as if each one carried the heart of Te Fiti.

"Sure, but don't lose any of the small pieces." Miranda clipped Ashton into his swing, then slipped into the kitchen to finish the corn bread.

As she slid the pan into the oven, Izzy dashed in. "Mommy! I love it. Can you zip me please?"

Miranda dried her hands and lifted the zipper. "A perfect fit. You look exactly like Moana."

Izzy beamed.

Olivia entered, holding the necklace with the emerald heart of Te Fiti attached. "Mom, could you help me put this on?"

"Hey. I didn't get one. I want it." Before Miranda reached Olivia, for the handoff, Isabella snatched the heart and scurried from the kitchen.

Olivia pivoted and zoomed after her. "Mo-om, tell her to give it back . . . Izzy, you're gonna get cursed for stealing that, like Maui."

Izzy screeched to a halt and wheeled around. "No, I don't wanna get cursed." As she closed the distance separating the two, she held the stone above her head with both hands. "I will restore the heart of Te Fiti."

Olivia put her hands on her hips. "You messed up. She tells Maui to restore the heart."

Izzy's arms lowered as her face pouted. "Uh-uh. Moana does it. 'Member, at the end? Maui leaves and her gamma lady comes up and says 'who you are?'" Izzy lifted the emerald into the air once again. "I'm Moana, and I'm gonna restore the heart myself!"

Miranda gave one more stir to the chili. "Izzy's right, Liv. The whole movie Moana tried to get Maui to do it, but in the end, she realized it was her journey to make."

Huh. Had she not watched the movie on repeat over the past few months, she would've glossed right over that part. She set down the spoon and moved toward the girls, kneeling down. "You know my favorite thing about that movie?"

Both girls turned to face her.

"Moana discovered her own path in life and her own purpose. She didn't get sucked into what society told her she should do. She listened to her inner voice. You two listen to your inner voice as you go through life."

Ashton cried from the swing, ready for his dinner.

Miranda stood, heading toward the baby. "You, too, little one. You need to follow your inner voice." She picked him up and settled into the chair to nurse.

"Hey, Mom." Olivia stood in front of her holding the emerald necklace.

Miranda lifted her head. "I can help you with that as soon as I finish feeding Ashton."

Olivia studied the emerald, then stared at Miranda with her deep hazel eyes. "What's your dream? What's calling you from inside?"

Miranda blinked. Sweet Olivia. So perceptive and wiser than her ten-year-old body. Her daughter truly was an old soul, perhaps sent to this family not to be taught by Miranda, but to teach her.

Her thoughtful question brought tears to Miranda's eyes. So often, her children acted as if she were more of a personal chef and maid than a real person with hopes and dreams of her own.

"I am a connector." Saying it now sent a jolt through her, much like that night she first filled out the circles.

She'd stuffed that experience away through the dark months. But now, in the presence of her children, saying the word out loud brought it surging to the surface, ready to take its rightful place as part of Miranda's core.

"Huh?" Olivia's scrunched up nose and questioning face brought Miranda back to the present. "What does that even mean?"

Miranda had to laugh. She knew her daughter's expressions enough to know Olivia was utterly underwhelmed by this declaration.

"It means, my dear Livy . . . " How could she explain it when she wasn't sure herself?

But as she opened her mouth, the words formed themselves. "I connect people to what they most need. As a mom, I connect each of you kids with what you need. I used to help build machines by combining different parts together. Once, I even drew plans for a drill to connect people in a small country in Africa to clean water, which would save them from walking miles every day to carry water to their homes."

"What?" Olivia's head tilted to the side. "Who doesn't have water in their house?" Her children didn't have a grasp on life outside their little bubble here in the United States. And why would they? They'd never traveled anywhere besides tourist destinations. And Miranda had only told them bits and pieces of her time living in Niger.

"Livy, it's hard to imagine when we have sinks all over the house, but millions of people don't have access to clean running water. They spend most of their days hauling water from rivers to their homes." Miranda motioned to the food they were about to feast on. "You've never opened our fridge or pantry to find it empty, but there are people around the world who don't even have a fridge, nor any food in their pantry, either. They often go to bed hungry."

Olivia's face clouded over. "How can we help? Can I share my food with them? Can we send some water to them?"

Miranda's hand flew to her chest. This girl and her oversized heart.

Isabella rushed over. "I wanna help too! I wanna share my food too."

"You two have the biggest hearts of anyone I know." Miranda stood up with Ashton and pulled them both into a hug.

Isabella pulled away and ran off.

Olivia followed Miranda into the kitchen.

When Miranda turned to face her, Olivia focused on her with an intensity Miranda hadn't seen in her eyes before. "Mom, I want to help. What can I do?"

"I'll tell you what, honey, I'll figure out a way we can help together. I'd love to help kids around the world get clean water, and I'd love to do it with you." She gave Olivia another squeeze.

"Count me in too."

Miranda startled and wheeled around as Brendon walked around the corner. Hadn't he been in his room? He must've been listening. A lump sprang to Miranda's throat. "Thank you, Brendon. I'd love to do something together. If we all put our heads together, I'm sure we could do some great things."

The oven timer buzzed. "Well, first I need to connect your bodies with some food. If we're going to help the world, we need to fuel ourselves." Miranda motioned toward the table where the plates still sat in a heap. "You can help now by setting the table."

Miranda grabbed a pitcher and placed it under the faucet. She lifted the lever, and a stream of clean, pure water filled the pitcher. A miracle right inside her own kitchen. How many people, her people, were trudging along the well-worn path right now to retrieve this precious liquid? Somehow, she would resurrect the decades-old promise to herself.

"Daddy." Olivia wiggled in her seat, her spoon clanging against her chili bowl. "We're going to give drinks to the kids!"

"Is that so?" Landon motioned to the pitcher he was using to pour water into their glasses. "Isn't that what we're doing right now?"

"No, not us, Daddy." Olivia giggled. "We're going to give water to the kids in Africa, so they don't have to walk all day to find it. Mommy said we could."

Landon turned to Miranda, his gaze asking for more information. "That sounds like a good thing to do." He spoke to Olivia but kept his eyes on Miranda.

Miranda opened her mouth to clarify, but Brendon spoke first. "Mom told us she's a connector, and she wants to connect people to clean water and food. Which I think is pretty cool."

Did she hear him right? Did Brendon call her . . . cool?

She focused back on what he was saying. "We aren't sure how we'll do it yet, but I thought . . . "

Who was this kid sitting across from her?

"About my Eagle Scout project."

Miranda almost choked on her water. *Act natural. Don't let your jaw drop.* They hadn't mentioned a thing about this since the ordeal. She'd accepted that it wasn't going to happen.

Yet, here he sat, talking as if he'd been planning it all along. She peeked at Landon. His quizzical stare told her this was news to him as well.

Brendon popped a piece of corn bread into his mouth and swallowed. "I think I want to help feed hungry kids. I'm not sure how to do it. Maybe a food drive for one of the shelters in town or fund a water project somewhere, something like that. I don't know."

Landon recovered quicker than Miranda. "That sounds like a great idea. Let's jump on the computer after dinner and check out some options."

"Cool, okay." Brendon spooned another mouthful of chili.

He was moving forward with his Eagle? On his own?

Her teenage son called her cool.

Please, don't be a dream.

Chapter Twenty-Four

Miranda lost count of the number of phone calls and emails she sent the following week trying to find a humanitarian group they could join. A few groups made mission trips, but almost none allowed children.

The shock of her children not knowing what billions of people around the world faced every day was a wake-up call. It drove her to find a way to help them become global citizens. They needed to do this as a family.

As Miranda waited in the school pickup line, she grabbed her phone. What more could she search? She'd exhausted all the terms she could think of regarding service and humanitarian work.

Whatever happened to the drill project? Her class had moved forward with the design she'd thought up before leaving school and produced a working prototype, but did they ever do anything with it after that?

She clicked on Google.

Human powered drill. Hmm, power drills? No, that wasn't it.

Human powered well drill.

The third headline caught her eye. "College Students Build Human-Powered Drill that Brings Fresh Water to Twelve Communities in Africa." Her jaw dropped.

Miranda clicked on the link, revealing a picture resembling the sketch she'd drawn years ago. Why hadn't anyone told her? The pang of hurt was quickly replaced by a surge of pride. It worked. Her brainchild was now a reality, finding fresh water for people halfway around the world.

"Hi, Mom." Olivia jumped in the car.

Miranda startled, then smiled. "How was school today?"

"I spilled ketchup on my shirt at lunch." Olivia twisted toward Miranda, exposing a big blotch of red right in the middle of the image.

A butterfly.

Miranda gaped at the shirt. The butterfly effect. One idea. One drill. One drawing. Even though she'd left school, the idea had grown wings and flown halfway around the world. A warmth spread throughout her chest.

"I know, it's bad. Do you think you can get it out? This is my favorite shirt." Olivia wiped at it with her fingers.

Miranda shook out of her daze. "I'm sure it'll come right out." She smiled as she merged into the street to drive home.

When they pulled in, the girls ran into the house. With Ashton sleeping soundly in his car seat and Brendon at a counseling appointment, she snatched this window of time. Sydney, her friend from the engineering program, would know about the drill. Her phone contacts displayed Sydney's number. Would it still be the same? *Please still be the right number.*

After three rings a familiar voice filled the line.

"Hi, Sydney, it's Miranda Williams—er, formerly Johnson. It's been so long. How are you doing?" As the only two females in the mechanical engineering program years before, Miranda and Sydney became fast friends, and their bond remained strong even after Miranda moved across the country. Marriage and family kept them geographically apart, and, for the past several years, the only communication they shared were Christmas cards and the occasional Facebook updates.

"It's great to hear your voice. We're doing great. How are things in tundra land? You're still in Minnesota, right?"

"Yep, still here braving the winters. How's California living?"

"As beautiful as ever. We need to convince that husband of yours that lawyers are needed here as much as in the permafrost."

Miranda laughed. "Come February, I might get on board with that idea."

With the window of time closing before the girls would need her, she jumped right in. "Did you follow up on that drill project after graduation? I read an article about a drill being used in Africa. Is that the same one you guys did for the capstone project?"

"Can you believe it? It's a funny story. After graduation, we all went our separate ways, and I didn't think much more about it. Then about five years ago, Dr. Scott contacted me to tell me he'd found a group in the field who wanted to try it out. I couldn't go on the trip, but Ray and Brian did."

Miranda pursed her lips. Ray and Brian. Though they'd never said it outright, through the years of the program, Ray and Brian both made it clear that mechanical engineering was a "guy field." No wonder they hadn't contacted Miranda to let her know her idea was still moving ahead.

Sydney continued. "Then, last year, my schedule freed up. John offered to hold down the fort at home, and you'll never guess where I got to spend a couple of weeks, two months ago." Sydney didn't wait for Miranda to guess. "Africa!"

Miranda's mouth dropped open and silence came out. She swallowed, then squeaked out, "You, the comfort creature? Which country?"

"I know, right? It was amazing. For the record, I no longer think you were crazy for living there."

Miranda's smile widened. How she'd missed talking with this dear soul. "What part of Africa?"

"We were in Tanzania putting in more drills. They're now up to twelve functioning drills there, with two more in the Republic of Congo."

"What? That's amazing."

Miranda didn't regret her decision to marry and start a family. Still, a small part of her longed to be a bigger part of this, to make an impact on hundreds, if not thousands, of lives.

No matter. Her dream had moved forward. "Syd, that's the coolest thing ever. I'm jealous you got to see the drill come to life. I'd give anything to be a part of that."

"Funny you should call right now. Some guy approached Dr. Scott about putting some drills in another country. I can't remember the name of it, somewhere by the Sahara. I think it started with an N?"

Electricity shot through Miranda. Could it be possible? "Would that be Niger by any chance?"

"Yes! At least I think that's what it was. Dr. Scott would know for sure. Do you have his contact information? I can send it to you if you don't."

"Go ahead and send it over."

"Will do. I know they wanted to start something but were hitting some roadblocks. Just a sec." Sydney's daughter spoke in the background, and then Sydney's voice came back onto the line. "Jenny has another crisis that needs attention. I better run. It's wonderful to talk to you. Give Dr. Scott a call. I'm sure he'd love to hear from you."

After hanging up, Miranda unbuckled Ashton and headed inside to check on the girls.

"Mommy, can I have a snack please?" Miranda peeled and sliced in record time, placing two plates of carrots and apple slices on the counter.

Olivia eyed the computer. "Hey, Mom, can I play Math Masters?"

Perfect. She could play, and Izzy would no doubt be mesmerized by the computer game. That should buy Miranda enough time for one more phone call. She headed upstairs with Ashton to get at least a little quiet while she talked to her old college professor.

Once settled in the chair with Ashton, Miranda stared at the number as her thumb hovered over the call button. Would Dr. Scott remember her? She would never forget him. As a college co-ed in mechanical engineering, she'd received all sorts of responses from professors toward females, not all of them favorable. Though many tried to hide it, their initial reaction of amusement, surprise, or even disdain toward Miranda on the first day of class usually told her everything she needed to know before they'd said a word.

When professor Scott had walked into the room the first day of calculus-based physics and eyed Sydney and Miranda, his genuine smile and nod brushed away her misgivings. He not only welcomed them both with open arms but made it his mission to make sure they both had every opportunity to excel in the program.

Later, Miranda had dreaded telling Professor Scott when she decided to leave the program to get married and move. Her decision could've pushed him to become calloused like some of the other professors, accusing her of fulfilling the stereotype of a woman who didn't follow through in the name of family. He surprised her again by being fully supportive of her decision and offering to help her in the future if she ever wanted to finish her degree. She thanked him at the time, but inwardly told herself she could never impose on his generosity. She was the one walking away.

And yet, here she was.

Miranda took a deep breath and hit the call button.

Good, voicemail. She left her name and number—and a quick rundown on who she was in case he'd forgotten—and ended the call.

Five minutes later, her phone rang.

It was him. "Miranda. Of course I remember you. It's great to hear from you."

Her shoulders relaxed. She wasn't such a nonexistent has-been after all. "Thank you for calling me back. Sorry for the long message. I spoke with Sydney and got excited about the drill projects."

"As well you should. If I remember right, you're the one who came up with the idea to make the drill in the first place, right?"

Miranda's heart thumped faster. He remembered. "It's always been a dream of mine. I can't tell you how great it is to see that it's come to life. Thank you for believing in the idea and moving forward with the class to build one."

"Let me fill you in on the next move. Steven Collins, the founder of a non-profit called Families Helping Families, approached me about six months ago. His good friend immigrated from Niger decades ago. Steven was so impressed with his friend that he wants to do a project there to honor him. The problem is, his friend died a few years ago, and Steve doesn't have any leads in that area."

Tingles shot through Miranda's body. *Don't scream. Don't drop the phone. Remain calm.* "I lived in Niger as a Peace Corps volunteer during college. There are a few people I still keep in contact with, and

I know several communities that could benefit from a water project."
Miranda flashed through her time in the Peace Corps. The villages.
The people. The vast desert lands that covered over eighty percent of
the nation, making water a rare commodity—and clean water almost
unattainable by the majority of the population.

"Is that right? Well, how about that? I think this might be an
answer to prayer."

"In more ways than you know, Dr. Scott." Miranda sniffed back
the tears that begged to release her gratitude.

He gave her Steve's number and they said their good-byes. But
before hitting the button. She said, "Wait, Dr. Scott?"

"Yes?"

Should she ask? Would it even be possible? She'd quit the program
once. Did she have the audacity to want back in? She had to at least
ask. "I know it's been a long time. Probably too long. But I wanted to
check about the possibility of . . . perhaps . . . finishing that last year
and getting my degree?"

She bit her lip. Her stomach gripped. Would he laugh at her? A
random student from the past wanting to jump back in. What a joke.

"I would love to help you with this. In fact, your timing is perfect.
We're working to start an online option for some of the classes in the
program. It's not quite functional, but I think we can work something
out to benefit both of us. We could have you help us test some of our
distance learning formats. A trip to Niger could certainly count for
some credits as well. Let me check some things on my end and see
what we can do."

Good thing this wasn't a video call. No one to witness her goofy
grin. The screams she kept inside exploded through her fist pump. The
jolt woke up Ashton, who let out a screech.

"Oh, sorry about that. I think my baby's ready to eat." When
Miranda hung up, she got Ashton settled and dialed the number Dr.
Scott had given her.

Before he answered, she knew.

They were going to Africa.

Now to get Landon on board.

Chapter Twenty-Five

The next morning, Miranda had the kids up and fed in record time, though it wouldn't make any difference how early they were ready. School started at the same time every day, and she couldn't head to the park any earlier than that. She willed the clock to tick faster as the excitement of the last twenty-four hours surged through her.

As the time to leave for school drew near, Miranda bundled Ashton into his car seat.

"C'mon, everyone, it's time to go."

Brendon and Olivia remained fixed on the computer. Olivia didn't turn as she answered. "Just a minute. Brendon's almost finished uploading a picture.

Miranda paused behind them and studied his work. The boy had talent. "That picture's amazing. I think I want to buy a copy. But now, you need to focus on school. You two have five minutes while I get the other two kids in the car, then you need to come out."

"We'll be there." Olivia's eyes stayed trained on the picture.

With the littles loaded in the car, Miranda walked back and stuck her head in the doorway. "Time's up, we need to go."

Chairs scooted across the floor, and the two grabbed their coats and backpacks.

As they pulled out of the driveway, Miranda eyed Brendon. "I had an interesting call last night."

His eyebrows lifted.

"I got offered a chance to help an organization build a drill and get water to communities in Africa."

Olivia piped up from the back seat. "Africa? Do you get to go there? Can I come?"

"I'm hoping we can all go." Walking the streets of her far away home with her children played like a movie through her mind. Miranda couldn't stop the smile that formed.

Brendon tapped the console. "Really? All of us? Do you think I could do something with the drill for my Eagle Project?"

She glanced over. His face held eager anticipation. "It's wonderful how you want to help with drilling on the trip. It's close to my heart. But is it close to yours? You should find a project that lights up your soul . . . like your camera does."

He raised one shoulder. "It's okay, Mom, I want to help with your project."

She squeezed his hand. "There are many ways you can help. You don't have to do it the same way that I do. It'd mean more for you and for those you are helping if you gave them something you love. It's like sharing a part of yourself with them."

"I don't know what that would be, though." He gazed out the window.

"What makes you come alive? From the outside, I see you light up every time you head outside with your camera."

"I love it. But I don't know how taking pictures of trees and sunrises can help a starving and thirsty family."

"You'd be amazed. Giving something as simple as a picture can fill them with hope. Most of the families I visited had few, if any, pictures. They loved looking at my pictures. In fact, when I left, I gave some families the pictures from my walls. I think that gift meant more to them than any loaf of bread."

Miranda stole a glance toward Brendon. His eyes were laser focused on her. Her heart melted. "In fact, you know what pictures of mine they loved the most?"

Brendon raised his eyebrows.

"My family pictures. They'd sit forever staring at the few I had with me. I don't remember seeing any family pictures out in the rural villages. What a wonderful gift. Something they would cherish forever."

Brendon's eyes widened. "Do you think so? A simple family picture?"

"I'd bet on it."

"That would be a great project." His whole face brightened, and she could see the wheels spinning. "I could bring some fold-up backdrops, or we could take outdoor shots. From the pictures you've shown me, they have a natural backdrop that would beat anything I could manufacture."

He talked rapidly as the ideas flowed. "And I could fundraise to get a portable printer. We could get some durable photo paper and frames to give them a quality family picture."

He spoke until they reached the high school, the most he'd ever talked on a drive to or from school. He'd found his thing, and the effect was magical.

On the drive back, Olivia peppered Miranda with questions.

"How long will it take to get there?"

"Is it hot in Africa?"

"I wanna help to. What can I do?"

Miranda glanced in the mirror. Olivia was leaning forward, her eyes shining. Miranda needed to temper this. She hadn't even broached the subject with Landon yet. "I'm sure you'll be able to help. But there are still a lot of things to figure out with the trip. We don't know for sure if we can go." Maybe she should've waited to say anything to any of them.

When they returned home, thirty minutes remained before the girls needed to leave for school. They headed outside to ride bikes around the cul-de-sac while she nursed Ashton once more. No hungry babies today. She wouldn't have anything stall this visit with Mindy.

Before she finished nursing, the door flew open. Isabella limped in, tears flowing down her cheeks. "Mommy, my toe got hurt. I have blood. I wanna Band-Aid!" The last part came out in a wail as she cocked her head back.

Miranda set Ashton down and opened her arms. "Come here, sweetie. Let's have a peek."

Isabella fell into her arms.

She gently lifted the small foot. A small scrape on her big toe trickled a little blood. If only Isabella would listen to one of the countless reminders to wear shoes on bikes. She fought the urge to say, "Told ya so," and got up to get the first aid kit. The wound matched the several other scratches and scrapes on other toes, for this same occurrence.

Miranda huffed. Would yet another lecture sink in where all the others had failed? Probably not. She wiped away the blood and replaced it with a pretty pink bandage.

Once it was secure, Isabella jumped up and bolted toward the door, but pivoted before she reached it. "Wait. I need shoes. They'll keep my toes safe, won't they Mom?" Without waiting for an answer, Izzy shot to the mud room and retrieved her shoes.

Huh, maybe something had sunk in from the previous lessons. With shoes in place, Izzy bounded out the door.

Ashton's screeches yanked Miranda back to the here and now. He was still hungry and let her know he didn't appreciate the rude interruption of his breakfast. She bent to pick him up, but her window of time had evaporated. She regarded the baby, then squinted at the clock. She needed to finish feeding him. Not only would the girls be late for their schools, but she'd be late for the park.

Once again, motherhood diverted her straightforward course, even for something as simple as a park visit. Deep breath. *The obstacle is the way.* She was at least learning patience, despite her internal kicks and screams.

The second Ashton pulled away, Miranda sprang into action. "Okay, girls, time to go. Can you please get in the car?" Miranda strapped Ashton into his car seat, picked it up, and headed into the garage.

As the door clicked shut, an unmistakable sound filled the air. *Oh no. This is not happening.* She inspected Ashton. Yep, the dreaded diaper blowout.

Please, diaper, work. Please keep it at least partially contained.

Miranda lifted one of his legs. No such luck. She sighed. Morning restart for Ashton. New diaper, new clothes, new blanket. Not even the car seat had been spared from his bottom blast.

The sight would've been comical if she weren't already frustrated. This was a blowout of epic proportions. Murphy's Law was in full force this morning: the earlier she was ready, the longer it took to walk out the door.

She let out a sigh then bit her tongue to keep the litany of not-so-lady-like words from spilling out. "Hold on, girls. Don't climb in the car yet. I've got to clean up Ashton."

The girls gawked at their smelly mess of a brother. Then started giggling.

Olivia glimpsed Miranda and stopped. "Mom, I can help. What do you want me to do?"

Miranda said a silent thank-you for this perceptive little soul. "I'd love for you to scrub out the car seat while I get Ashton cleaned up."

"Okay!" Olivia responded with such enthusiasm, one would have thought someone told her there was a present waiting for her inside.

Isabella shoved her way into the scene. "I wanna help."

"That'd be great, Izzy." Miranda turned toward her, careful to keep Ashton at arms distance. No need to dirty herself as well. "Could you run inside and grab the diapers and wipes for me while I get these clothes off?"

"Okay, Mommy." Isabella scurried after Olivia, grinning widely.

"All right, little guy." Miranda turned her attention back to the stinky poop bomb. "Let's get you cleaned up."

He cooed back at her, oblivious to the havoc he'd caused.

Miranda followed the girls back into the mudroom and pulled a towel from the laundry hamper. She laid Ashton down on it. "I got this. I'm the fastest diaper changer in the world. We can still salvage at least part of the morning."

Izzy charged in, holding a fistful of wipes and a new diaper.

"Wow, that was fast. Thank you, sweetie." Miranda held her breath and went to work, peeling clothes and wiping him. Luckily, yesterday's finished laundry sat out, waiting to be folded. She dug through and grabbed an outfit for Ashton. It wasn't the "dapper little man" outfit she'd picked with care earlier that morning, but he was covered and clean. Good enough for today.

Olivia scrubbed furiously on the car seat. "Thanks, Liv. That's good. Here, why don't you swap me. You hold Ashton, and I'll finish."

Olivia took Miranda's offer and kept Ashton entertained while Miranda scrubbed a bit more on the seat.

When the car seat also graduated to "good enough," she washed her hands, threw a small towel over his seat and strapped him in for the second time.

"Well, little man, that should clean you out for the better part of this day. No more surprises, okay?" Miranda tickled him under his chin. He responded with a huge, gummy smile, revealing his deep dimples.

Olivia leaned over him next to Miranda. "Mom, wouldn't it be funny if he had another blowout right now?"

"Nope. Not funny at all." Miranda tapped Olivia's nose. Then she picked up the car seat. "Let's try this again, shall we?" They climbed into the car and headed toward the girls' schools.

After the last drop off, Miranda checked the clock. She was hopelessly late for the usual meeting time at the park.

Please have Mindy wait for me.

As she pulled out of the preschool lot, a light flickered on the control panel. *Seriously?*

She was driving on fumes. Yesterday, she'd planned to fill up after the school runs. But phone calls followed by daydreaming about summer had engulfed the remainder of the evening. And the tank remained empty.

"Augh!" Miranda slapped the steering wheel. *All I want is one hour at the park. Is that too much to ask?* In the grand scheme of things, this was nothing to complain about. Still, why couldn't she have this small window of time? Ugh. And why was she so worked up about something so trivial? The fuel light glared at her, and she snarled back. What was wrong with her?

She took a breath and turned into the nearest gas station. She jumped out and became a one-woman Indie-500 pit crew. As the fuel flowed, the unmistakable snuffle of crying floated through the air from the other side of the pump.

Miranda peeked around. A girl no older than twenty tried in vain to break into her car, where her keys, phone, and purse lay together on the front seat, safely locked in.

Before she knew what she was doing, Miranda walked to her. "Hey there, it looks like you're having a worse start to your morning than I am. How can I help?"

The girl turned and wiped her tears as relief flooded her face. "I could use some help. I just started college here and am on my way to a job interview. I stopped to get gas and, like the airhead I am, locked the door out of habit, but I forgot to grab anything. Now I'm stuck here with my money locked inside a car with no gas. I'm gonna be late for my interview. I need this job." Her voice trembled as tears again slid down her cheeks.

"It's okay. We'll get you there. And get into your car. Do you have a spare set of keys in your apartment?"

The girls wiped her tears. "Yes, but I don't have the key to my apartment, and I think my roommates probably left by now."

"Okay. Use my phone to call your roommates to see if anyone's still there. While you do that, I'll fill up your car. Then I can drive you to your apartment to get the keys and bring you back here so you can make it to your interview."

The girl's face brightened as she took Miranda's cell phone. Then she sheepishly peered back at Miranda. "I don't have any numbers memorized. They're all on my phone."

Miranda placed her hand on the girl's shoulder and stared into her eyes. "It'll be okay. What's your name?"

The girl sniffled. "K-Katie."

Miranda smiled. "I'm Miranda. We're going to figure this out. Jump in my car. We'll drive to your place. Maybe we can catch one of your roommates."

As soon as both gas pumps popped to a stop, Miranda hopped into the van. Continuing in her Indie-500 mimic, they squealed out of the gas station. Following Katie's directions, she took off for the apartment building a mile down the road.

As they turned the corner into the apartment complex, Katie pointed. "There's Joanna!"

Miranda rolled down her window. She waved like mad at a perplexed-looking girl driving a red Mazda toward them. Miranda stopped, and Katie rushed out, waving. When Joanna recognized her roommate, the confused stare turned into a smile.

Joanna parked her car. Miranda waited while the two girls ran to the apartment, and then Joanna left. Katie emerged seconds later, keys in hand. Miranda dropped her back off at her car with ten minutes to spare for the interview.

"You have no idea how much you saved me today. You were an answer to my prayers. Can I pay you for the gas?" She looked toward her purse in the car.

"Don't even think about it. I was a freshman in college once, too. It was my pleasure. You go nail that interview." Miranda hugged her, and the girl dove into her car and sped away.

As Miranda climbed back into the van, she spied the clock. No way Mindy would still be at the park. She probably thought Miranda had stood her up again. Miranda sighed. She'd drive by anyway and at least check it out.

On the way, the previous hour's events replayed in her mind. How strange that she happened to be at that exact gas station, not her usual one, at the precise moment the girl would need help. Miranda wasn't the only one in the world who could've assisted the girl. If she hadn't come along, surely someone else would have stepped in. Yet the question lingered. Had the struggles of her morning been used to put her in the position to help?

But why me?

As with all her talks with God, His answer came in a sweet, silent thought. Light as a breeze, it flowed through her mind. *I wanted to see if you're ready.*

What did that mean? Ready for what? She must be delusional and talking to herself. She shook her head as she turned into the entrance of the park.

Miranda's gaze zoomed to the bench and she gasped. A smile crept upon her lips as every cell in her body relaxed. Her friend sat casually on the bench, like every other visit.

Miranda grabbed Ashton out of his car seat, perhaps a little too quickly. He woke with a start and whined.

"Oh, no, you don't. You've caused enough ruckus for one morning." She snuggled him into her shoulder, grabbed the diaper bag, and hurried to the bench.

Mindy was pleasant, as always, with her greeting. She reached for Ashton as Miranda walked up. "You get to snuggle this new little life all the time. I need my turn."

CHAPTER TWENTY-FIVE

No argument there. She gently handed him off and took her place next to Mindy.

"No glasses today?" Miranda pointed to Mindy's glass-less eyes.

Mindy laughed and shook her head. "No glasses today. With the season changing, they aren't as necessary for now."

Before another lesson, Miranda had to share the good news. "You'll never believe what's happened over the past week. It's been one miracle after another."

Her enthusiasm bubbled over as she recounted the previous week's events. Brendon's impromptu performance, their family Halloween theme and, most importantly, the call to Sydney that led to a potential trip twenty years in the making.

Mindy listened, leaning closer with her hands clasped as each new detail spilled out. "That's fantastic." She clapped as her smile grew wider. "I can't believe it's all come together like this. Such marvelous news. That trip sounds like it will be out of this world. Might be a bumpy road to get there, but it will be worth it. All of life's great quests are."

Huh. It had all fallen into her lap so easily, Miranda couldn't imagine many hiccups. Once Landon got on board . . . She'd need to explain everything to him. Prep him before one of the kids jumped the gun.

Mindy leaned toward her. "And Brendon singing and dancing? That would be a performance worth paying for."

Miranda shook from her daze and laughed. "If I didn't think it would've shut him down in a heartbeat, I would've grabbed my phone and recorded the whole thing."

"Sometimes, the memory of such historic activities is best kept to the retelling of them by the eyewitnesses." Mindy's eyes sparkled. "I have a hunch this will be one re-enactment that will live through the history of your family for generations to come."

"You're right about that one." Miranda recalled again the memory of that perfect night together. The singing. The planning. The beauty of it all.

She patted her friend's leg. "Thank you for waiting this morning. I'm sorry I was late. It was one of those 'everything that could go wrong did' mornings."

"Or, perhaps things going right to get you where you needed to be?" Mindy half smiled, her bright eyes twinkling.

Miranda hadn't mentioned anything about the gas station. Who was this woman?

"Often, the muck we wade through is God putting us right where we need to be, right when we need to be there. We rarely see it that way and lose many opportunities to partner with Him in helping others."

"You mean, by not wearing the 'eternal eyewear.'" Miranda leaned over and nudged Mindy with her shoulder.

"Precisely."

Ashton woke with a jolt and whimpered. Miranda lifted her hands to take him, but Mindy shifted him to her other shoulder and rocked him, lulling him back to sleep.

"You're not only the sunscreen whisperer but the baby whisperer as well."

"Once a mother, always a mother." Mindy winked at Miranda. "I don't want to give him up yet, so I better keep him content while he's with me."

"And like a mother, you've given me such sage advice. I can't thank you enough for how much you've taught me. You've made me look deeper at things than I ever would've done on my own. I can't wait to hear your next bit of wisdom."

Mindy smiled her familiar warm, all-embracing smile. Her eyes filled with tenderness. "My dear, you have everything you need."

What? No. There would be more. There always was. Something that sounded utterly off the wall at first but then wove its way into a perfect lesson that was just what Miranda needed.

She sat there, waiting for Mindy to continue.

Silence reigned between them.

"Are you serious? You can't be. You always have some great lesson—or story or experience. I could use one right now."

"You have everything you need."

Miranda's jaw tightened. After the morning she'd had, she really needed a new thought to ponder. How could Mindy be done?

"It doesn't feel that way." Miranda swallowed hard. "I'm barely scratching the surface on how to make this whole journey through life work. I have no idea how to make all the moving parts come together.

How do I fuse working on myself with nurturing and raising my children, and being a good partner for my husband, and—"

"You don't have to figure it all out right now. That's why it's called a journey. But from our visits here, you now have all the pieces you need."

Miranda felt her face flush. "What're you talking about? I don't have any pieces. I'm a hot mess. We've talked about so many random things. How do I put them all together?"

Mindy's relaxed arm rested on the back of the bench and she smiled that warm smile. "Take some time over the next little while." She paused, her words unhurried. "Think through our discussions. Connect the concepts and you'll find everything you need."

"Why do you keep saying that, as if you know exactly what I need? You hardly know me at all." Miranda's throat tightened. She pinched her lips together.

She took a deep breath and closed her eyes. "I'm sorry. Things are still hit and miss at home. Sometimes I get it right, but then I mess up and take three steps back. Your words of wisdom get me back on track."

Her voice sounded shrill in her ears. Like Izzy begging for one more cookie. This couldn't be happening. These visits couldn't end. She'd always known they wouldn't last forever. Mindy wasn't from around here. Miranda had tried not to think about the time when there wouldn't be anyone to greet her at the park. Someone who perceived the fears she'd never voiced and answered questions she couldn't ask. "Are you going back home?"

"We'll all go home sooner or later, won't we?"

Now, Mindy was avoiding the question. Miranda clenched her teeth. "I suppose we will. But while we're here, I still have questions. So many things I don't know." It was pointless to push. Her heart told her this was the last bench visit.

"Never stop questioning," Mindy said. "The greatest answers lie behind the biggest questions." Her even tone didn't flinch despite Miranda's watery eyes. "Sometimes, it takes backing up and looking at things from a different angle to see the connection."

What's that supposed to mean? She quickly dipped her head as a renegade tear escaped her command and slipped slowly down her cheek. She wiped it away as she brushed her hair out of her face. "I guess I'll have to try that." She had no desire to attempt it. At least not on her own.

She changed the subject. Maybe she could keep the visit going. "How's your family doing?"

"They're doing better than they think. Struggles still lie ahead, but they have all the tools to work through anything that comes their way."

Miranda wanted to roll her eyes. *Here we go again. Why does she keep saying that?* Her smile faltered as fear crept up her spine. She nodded as she rubbed the side of her neck.

Ashton stirred again, and Miranda stood at the window of escape. "Thank you for all your help and great lessons. I better get him home. I still need to clean his car seat. He had a diaper blowout before we came here. I should do that before I pick up Isabella so we can run some errands before the other two get home from school."

Mindy accepted her excuse unfazed. "Of course. It's been my pleasure to meet with you." She rose and paused before turning. "Think through our talks. See how they connect. Remember, God has a purpose for you. A specific purpose. He'll always be right by your side to walk you through that purpose."

"I think you have more faith in me than I do."

"It's there. Don't force it. Life's journey is not a sprint. Run the race with patience." Miranda knew the scripture well. The verse had pushed her through many cross-country races and half marathons. It helped her pace herself and also push herself at the same time.

"I'll try to remember that." The lump in Miranda's throat forbade her from saying more. She stood, gave a final wave to Mindy, and headed to the car.

Chapter Twenty-Six

Miranda drove halfway down the block before she let the tears fall. In some ways, it was like she'd lost her mother all over again. Under Mindy's tutelage, she'd spent the past several months learning and growing in ways she would never have imagined possible. Mindy not only encouraged and uplifted her, but in some ways, she saved her life. Quite possibly her family as well.

How could it be over? How could she have everything she needed? A great start on a new outlook on life, yes, but the direction she should go was not clear. Why would Mindy think otherwise?

She took a deep breath. The visits were over. Nothing she did or said could change that. A dull ache entered her stomach and crawled up her chest.

She pulled into her driveway and retrieved Ashton. She unhooked the cover to his car seat to wash it. A glance at her watch revealed she wouldn't have time to get it washed, dried, and replaced. She needed to grocery shop at some point today. She hadn't exactly lied to Mindy.

The full cleaning would have to wait until after preschool pick up and the store. With the thirty remaining minutes before Isabella's pick up, she'd feed him again. She crumbled into the oversized rocking chair. While Ashton nursed, she focused on what Mindy directed her to do—go back and review the previous visits and topics.

With no pen or paper, she combed through her memories to the stories and examples Mindy had shared. Obstacles, master of one, finding her core.

What were the others? Her mind clouded over. How could Mindy decide now to be done?

She took a deep breath. *Stop. It's no use questioning now. She's gone.*

Miranda had much to be grateful for. The lessons. Brendon's life. His starting to find happiness. Her family. The possibility of Niger.

The phone alarm rang. Time to put the pondering to rest for a while. She gently lifted a now sleeping Ashton and returned to the car.

She pulled out and headed towards Isabella's preschool, thinking about the trip.

Was she ready to organize and carry out such a huge undertaking? Taking care of the physical details wasn't the problem. Computer searches and clicks could reserve airline tickets and hotel rooms. The underlying question elbowed its way into her mind. Was she firm enough in her core to drag her husband and children halfway around the world to fulfill her dream? And what would Landon think? After their last big talk, he seemed open to pursuing new avenues. She'd find a way to bring it up with him.

Mindy would've been able to put her doubts into perspective. The wise teacher had helped her find the beauty that came from being true to who she was meant to be, even while fully engaging in her role as a wife and mother.

Engage. Another one of the topics. What were the other ones?

———————

"Daddy!" The girls ran to greet Landon in their daily greeting ritual as soon as he opened the door that evening. In the midst of the tickles and hugs, Olivia jumped up and down. "Guess what, Daddy. We're going to Africa!"

So much for easing into the discussion.

Landon eyes found Miranda's, the questions evident. "Oh, really?"

Miranda's stomach dropped. If only she'd kept quiet this morning, it would've bought her some time to feel him out first. "It's not a sure thing. But I got an offer to help an organization, Families Helping

Families. They're focusing on drilling projects and want to do some in Niger. With my connections there, it's a natural fit."

"Can we go, Daddy? Please?" Isabella mimicked Olivia's bouncing.

Miranda patted Isabella's head. "Nothing's decided. It's just an idea. You two go wash up for dinner."

She studied Landon's face as the girls ran off. His smile turned to a grimace. Her stomach clenched. This was not how she pictured sharing her dream.

He folded his arms, his eyes turning hard. "When were you planning to fill me in on a trip that involves taking our family halfway around the world?"

"There's no set trip. At this point it's only in the talking phase. I just found out about the possibility yesterday. I mentioned something to Brendon this morning, and the girls overheard. That's all. I was planning to talk to you about it tonight."

Brendon jogged down the stairs. "Dinner smells good. I'm starving. Hey Dad."

Landon stared at her with intensity for a moment longer, then outfit himself with a proper smile and turned to face Brendon. "How was your day?" He walked over and gave Brendon a quick hug.

Brendon shrugged. "Okay."

Miranda walked back to the kitchen and set the soup on the table, a pit growing in her stomach. Hopefully, they could regroup through dinner.

Landon handled the bedtime stories and Miranda did the tuck in. After she laid Ashton in his crib, she slipped downstairs where Landon surfed the channels.

She eased onto the couch next to him. "Brendon has a big English project due before Thanksgiving break. He's up slaving away on it in his room."

The images on the TV changed as Landon continued to click the remote.

Not an ideal way to bring this up, but she had to do damage control. She cleared her throat. "Hey, honey. I'm sorry."

Landon set the remote on his leg. "I just felt a little blindsided by it all." He tapped the side of the remote as he faced her. "Look, I'm on board with you finishing your degree. If that helps you feel better, then I'm all for it. But going to Africa? All to fulfill some random void? Taking a few online classes is one thing. Taking our whole family halfway around the world is a bit extreme, don't you think?"

Miranda bit the inside of her cheek. Concentrated on breathing. Heat rose through her neck into her cheeks. "I get that it's a big undertaking. But—"

"It's just not gonna work. Now is not the right time. You don't have a current passport. The kids don't have any. We'd all need to get a bunch of vaccinations. I don't think you realize what goes into making a trip like this happen. I know it pulls at your heart because it was a place you lived. But it's just not feasible for us right now. My caseload is high, our kids are little. Plus, everything with Brendon . . . it's not a good idea." He pecked her on the cheek and stood up, stretching his arms. "I'm tired. Let's head to bed. I've got a big case to wrap up tomorrow. I'll probably be late again." He clicked off the TV and headed to the stairs.

Miranda sat for a moment longer. What just happened? Her ribs cinched around her chest as her breath hitched. *I guess the discussion's over.*

For now.

The following day, Miranda tried to put the trip out of her mind. But images of Niger invaded every thought. Mothers and children walking for miles on the dusty trails under the scorching sun to scoop water from a muddy river, then making the long trek back, their backs bowed under the weight of the full containers. As she turned on the kitchen faucet to get a drink for Olivia after school, the readily falling water mesmerized her. Images of gears and drill pipes, hooking into the drill collar as the bit bored into the ground filled her mind. She clearly pictured the pieces—the discharge line, the wheel connected to the gear shaft. Powered by a wheel turned by humans, not reliant on the spotty electricity connections in the village.

She shook her head and handed the cup to Olivia. Letting go of this opportunity would not be easy. Leaving the girls with their snacks, Miranda sat down to nurse Ashton. She needed a change of focus. The lessons from Mindy. Master of one . . . Engage . . . Butter flies. How did they all connect? Still nothing. The more she thought about the concepts, the more jumbled they became.

Brendon bounded down the stairs. "Hey Mom, I forgot to tell you, I was talking to my English teacher about my project and she said she has a portable printer she could donate for us to use." He plopped onto the couch. "Oh, and I found a website that you can order frames in bulk for pretty cheap."

This, from the same boy who, last spring, had scowled at the mention of *Eagle Scout*. How could she tell him the trip prospect had been slashed? She couldn't. "That sounds great. I bet they would do a discount for a humanitarian project."

His eyes grew wide. "You think so?"

"Most businesses are happy to help, if you explain what you're doing."

"I didn't even think about that. I'll go check to see if there's a number on the website." He popped up and traipsed toward the computer, but looked back at Miranda. "Hey Mom, could you help me with something? Mr. Fink said he thought it was a good idea and I should start working on the proposal." Oh man, he'd already told his scout master about it.

What was she doing? Planning with Brendon when Landon objected? She opened her mouth to break the news, but clamped it shut. Brendon was so excited, lit up for the first time in months. She couldn't do it. Not yet. She had to try to make this work.

As Miranda fell into bed that night, she replayed the past few days. As she pulled the covers up around her neck and forced her eyes closed, the struggle kept her awake. The factors that led to the possibility of the trip were too coincidental to brush off. She was supposed to go back.

Why couldn't Landon see how important this trip was? Her entire married life, Miranda had shifted her needs to the side to support others. She stood by Landon through law school and helped him get settled in his career. Then as a stay-at-home mother she fulfilled the needs of her children. Was she audacious enough to make everyone now shift their lives to help her live her dream? If only she could have one more visit with Mindy. If ever there was a time to have the woman help her make sense of things, this would be it.

The next morning, Miranda woke with the questions still on her mind. She pushed them aside as she stepped into the shower. Thanksgiving was only a week away, and she'd hardly made a dent in her to-do list. She had to focus and get into the here and now. She mentally started a checklist for the holiday.

But as the water splashed around, so did her thoughts. She lashed out to God. "Why do I feel this unnatural need to pack up my family and drag them through the deserts and mountains of Niger? I had my time when I lived there, single, alone, only myself to worry about. But now I have more lives sitting on my shoulders. Why do I think I can go play superwoman and save the day drilling water?"

She couldn't ignore the non-coincidental moments. Nor could she deny the feelings that had stirred deep inside throughout her visits with Mindy. The decision about the trip seemed so right when she spoke with Steve from Families Helping Families on the phone. As if the path of engaging with her talent was being laid out before her. But was it all supposed to happen right now? Maybe Landon was right. It was a big undertaking, and she was neck deep in motherhood. Her youngest wasn't even a year old. Maybe she should push pause on this whole endeavor and wait until the kids got older.

She was only one person. One lowly mother. What difference could she possibly make in the tidal wave of world suffering?

Each person you touch is worth the effort. The thought meandered into her mind so softly, she almost didn't recognize the words.

But I'm a mother. How can I justify splitting my focus to put together a community water project and get a whole program up and running in the next nine months?

Nursing your baby will give you all the planning time you need. You've been given this time to use for a purpose. Again, the message came so softly it almost didn't register.

Isn't this me trying to relive my glory days from the Peace Corps? That was almost twenty years ago. I need to move on and be okay with putting all my energy into my own children.

I sent you there then so you could help them now. They are all my children. They need your help.

As soft as a sunrise, Miranda's core settled into her heart and mind. Then a shadow crossed her heart. *But what about Landon? I can't do this without his support.*

The Lord shall fight for you, and ye shall hold your peace.

She paused. Yes, the Lord could do miracles. He'd parted the Red Sea and fought for the Children of Israel. But could he part Landon's heart?

Chapter Twenty-Seven

"Mom, can you help me tune?" Olivia held out the half-sized student violin to Miranda.

Miranda turned from the sink and wiped her hands on a dish-cloth. "Sure. Could you get me the tuner? Let's see if we can get the strings to cooperate."

They were a few months into lessons, and it was going surprisingly well. Olivia possessed a knack for it and had cruised through the ini-tial techniques. She now played real songs. It wasn't pretty, but each day she improved.

As taught by the teacher, Miranda watched the needle on the tuner and twisted the tuning pegs slightly to tighten each string and bring it into the right note frequency.

"I think that'll do it. Try it out and see how it sounds to you." She handed the violin back to Olivia, who quickly put it into position on her shoulder and played a scale up and down the strings.

Miranda coached her through the different parts of her practice as she mixed the meatloaf for dinner. As she listened to Olivia work through a new part in her song, she heard the struggle come out in the notes. They wavered and jolted at first. Olivia would hit a wrong note, stop, adjust, and try again. After mastering one note, she'd add another. Then she'd practice a measure. Then group several measures together.

After twenty minutes, Olivia mastered a small section in her new song.

"Hey, Mom, listen to this!" Olivia played through the section beautifully.

"That sounds wonderful, honey. You worked hard on that phrase, and now you've got it."

"I like this part." Olivia replayed one section where her bow and fingers slid from one string to the next, then back again.

"It's tricky, and I didn't think I'd be able to do it when Miss Shannon showed it to me last week. But now I like how the strings go together."

"All of your practice is paying off. You play that part great now. Good job, honey."

Olivia beamed as she put her violin away.

"Could you please round everyone up? It's time for dinner."

"Is Dad going to be late again?"

Miranda put on an oven mitt and squished a potato in the oven. It easily caved to the pressure. She pulled it out along with the rest of them. "He might be honey. He's been—"

The front door swung open and Landon bounded inside. "Hey everyone, I'm home." The girls squealed as he greeted them with the tickles and hugs.

His smile almost reached his ears and his eyes sparkled as he sashayed into the kitchen. "I have big news."

Miranda set the meatloaf on the table and glanced up. "What?"

His smile widened even more. "My proposal got accepted for a session at the ABA Annual Convention. You're looking at the speaker for the plenary session." His puffed-out chest almost popped the buttons on his shirt. "They also nominated me for a position on the board. I can't believe it! I knew I had a good chance for the session proposal, but I didn't think the board position would come for another year or so."

Miranda swallowed past the lump in her throat and pasted on a smile. "I'm proud of you. This is a big accomplishment. You'll do a great job." She brushed past him and retrieved the butter from the fridge, then walked to the stairs. "Brendon, girls, dinner."

Landon retreated a step. "Am I missing something here? This is a really big deal. You know how long I've been working for this."

"Yes, you've been working hard. Extra hours. Extra conferences. Making the right connections. I'm happy for you." The hollowness in her voice echoed in her ears.

Ashton cried from his bouncy seat and Landon scooped him up. "Is something wrong?"

Miranda slammed butter on the table and whipped around. "Wrong? No, nothing's wrong. You go ahead and reach for the stars. Speak. Travel. Advance your dream. I've been by you every step of the way . . . for almost twenty years."

"Yes, of course. You know I appreciate that." Landon's words came out slowly.

"Do you? Did you even think about discussing the board appointment with me before accepting? I'm guessing it'll mean more time away from the family." Her insides boiled.

"I'll need to stay late twice a month for conference calls starting in January, but that won't be a big deal." Landon shrugged. "It's only twice a month."

Miranda raked her hands through her hair. Breathe. "See. You don't even think twice about what it entails on the back end as you go on trips and stay late at work. It's a given that I'll be here to pick up the pieces and make everything run smoothly. But the minute I want to do something for me, that might be a little out of your comfort zone, you refuse to even discuss it."

"We did discuss it. We talked about it last night."

"No, *you* talked about it last night." Ashton lunged for her, and she pulled him into her arms.

The girls bounced down the stairs with Brendon following behind. Miranda lowered her voice. "We can finish this later."

The girls monopolized most of the dinner conversation, thankfully covering the brooding silence between Miranda and Landon. Throughout the discussions, Miranda formulated her counterarguments. How could she make him understand? This was something deep in her core. It all came together so beautifully during her visits on the bench. Why did it now seem so jumbled?

As the last bites were taken, Isabella jumped down and ran toward the family room. Miranda stood up and collected her plate. "Not so fast, Izzy. You three are all on dish duty tonight. Dad and I need to have a quick talk upstairs."

Landon flashed a glance her way and narrowed his eyes. She had to do this now, before she lost her nerve. She carried a sleeping Ashton upstairs and laid him in his crib, then joined Landon at the foot of their bed.

Miranda sighed as she sat down. Where to start? "Honey, I'm sorry I wasn't more excited for you tonight. I know it's a big accomplishment. I'm happy for you." She fidgeted as he folded his arms. Clearly, he was waiting for the "but."

"Finishing my degree is more than taking a few online classes. I walked away right when we started the capstone project. A project I conceptualized, but never got to see finished because I moved with you across the country to support your dreams. Is it too—"

"Dreams that now support our family." His green eyes darkened. They may as well be in a courtroom. He was in full rebuttal mode.

"I know they support the family. And I'm forever grateful for that."

"Are you? All these years, I've worked hard to support us. So you can stay home and live your dream. The dream that you've told me from day one was to be a full-time wife and mother. Now, right in the middle of it, you change the game. It's suddenly not enough for you. Can you see how that feels on my end? Everything that I've worked to give you is now not enough."

No argument she made would stand up against his years of debate experience. But she had to try. "Yes, and I can see how this came as a surprise. But this trip could not only fulfill my graduation requirements—it's a way I can use my talents to help bless the lives of others."

"Why can't you be content with blessing the lives of your kids? Why is that not enough anymore?"

It was a good question. One she'd posed in her wrestle with God. "Honey, God has more children than just ours. I can use my talents to both bless our own children, but to also bless His children across the world. She shifted on the bed. "This experience could have long-term positive effects on our kids as well."

Landon shook his head, the hard sheen still clouding his eyes. "Our family's been through so much this year. Why does your fulfilment have to include this crazy trip? I'm sure there's another way to fulfill the degree requirements. Plenty of people get an engineering degree without traipsing off to Africa. There are so many costs involved in something like this, and it's not like getting your degree will bring any money in . . . "

Heat surged through Miranda's veins and the pulsing of her heart throbbed against her temples. She swallowed her urge to scream and instead took a deep breath, deliberately slowing the pace of her words. "Yes, this trip will cost a lot of money. And my degree will be an investment that won't be recouped financially. How is that different from the contributions I've made to our kids by staying home with them? The ROI is not always about money." She folded her arms and met his steeled expression with her own. "I may be just one woman. One mother. But I have something unique to offer, that could help entire villages. I want to teach the kids that I can pursue my dreams also. Not just you. And help them grow in their compassion for others in the process. What better way to do that then by actually showing them? And taking them to Niger?"

The hardness in his eyes softened slightly. "Honey, I get it. It would be really cool to take the kids to your old home. I get that . . . " He reached over and patted her leg. "I just don't see how we can pull this off. With this new board position, and my session to prepare . . . " His words faded to the background as an image filled her mind. Mindy's three circles of control, influence, and concern. Miranda shook her head. Landon still wasn't on board and she couldn't control him, only herself.

Olivia stuck her head in the door. "Mommy, the kitchen's clean. Can we do scripture share?"

Miranda swallowed past the lump in her throat and smiled. At this moment, that's precisely what she needed. To do what she could control in this situation. And right now, prayer was the only thing that might change Landon's heart. "Sure thing, honey. Can you round everyone up?

The kids piled into their bedroom. Landon transformed back into jolly dad mode. "Let's see, whose turn is it tonight? Liv, I believe it's yours."

She nodded, her Bible already open to Exodus chapter 19. "We had a lesson in Sunday School about when Moses got the ten commandments." She read verse twenty. *". . . and the Lord called Moses up to the top of the mount; and Moses went up."* Olivia raised her head. "We went on a mountain climb in class. Well, it wasn't a real mountain. You know that hill by the church playground? The one we go sledding down? We went out there and climbed up, and at the top we got some treats. Our teacher told us that even though God had something to give to Moses, Moses needed to work to get it. God didn't just put the commandments outside Moses's tent. Moses had to climb a mountain to get the blessing. Sister Clark said that even if we know what God wants us to do, it doesn't mean it will be easy. We still have to overcome challenges to do it."

"Thank you, Liv. That was a great scripture and example. Who would like to say the prayer?" Landon knelt by the bed and everyone followed suit.

During the prayer, Liv's words echoed in Miranda's mind. The past few months had definitely been an awakening to God calling her. Yet she'd been waiting for the answers to come to her, not doing the work to seek them out. She needed to get to the bottom of Mindy's coded messages and find what it meant for her life. If she was to go to Niger, she'd climb that mountain to convince Landon. If there was another way to fulfill her purpose, she needed to find out.

———

Ashton's midnight feeding provided the perfect opportunity for Miranda to start her climb. She took the hungry baby downstairs to the recliner and he quickly settled into nursing.

Miranda started at the beginning.

The first visit. She chuckled at how annoyed she'd been when Mindy sat next to her on the bench and started a conversation. Man, if she could only go back and shake herself in that moment. She'd tell herself to get out a paper and take good notes because the words she was about to hear would change her life.

They talked about the butterfly effect. Simple, but profound. She never would've guessed that shoveling someone's driveway on a whim could lead to saving a life, thus touching every life that the person touched.

Miranda thought about the people Mindy had mentioned. Time to dig into the overdue assignment. A click on her phone revealed the names. Norman Borlaug and Moses and Susan Carver. Another click on Google told her their story.

When raiders invaded the Carver farm in 1864, stealing horses and slaves, Moses and Susan were instrumental in saving, and then raising, one of the infant slaves as their own son, George Washington Carver. In addition to all that he did in his own right, George touched the life of a young Henry Wallace, and shared his love of botany with the child. Henry Wallace grew up to become the Secretary of Agriculture, then Vice President to Franklin D. Roosevelt. He convinced President Roosevelt to build a botanical station in Mexico. He then convinced Norman Borlaug, a young recent graduate, to leave his secure job at DuPont and travel to a dilapidated building in rural Mexico with a bare-bones staff.

Over the next two decades, they developed resistant strains of wheat, corn, and rice. These developments are credited with saving the lives of well over two billion people around the world.

Miranda sat back and absorbed the magnitude of this link. A link that began with one woman, who raised one child.

Susan Carver chose to go deep into the life of one child. She had no way of knowing the long-term effects of her choice. But did that make her impact any less heroic?

Go deep. Miranda had gone deep; Jess had gone wide. Both ways mattered. Miranda grabbed her phone and pulled up the last text stream with Jess. There, staring at her from the screen, was Jess's final observation.

An apology was long overdue.

Jess. Where do I even start? Perhaps with a big, I'm Sorry. Though even typing the words, I know they fall short. Your text and assessment of me was spot-on. If I'm honest with myself, I haven't come to terms with my decision to go deep. Though it's hard to admit out loud, I've been jealous watching you and Steve travel the world, make an enormous impact, and receive instant accolades. That was the emotion behind my hurtful text. What you're doing is amazing. I'm in awe at how much you both have dedicated your lives to helping countless others.

I'm so sorry. I miss you.

She set the phone down and released a sigh as the tension drained from her shoulders. Even if Jess stayed upset with her, the act of owning her emotions, and admitting them to another person, lifted a massive weight from Miranda's shoulders.

Her phone dinged, and Miranda grabbed it.

The phone number you are trying to reach is currently out of network and will not receive the message until it returns to a network-covered area.

That's about the type of response she'd get after pouring her heart out. She thought their fieldwork was to southern Greece, but they must've gone to another area after that. She'd have to settle for Jess getting her message at some point in the future.

Miranda switched Ashton to the other side, and he continued to nurse with a vengeance, probably building up for another growth spurt. Miranda studied his perfect frame and sat in awe at this human she and Landon had created together. So tiny, yet he occupied such a large part of her heart. As did all her children. How could our country ever have condoned the act of ripping children away from their mothers based solely on the color of their skin?

Had she lived in the dark days of slavery, would she have had the fortitude to stand against it, like Harriet Beecher Stowe? One brave woman, a mother, who engaged by utilizing her unique skill set. Like Miranda, Harriet didn't know exactly what her skill set was nor how she could help. But she knew she needed to. Her sister-in-law had urged her on. In a letter, Harriet's sister-in-law wrote, "If I could use a pen as you can, I would write something that would make this whole nation feel what an accursed thing slavery is." That statement nudged Harriet forward.

What she thought would be a six-month project, took over a year to complete, published in weekly installments. Her inspiration came little by little as she engaged with a pen and paper, consistently sitting down to write and let the story grow.

The reaction to the book was almost instantaneous. The first printing of five thousand copies sold out in a matter of days. Within the first year, *Uncle Tom's Cabin* had sold over three hundred thousand copies, with even more throughout Europe.

Miranda paused. How amazing that one person—one mother—could change the trajectory of an entire nation by engaging with her core.

Finding her core. The third lesson. Though she was still growing into her own purpose, she felt some peace knowing she was on the right track. She rehearsed Mindy's words to see the process as a marathon, not a sprint, and let it come one step at a time. Was she ready to make the next step and push Landon to return to Niger? God's words—*I sent you then so you could help them now*— still rang in her heart and mind. But one big obstacle stood in her way. Convincing her husband.

Obstacles. Miranda had devoured *Beneath a Scarlet Sky*, the book Mindy recommended. Through several midnight feedings, Miranda became the pupil of a life forged by war. Pino Lella knew plenty about obstacles opening new doorways. A teenager when war exploded at his door in Milan, Italy, Pino's obstacles pushed him into the perfect position to help turn the tide of the war in Northern Italy. Drafted to fight in the war for his enemy, Pino donned the dreaded swastika uniform, and believed all his previous anti-German efforts were in vain. When the allied forces recruited him as their spy, he realized this new position would allow him to be of greater use than he could ever have imagined. The power of one person—a mere teenager—had far-reaching effects. He couldn't control the actions of the German general for whom he was chauffeur, but he could control what he did with the information he gleaned.

Control . . . master of one. The fifth lesson Mindy had shared with her.

Simple to understand. Difficult to implement. Some of her fights with Brendon sprang to her mind. The center of each encounter was a fight for control. She had tried to control not only her life, but his as well. Tried to master the lives of everyone in the family.

To what end? To build the false image of an ideal family. What good would that do when they were internally crumbling? Wasn't that still what she was doing with her kids? Landon wasn't on board with the trip, and she was trying to force him into her thought pattern.

And the kids. She hadn't told Brendon the trip was in limbo. She'd made everything seem so perfect.

It was time to stop. The only thing she could control was her own behaviors and reactions, and she needed to do that. She must face the fact that it wasn't going to happen. At least not now. She needed to stop trying to control Landon and come clean with Brendon. She'd help him figure out another project. The trip could come later. After this many years of waiting to pursue her passion, she could wait a while longer.

But she couldn't let it drop. Not again. She knew it would happen. She would find a way. Somehow. Maybe not this year. But it would happen at some point.

Ashton stirred and yawned. Miranda followed suit. She glanced at her phone and moaned. Nearly 2 a.m.

How could she have let herself stay up while Ashton slept? She slowly stood, careful not to wake him. She needed to salvage every second of sleep possible before the rest of her family rose to start another day. As she tiptoed up the stairs, she tried to recall that last lesson from Mindy. What was it? Her sleep-deprived headache blocked any further information flow.

Miranda gently kissed Ashton's head and laid him in his crib. As she softly slid into bed, she drifted off before remembering anything more.

Chapter Twenty-Eight

"Mom! It's morning time. Mom. Mom! Mommy!" Isabella had two settings—on and off. When she woke up in the morning, it was time for the entire house to follow suit.

Miranda didn't open her eyes. "Honey, it's Sunday. You don't have school today."

"Mommy, wake up." A poke in the eye urged Miranda to move. Her sweet moments of slumber were officially over.

She scuffled to the bathroom and sloshed into the shower. Maybe the water could revive some of her mental capacity. No such luck. She climbed out more tired than she'd entered.

"Time for breakfast. Everybody downstairs, please. Come and get it while it's hot." Landon's voice climbed the stairs. Thank goodness for their weekend tradition of Landon cooking.

Miranda snitched a wad of perfectly cooked hash browns as the three kids bounded down the stairs. "Once again, you've created a breakfast masterpiece." Her mouth watered at the spread of hash browns, eggs Benedict, and fresh fruit, rounded out with biscuits and gravy. No grumbling would come from their stomachs during the church service.

She turned to Brendon. "You look sharp. I like the new suit." He'd outgrown his other one with a growth spurt last spring. It was one excuse he'd used to complain about why he shouldn't have to go to church. If only she'd known the real reasons.

"Thanks." His head bobbed a little. She wouldn't blame him if he never set foot in the building again. Seeing him stand here, dressed and ready to go, made her mama heart swell. This boy—no, young man—of hers possessed such strength.

She sat next to him and spoke, below the chatter of the girls across the table. "You don't have to go if you don't want to."

He smiled and nudged her with his shoulder. "Remember, I control my response. His words only have the power I give them."

How did she get so lucky to have this boy in her life?

After prayer, the clinking of silverware and chewing filled the air.

Miranda soaked in Brendon's newfound enthusiasm. She had to give it one last shot. Even if the trip wasn't happening this year, she had to explain to Landon the importance of at least keeping it in the realm of possibility as she finished school.

She cleared her throat. "Honey, could we talk in the office for a minute?"

"You bet." He got up and led the way. What she would say when they entered, she had no idea. But she had to say something. She could relinquish the timing and the trip, but not the dream. Not this time.

When she closed the door, he pivoted around and took both of her hands in his. "This really is a dream of yours, isn't it?"

Miranda nodded her head. *Isn't that what I've said over and over?*

"I owe you an apology."

"What? Why?"

"I haven't been fair to you. You've stood by my side and supported me through every phase of my career and goals. I never considered the fact that you might have goals of your own. Goals that had to do with something other than the kids."

"Thank you. I really appreciate—"

"Let me finish . . . If you want to make the trip to Niger work, then I think we should try to make it happen."

The knot in her stomach dissolved into butterflies. "Really?"

He nodded. "Remember Olivia's talk last night? About Moses climbing up the mountain?"

She nodded. Was this really happening?

"You've climbed countless mountains for me. It's time for me to reciprocate."

Miranda jumped into his arms and buried her head into his shoulder. "Thank you. I can't tell you how much this means to me. I love you." *Thank you, Lord, for fighting this battle.*

"I love you too." He pulled back and gently kissed her. "I love you now and forever."

She grabbed his hand, unable to contain her giddiness. "Let's go tell the kids." She sprang out the door, pulling him along.

"Kids, guess what? We're going to Africa!"

———————

They piled into the car in record time. About halfway to the church, Miranda turned to make sure the church bag was in the car. "That's an interesting choice of footwear you have there, little one." A sparkly white sandal adorned one of Izzy's feet, a pink cowgirl boot housed the other.

"They're so cute. I love my shoes." Isabella wore a gleeful grin.

"But they don't match." Olivia giggled.

"But I love them both. I want to wear both of them." Isabella beamed, still not showing the least bit of apprehension for her unique choice.

A few months ago, Miranda would've made them turn around. Even at the expense of being late, she wouldn't dare walk in wondering what all the other mothers thought about her daughter's eclectic style.

The emerging Miranda laughed and grabbed her phone to take a picture. "This'll be a great one to keep in the archives." The frame captured both the shoes and Isabella's beaming face.

"Izzy, you're going to go far in life." Landon peeked at her through the rearview mirror. "You have a world of determination scrunched into a tiny body. I can't wait to see who you become."

That's the missing topic I couldn't remember. She let her mind drift back to that day on the bench, a whole new perspective on seeing the world—and her children. She'd learned to see her children not as they were in the moment but as the people they had the vast potential to be.

That must be how God sees me. How He sees everyone. She rubbed her chin. *Huh. I bet God looks at this whole earth-phase of our existence as a preschool phase in His eternal time frame.*

God must look at her the way she looked at her children. At each of their milestones, she cheered like crazy. The sitting up. The crawling. The walking.

Regardless if it was her second, third, or fourth child, each of these events held the same significance. And she cheered just as loudly. She imagined God watching and cheering for each individual accomplishment of each of His children on their personal journeys through life. Cheering for them, even through their mistakes, knowing they could become much more.

For a moment, Miranda caught a beautiful glimpse into how happy and proud her Father was of each step taken by each child. He loved His children collectively. But in that moment, the individualized love and concern God held for every person, including herself, touched her core.

A warmth enveloped her, like an all-encompassing hug. She held a deeper level of love and concern for each of her children, separate and unique in its completeness. She stopped trying to put words to it and instead sat and basked in the quiet quintessential moment of grace.

Chapter Twenty-Nine

As Miranda drove home from the morning drop-offs, her mind drifted again to the bench. She had yet to discover the overarching connection between all the lessons.

Did Mindy mean to incorporate them into different circumstances in her life? Relinquishing control helped her reach resolution with Landon. She'd already envisioned the butterfly effect of her kids taking this exciting trip . . . but something inside told her there was more to it than that.

But what?

She went through them again in her mind.

Still nothing.

She huffed and put them out of her mind. There was no time for this right now anyway. Thanksgiving was days away, which officially ushered in the Christmas season and all of the hustle and bustle that included.

That night, as she nursed Ashton, the nagging feeling crept in again. What was she missing? She laid him in his crib and pulled out a notebook. She needed to figure this out. She started writing . . . Butterfly, Engage, Core, Obstacles, Master of One, and Eternal Eyewear. They all held such meaning to her on their own, yet she couldn't see the connection.

She doodled around with them, drawing pictures, writing them in different positions. Writing little notes about them.

She turned to a new page and wrote them as a list:

Butterfly

Engage

Core

Obstacles

Master of One

Eternal Eyewear

She studied the list, squinting her eyes. What was she missing?

As if she'd been wearing 3-D glasses, letters lunged from the page. She gasped, closed her eyes, and viewed the list again. There, vertically, the six words came together in beautiful alignment. The first letter in each row fused together. It had been there all the time, hidden beneath the layers of each topic.

BECOME.

Become. A current of energy surged through her, tingling her neck. How had she missed it before?

Hot on the heels of the discovery bounded the follow up. Become what?

True to Mindy's nature, she once again kept the key to full understanding dangling just out of reach.

What was Miranda supposed to become? A connector? An ambassador for fighting the world's water problems? A wonder mom? The question lingered with her throughout the night and into the morning.

After getting the kids off to school, their last day before Thanksgiving break, Miranda drove the familiar route to the park.

It was a long shot. Still, she hoped to see her dear friend and mentor.

She prayed for it. One more talk with Mindy. She longed for that as much as she ached for one more hug from her mother.

As she rounded the corner, her heart sank. The bare trees echoed the emptiness of the park. The overcast skies matched her mood. The clouds, like her, were on the verge of dropping their tears toward the dying brown earth.

Even as she pulled Ashton from the car and moved toward the bench, she knew.

There would be no miracle today.

No friendly and familiar greeting waited for her this time. Loneliness surrounded her like a shroud, emphasized by a hollow thud as she slumped onto the bench.

November had been unusually warm, with no early snow. Today, however, a foreboding breeze blew in a warning that frigid days were near.

Snuggling her four-month-old, Miranda shielded him against the biting north wind. Ashton cooed and smiled at her, flailing his newly found arms. He grabbed at anything within his reach. His greedy hands grabbed Miranda's cheeks and pulled her close. Even his darling dimples and exuberant smile couldn't lift Miranda from her slump. The vacancy on the bench mocked the empty space in her heart.

Miranda lifted him up, admiring his bright blue eyes. "Well, my little one. Maybe some questions aren't meant to be answered. At least in the time frame I want. If she's not here, how about I ask you? What am I to become?"

Ashton responded with coos and gurgles.

"When it comes to you and your siblings, I see endless possibilities for your future, for you to *become*. Yet, for myself, it's a vast unknown. Who should I become?"

He arched his back, signaling his hunger.

"Is this your final answer?" She set him up to nurse. "Are you telling me I am to become a professional nurser?"

He drank the sustaining nutrients, then quickly fell asleep, wrapped snugly in his favorite fuzzy blanket. The sky shifted from gray to charcoal, threatening to erupt. With the dropping temperature, it might be flakes that fell this time. She should take Ashton home, yet she continued to sit in a silent and sullen protest.

Thank goodness for the distraction of the holiday season. She could busy herself in the preparations and anticipation of seeing her children happily exuding a contagious giddiness. She also had the trip to look forward to. Ironically, feeding that part of herself didn't take her focus away from her role as a mother, as she feared it might. For years, she'd been physically present with her children and husband, but she had secretly resented them for absorbing all of her time and energy. After giving all of herself to them, there was nothing left for her. Fueling her passion somehow also gave her the energy and ability to more fully engage with her children.

Engage. Core.

Become.

The word shot through her again. She studied Mindy's empty spot on the bench.

She hugged Ashton closer as she dropped her head and silently screamed. *Become what? What am I supposed to become?*

She shifted the blanket, checking to make sure Ashton was still bundled and asleep.

"You become you."

Miranda snapped to attention. She knew that voice.

She shot a glance to her side. The spot remained vacant.

She twisted around.

Nothing. She scoured the proximity. She was still the only person crazy enough to be sitting alone at the park on a day like today.

Great. Now I'm losing it. And losing it with captain obvious comments. "You become you." What does that even mean?

"You become you."

It was so clear, Mindy must be right behind her.

She twisted again but only the mist forming in the air greeted her.

She gazed at the ever-darkening sky. So much like the shadowy clouds that greeted her upon arrival in Niger all those years ago.

As she studied the clouds now, she stepped back in time, walking those village trails. The previous years scrolled through her memory. Years filled with joys, struggles, and everything in-between. It all flashed before Miranda in a heartbeat.

The person sitting here on the bench was both the same and different from the girl who first walked under those darkening skies in a country so far away, on her own personal adventure into the great unknown years ago. She'd grown in so many ways. There was still more growth in store.

"Through each experience, you became the person you were yesterday. Each day you live adds one more piece of the person you have yet to become."

Miranda didn't turn this time. Mindy wasn't there. Maybe she was going crazy.

Crazy enough to talk back to the voice. "But who am I supposed to become?"

"You become you."

"You said that already. What does it mean?" She could only imagine how she appeared, having a one-sided conversation.

"You become you. There's no one else in the world you are meant to be. You walk forward daily, submitting to internal change, engaging in the struggle to live your core, achieving mastery of the only person you can—yourself. All while keeping the eternal perspective in place. You release yourself from the comparison game and allow grace to govern your journey." Mindy's voice was calm and reassuring. No hint of judgment or impatience with Miranda's continuing doubts and questions.

"How will I know when I become what I'm supposed to be?"

Mindy's voice continued. "You become who God created you to be. At the end of the journey, you become me."

Miranda blinked. Then blinked again. "Wait, wait, wait. What are you saying?"

Silence surrounded her.

"Oh, now you go silent? You haven't had a problem with comebacks before. Are you saying . . . what I think you are . . . ?" No. This was absurd. "I wished so badly to have one last conversation with you that I conjured up this entire exchange in my obviously overtired brain."

Yes, that was it. "This whole interchange has been one gigantic figment of my overworking imagination."

She smiled, congratulating herself for being able to wrap it all up so—

"No, this isn't absurd, and you didn't conjure this in your imagination." Mindy's voice was so clear it made Miranda jump.

"Okay, now I'm thoroughly confused. What are you talking about? And why am I still having this conversation?" She chided herself for listening to this improbable friend.

"You're still having this conversation because part of you knows. A piece of you recognized me. The same was true for each of your girls."

Miranda pictured the way Isabella had run up to Mindy, and how even Olivia had leaned in for a hug.

Mindy had so easily soothed Ashton. And what about her own feelings of being drawn toward something in Mindy that she couldn't identify? It was in the way Mindy could almost read her unspoken questions. The way Mindy helped Miranda express those forbidden feelings, which released the shame that had plagued her for years.

Even as the pieces fit together, Miranda shook her head at the impossibility of it all.

"Am I on some sort of candid camera or practical joke episode? This is real life, not some time and space warp episode of *Star Trek*. It's not possible that you could be my future self."

"Just because it doesn't seem possible, doesn't mean it's impossible. Many things to the natural mind are impossible, yet to the Great Creator, they are simple. He works in unique and creative ways. In ways that affect every aspect of your life—and the lives of everyone else walking the mortal journey. It's human nature to be oblivious to most of these occurrences. He never forces us to see nor to participate."

Miranda opened her mouth to object, but her heart whispered to open her ears instead.

"It was your choice from the beginning. You could've put in your earbuds on the first day. You didn't have to return after Brendon's brush with death. You were never pushed or cajoled into any action beyond what you were willing to take."

Miranda let this sink in. Once again, Mindy—she still couldn't bring herself to embrace Mindy as her future self—distilled a confusing topic into something not only understandable, but believable.

"That makes sense. In a completely confusing sort of way."

Countless questions flooded her mind. She imagined the woman. Was that what she would look like later in life?

And then all the things Mindy had said about her own family bubbled up in her memory.

Miranda's family.

Would Brendon continue to gain confidence and move forward? Were there any big catastrophes she could help them avoid?

Before she voiced any of her questions, Mindy spoke. "That's not how this works. I helped you see what you already had inside. What you do with this insight is up to you. Besides, what's the fun in reading the book if you already know how it ends?" A soft laugh floated in the air.

Are you laughing at me? My future self is laughing at me. "Okay, now I know you can't possibly be future me. The future me would let me read the last page."

"There's always time to change that. You should try it with your next book. The journey becomes much more exciting."

With that, Mindy disappeared. Miranda could feel her leave like a final leaf floating softly away in the breeze, signaling the tree to enter a new season.

Miranda sat alone, but no longer lonely. The cold no longer bothered her. A warm peace filled her soul. She lingered on the bench as soft, white flakes slowly descended to the earth.

A new season ushered in.

Chapter Thirty

Thanksgiving morning dawned white and beautiful on the outside with laughter and excitement on the inside. Miranda and Landon prepped the turkey, then busied themselves with the side dishes. Company would be there in the early afternoon, and they had a lot to do before then. As was tradition, they invited all the college kids in their congregation from church who weren't heading to their own homes, which turned the day into one big celebration.

Miranda left Landon peeling potatoes to answer Ashton's cries for his own Thanksgiving feast. She slowly rocked Ashton with the sounds of the Macy's Thanksgiving Day parade projecting from the TV. She surveyed the scene in her home, her universe, and her heart skipped a beat. Brendon and Olivia were outside, snapping pictures of the snow-covered trees. Every so often, they'd come inside to show Miranda or Landon their favorite shots. Isabella paraded up and down the stairs, modeling a different princess dress each time. Landon sang along with each song from the parade. She soaked in every ounce of these moments.

Mindy's final council rang true. She was glad, for once, that she hadn't received the last-page details from this book.

Her book.

Had she known, she'd be fretting over any future catastrophes, trying to manipulate things to help them avoid more heartaches.

Heartaches and trials would come, no doubt. But when they did, Miranda could view them as stepping-stones on the journey to become who they needed to become.

"Hey, honey, can you believe we're going to be there in six months?" Landon's voice brought her attention back. On the screen was a group of dancers portraying an African scene from a new Broadway show.

"I can't wait." Miranda stared at the screen, mesmerized by the ritualistic movements that so closely characterized the dance style she'd become accustomed to in her time in Niger. It hadn't been a waste after all, but a building block of who she was. Of who she would become. She'd fully open the gifts and passions she'd buried for so long and allow them to also be a part of herself. Part of her contribution. Her mark on the world.

She could focus both on her home and across the world. The two could coexist. They were meant to coexist. Those parts of her made her whole. It didn't have to be that way for every person, but it did for her. Her soul settled.

"Mommy, can we take some fudge over to Miss Elizabeth?" Isabella stood before Miranda holding two squished pieces of fudge, one with the corner bitten off.

"That's a great idea, honey, but maybe some new pieces would work better." Miranda followed her to the kitchen and cut some fresh pieces. The two girls then accompanied her across the cul-de-sac, their prints squishing in the fresh layer of snow that coated the earth.

Elizabeth opened the door surrounded by her grandchildren. Her face lit up at the two girls and Miranda on the doorstep.

Izzy shoved the plate of fudge forward. "We made you some fudge. It's yummy. I got to lick the bowl with Bwendon."

Elizabeth's brown eyes twinkled as she took the plate. "Thank you. This looks delicious."

She handed the plate to the girls who pivoted and ran back to the kitchen.

She turned back to Miranda. "How did the Mom of the Year nominations go?"

Mom of the Year? How did she . . . ah yes, the committee. That dreadful day . . .

She lifted one shoulder along with a corner of her mouth. "I decided not to do it. It wasn't . . . me. But thank you for your help with the committee members that day. And thank you again for all of your help during that time." Miranda retreated a half step. "Well, I'm sure you want to get back to your family, so we won't take any more of your time. We wanted to wish you a Happy Thanksgiving."

Olivia and Isabella wheeled around and bounded down the porch steps, jumping into the growing mounds of snow.

Miranda followed suit but twisted back before the door clicked. "Elizabeth . . ."

Elizabeth pushed the door open again, a smile lighting up her face. "Please, call me Liz . . ."

Liz.

Of course. Miranda's mind shot to one of the park visits as a smile stole across her face. "When things settle down from the holiday, I'd love to have you over for hot chocolate some time."

Liz's smile widened. "I'd love that. It's a date."

———

At one-thirty, the first guest arrived. They never knew exactly how many people would show up each year. They left an open invitation with the college kids in their congregation, which included any friends or roommates as well. Miranda couldn't stand the thought of anyone being left alone on Thanksgiving. As people came in, she and Landon added to the place settings, breaking out the plasticware when the glass plates ran out.

The familiar faces of the college kids poured in, commenting on the delicious smells that wafted to the doorway from the kitchen.

The doorbell rang again, and Miranda opened it. "What? How are you?" There on the doorstep stood Katie, the girl from the gas station several weeks earlier.

Katie stepped back. "How crazy is this? I was sure I'd never see you again to thank you for saving me that day."

Bethany, the girl from Miranda's congregation who had invited her, peered at them, her brows knitted together.

Katie turned to Bethany as they walked into the house. "Do you remember me telling you about that day I was on my way to the interview and had so many things go wrong? This is the woman who swooped in to save the day." She stared at Miranda as if she were seeing an angel. "I can't tell you how grateful I am for your help that day." Her eyes got misty. "I was struggling. I was homesick, and my class load was crushing me. That morning I thought about dropping out and heading home. You walked up as if sent from God Himself."

She peered at Bethany while pointing toward Miranda. "Then she appeared from out of nowhere and had me back on course before I could even finish the thought."

Katie looked back at Miranda. "Your calm convinced me that if I get into the nursing program, I want to help people in traumatic situations find the calm amidst their storm. *Thank you* doesn't quite seem adequate for how much you helped me. I only hope to be able to pass it on someday."

A lump formed in Miranda's throat. She smiled as she imagined Mindy's knowing "Mmm, I told ya so" as she once again thought of the butterfly effect and the power of one seemingly insignificant person. Simple in concept, profound in possibilities.

In all, they welcomed ten college kids. Their talkative nature, combined with Miranda's own kids, produced a healthy cacophony of loud conversations and bellowing laughter. The entangled buzz echoed sweetly in Miranda's ears.

During the dance-off, Olivia picked up Miranda's phone.

"Mom." Olivia brought it to her after the song ended. "Jess texted you."

Miranda grabbed the phone and slipped into the office as the next song started.

Mindy, just landed and got your message. Made me cry. You know I love you forever. Gotta go. Hang some stockings for us, we're coming home for Christmas.

**Miranda. Sorry, autocorrect hits again.

Mindy? She'd called her Mindy?

Miranda's thumbs jumped to the screen. As she typed, another message from Jess chimed through. *Oh, one more thing. Olivia sent an email about your trip to Niger. That's awesome! Steve talked with his boss, and they pledged to fund the drilling for two villages. You are my deep diving hero.*

Miranda stopped typing, and her hand flew to her open mouth. She leaned outside the office door. "Landon." She beckoned him away from the group. When he joined her, she held the phone up for him to read the good news.

"Who's Mindy?"

Miranda's smile only widened. "It's me."

Epilogue

"Mom, your phone's ringing." Olivia held it out to Miranda, who handed the star to Isabella. Landon then lifted her to position it on top of the tree.

"You can let it go to voicemail, honey. We aren't quite finished."

Olivia set the phone down and resumed hanging the stockings on the mantel. Brendon placed the final ornament on the tree as she hung the last stocking.

Landon strode to the light switch on the wall. "Are we ready for the grand lighting?"

Brendon picked up the end of the Christmas light string. "Hit the switch, Dad."

Landon flipped the switch, and darkness filled the room. Brendon plugged in the string of lights, and a soft colorful glow enveloped the room, punctuated by oohs and aahs from the girls.

Izzy's hands cupped her cheeks. "Look at all the colors. It's magic. This is the bestest day ever!"

The family sat on the floor gazing up at the festive tree and drinking hot chocolate, basking in the warm glow of their unity and love.

Miranda glanced at her phone. A number one above the phone icon signaled a voicemail. Oh yes, the phone call. She picked it up and clicked to listen to the message.

"Miranda, this is Penelope. It hasn't been officially released yet, but I couldn't wait to tell you. You are the newest Mom of the Year for the state of Minnesota!"

Miranda pulled the phone away and peered at it in confusion. What was she talking about? She backed the message up. It couldn't be right. She'd texted Penelope and told her she wouldn't be moving forward with the nomination process. She'd thrown away the application.

This had to be a mistake. The irony of it hit her, and she laughed out loud.

Sitting next to her, Landon nudged her shoulder. "What's so funny?"

"I got the craziest phone call. The committee for Mom of the Year said I won. The only problem is, I never applied." She put the phone away, shaking her head. "They made a mistake and got me mixed up with someone else."

A mischievous smile played at the corners of Landon's mouth. Miranda surveyed the room. All eyes on her. All faces sporting the same smiles.

Olivia broke first. "We did it, Mom. We submitted your application."

Miranda's eyes widened as her mouth gaped open. "You *what?*"

"Well, it was Brendon's idea." Olivia spilled it all, bobbing in her spot to punctuate the details. "He dug out the application from the garbage and said we should all fill it out for you, that you were the best mom in the world, and we needed to let everyone know. We all wrote on it, even Izzy told them about your yummy chocolate chip cookies."

Miranda opened her mouth to speak, then closed it again. She looked around the room again. Her heart almost burst. "I . . . I don't know what to say."

Landon wrapped his arms around her. "You say, I accept."

She held her arms out, and they took the hint. The older three set their hot chocolate mugs down, then ran over and dogpiled her. Even Ashton chimed his approval from his baby swing. Landon zipped over and picked him up, then placed him on the top of the pile.

———

The credits rolled on *The Polar Express*, the first of many Christmas movies they would watch by the glow of the Christmas lights. Miranda gathered some of the mugs. "Okay everyone, time for bed."

Landon scooped up a drowsy Izzy, and Olivia followed him up the stairs as Brendon carried the rest of the mugs to the sink. Miranda rinsed them, then followed the rest of the bunch for scriptures and prayer.

As they gathered in Miranda and Landon's bedroom, Miranda opened her Bible to Luke. Chapter two was a popular choice for scripture share in the nights leading up to Christmas. "We usually start at the beginning of Christ's life for this season." She scanned the verses, then flipped forward a few chapters. "But tonight, I want to start at the end, when Jesus faced Pilot, days before His death. In John chapter eighteen, verse thirty-seven, Christ declared to Pilot, *'To this end was I born, and for this cause came I into the world.'*"

She regarded the young faces of those sitting around her in their bedroom. The faces she brought into the world. "As we go through this season and celebrate the life of our Savior, I want you to also ask yourself, to what end *you* were born?" She studied them again. The wisdom poured into her from Mindy bubbled to the surface, begging to cascade into her children.

The time would come, the lessons would be shared, when they were ready to receive. For now, she gave the first piece. "Each of you came here on purpose. For a purpose." And so did she.

Miranda and Landon tucked the kids into their beds, then settled in for the night. As she allowed her body and mind to relax into sleep, moments from the bench played before her. Mindy flashed before her mind. She'd managed to share enough personal insights to teach the lessons yet kept the details of her past—Miranda's future—at bay. She'd shared very little about the childr—

Miranda's eyes shot open as she sat up like a bolt.

"Twins?!"

Acknowledgments

I cannot begin to extend adequate thanks to those who spent time and energy helping develop this book into what it is today. From critique partners (thank you Carrie Walker, Andra Loy, and Steve Petersen) who painstakingly combed through sentences and paragraphs to wordsmith and tweak in ways beyond what I could personally do, to all of the beta readers who gave such valuable input and helped me see the book through other eyes. You all had such a hand in molding the story.

Thank you to the editors of different renditions of The Bench: Jenny Proctor, Robyn Patchen, Teresa Lynn, and especially Valene Wood from Cedar Fort. There is no way this book could have become anything without your help.

Courtney Proby's cover design captured my vision of the bench beautifully. Thank you to Angela Johnson and the rest of the team at Cedar Fort. Your work astounds me.

To my family, who spent way too much time staring at the side of my face while I plunked away on the computer working on draft after draft. Thank you for believing in my dream.

A Letter from the Author

Though this is a work of fiction, the internal journey of Miranda has very much been my journey. I vividly remember receiving my own impressions and soul rumbling, knowing there was something I was to be doing . . . but not knowing exactly *what* or *how* to do it. After much thought, prayer, and even pleading, somewhere in the middle of the mountains in Guatemala, pregnant with baby number seven, I came to first understand and then to embrace my role as a nourisher of body and soul.

As a nourisher, I work with Care for Life in forgotten communities around the world where we work alongside local families to alleviate suffering and instill hope. To this end, the proceeds from *The Bench* are utilized to bring hope and healing through family programs throughout the world. To find out more about this journey, visit **http://www.familypreservationprogram.org**.

Your purchase of this book is helping to bring this about. Thank you for being part of the solution.

Sincerely,

Jen

Jen Brewer is a nourisher of bodies and souls. When she's not caring for her children or planning date nights with her husband, you will find her writing, speaking, or building up forgotten communities in Guatemala through digging gardens and nutrition education. Born and raised in Burley, Idaho, she now claims Minnesota as home, but has instilled within her children a love of all things potato, and misses her western mountains terribly. Some of her other works include *Stop Dieting and Start Losing Weight for Good*, *Be the Chocolate Chip*, and *The Kindness Snowflake*. You can follow her work in Guatemala and find her latest and greatest happenings at **www.jenbrewer.com**.